The Virtuous Saint

By

Johan Minto

© Copyright 2009 J. Minto

All rights reserved

This book shall not, by way of trade or otherwise, be lent, re-sold, hired out, or otherwise circulated without the prior consent of the copyright holder or the publisher in any form of binding or cover other than that in which it is published and without a similar condition including this condition being imposed on the subsequent purchaser

ISBN: 978-0-9558557-5-7

MMIX

Published by
ShieldCrest,

UK: Aylesbury, Buckinghamshire, HP22 5RR
USA: Morrisville, NC 27560
www.shieldcrest.co.uk

To my extraordinarily brave, humorous, independent, and lovely Mum who passed away whilst this novel was in the first throws of being written. She was always my inspiration and even now she continues to be so.

ABOUT THE AUTHOR

Johan Minto was born in Scotland but from the age of thirteen until the present day she has lived in her beloved Yorkshire with her husband and three children. She has travelled extensively across Europe, North Africa, and America savouring the delights of the variety of people's traditions and food and drink.

The Virtuous Saint is the first novel of a trilogy of books which the writer has written and has taken almost two years to complete. She has also written one other contemporary novel.

Other books by the author

Marcus Hoag Trilogy

The Heliopolis Scrolls

The Jesse Tree

The Babysitter

AUTHOR'S NOTE

The Virtuous Saint is a work of fiction; however the historical facts surrounding Saint Benedict and his Regula Monachorum can be read from the dialogue's of the Saint Gregory I.

Also the Cathedrals and Minster that are personified in the story is, I must say, spectacular works of fine art and once the reader has finished reading this book, I guarantee, like the Canterbury Cantors, you will want to visit these wonderfully sacred bastions of divinity to appreciate exactly what the writer was trying to convey.

List of Characters

Dr. Marcus Hoag	-	Adventurer/Antiques
Paul Hoag	-	Dr. Hoag's Son, Student
Dean John Graham	-	Temporary Dean of University
Christine (Chrissie) Greenwood	-	Dr. Hoag's future wife
Louise Pendleton	-	Paul girlfriend FBI Agent
Danny Firth	-	Friend of Dr. Hoag
Mike Winterbottom	-	Friend of Dr. Hoag
Dean Alexander	-	Dean of University
DI Kent	-	Detective from London
DC Logan	-	Detective from Dublin
Dr. David Connor	-	Son of CG & DF
Msr. Marc Connor	-	Son of CG & DF
Giovanni Mancini	-	Vatican Museum Curator
Lou Quarry	-	Private Detective
Benedict	-	Abbott of Montecassino
Romanus	-	Monk/Benedict's friend

CHAPTER 1

Saint Peter's University New York
June 10th 1980

The guard at the university gatehouse scanned the invitation bar code with his hand held identification gun and handed it back to the visitor. "Your invitation is in order Dr. Hoag. Have a good day sir."

"I intend to Pete." As Dr. Hoag slipped the card into his inside jacket pocket he asked the guard. "How long has it been?"

"It's been a while sir. Must be what? A good two years since I saw you last."

"Too long Pete, retirement feels good, you should try it."

"I got a couple of good years in me yet Doc. Tell Paul to have a good day sir."

"Sure will Pete," and with a wave Dr. Hoag left the guard at the gate and drove his old Chevrolet up the long drive, which took him past the chapel on the left with the lake in the background. There were strict rules regarding sailing on or swimming in the lake, but the students had their own philosophy on rules, they were simply made to be broken, and Marcus Hoag sure broke a few in his time here. He slowly passed the science blocks on the right then carried on into the campus car park.

Marcus, a young looking 55 year old, with short fair hair, tinged with grey on his short side burns, and a slight paunch around his middle, from the time his wife died five years ago, he thought, why punish myself in the gym anymore. So he cancelled his subscription and tried to live the life of early retirement.

Marcus pulled into the car parking space opposite the science library building and thinking about his only son, he looked forward to seeing him. They hadn't seen each other for almost a year, but spoke briefly on the phone last New Year, wishing each other all the best; they both had, or so he thought, busy lives. Paul wanting to spend Christmas with his friends skiing in the mountains and Marcus had a meeting at his local bar, namely with a Jack Daniels whisky. Not that he was an addict; he just enjoyed how the taste made him forget the past.

He walked through the car park and across the grass, continuing on past the rhododendron bushes with incredible blooms as big as his head. Marcus looked up at the impressive building that loomed in front of him, and as he remembered his last year in the Saint Matilda 400 student dormitory, an immense feeling of nostalgia and pride flooded through him. Its grey granite walls were four stories high with small towers on each corner, but the most impressive part of the building was the entrance. Two large solid doors, standing open at the top of six, half circle steps, set into an almost cathedral like archway.

As Marcus was looking up in amazement at the beauty of the workmanship, he spoke quietly to himself. "Why hadn't I noticed all this before?" Just then he heard a familiar voice behind him. He turned and saw Paul running from the gymnasium and crossing the car park with a flat, black graduation cap in his hand, and casually draped over his shoulders, a black billowing gown and silk hood, he was grinning from ear to ear. His son, thought Marcus, looked as he himself had done when twenty-three years old. Well! Almost, Paul was a little taller, and more athletic, a lot more athletic, with a shock of blonde hair, a little too long, but hey! He was young. Marcus could see his wife Alice in his sons sea green eyes. It was uncanny the way his mouth spread across his face when he laughed or smiled, the same as she had.

"Hey dad, changed a bit since you were here, huh!"

Marcus took Paul's outstretched hand in both of his and shook it vigorously. He didn't realize just how much he'd missed his son, and the feeling almost overwhelmed him. They patted and punched each other playfully on the shoulders, both remembering times gone bye. "Come on then," he said to his only son. "Show me round the old place again."

With Paul's left arm around his father's shoulder and Marcus a little shorter than his son put his right arm around Paul's waist, they both walked up the steps and through the ancient archway into the quadrangle, past the benches dedicated to deceased saints, scholars, and masters. Passing the flower borders and on through the opposite archway emerging into another quadrangle, but smaller than the first, and followed the path to the right through another small archway with a three story building and bell tower in front of them, but this building looked more like the threatening shape of a mausoleum.

This was the graduation hall or to give it its correct name, Saint Andrew's Hall, the plaque on the wall read:

Saint Andrews Hall
Built 1700
Converted in 1950

They entered the building together father and son, each with their own thoughts of what the afternoon would bring. Paul worried about going up to accept his degree in front of all his friends and the Dean, but Marcus was remembering his stupidity, just before he accepted his. No doubt the Dean, Dr. John Alexander Ph.D., will remind him of what he thought was foolishness. If he hid at the back of the hall the Dean just might not see him. Huh! Thought Marcus, he was deluding himself and he knew it, Dean Alexander had eagle eyes.

"Are you nervous?" asked Marcus.

"I'd like to say no, but my hands are shaking, so I guess it's a yes. Was it the same for you dad?"

Marcus smiled as he looked down at his shaking hands. "Just the same son, just the same, but a Jack Daniels would go down pretty well just about now."

Paul nodded his head; he knew what would happen once his father had a JD he probably wouldn't stop at one. Instead, he asked. "What about a cup of tea?"

"Sure," said Marcus, and smiled knowingly at his son. "That's just the thing to calm the nerves."

Paul smiling at his fathers feigned nervousness walked away and headed for the nearby refectory. Just as Paul disappeared through the doorway Marcus saw something he thought he would never ever see again. In his eye line he spotted the stain glass window, which he broke, just before he accepted his degree. It had been repaired, but he could still make out the broken pieces, but wait a minute, he thought to himself, something's not right I need my notebook. "Damn!" he cursed aloud. "What did I do with it?" He searched his pockets and found only the invitation card and a few other bits and pieces, and then he realised he'd left it in the car, and that was in the car park.

"Thirty years ago," a voice boomed behind Marcus. "It took a stain glass specialist a week to repair that window, and the student still hasn't paid for it."

Marcus didn't look round, but said with a hesitant grin on his face. "Thirty years is a long time Dean Alexander." Marcus turned to face the Dean and almost proffered his hand, but with a look of surprise and expecting to see Dean Alexander, changed his mind and kept his hands hidden inside his jacket pockets. The man he saw was the most hated person he'd ever had the misfortune to meet.

John Graham and Marcus weren't exactly best of friends and Graham also kept his hands out of sight behind his back. He looked like a seven-foot giant to Marcus's five foot eight and with a girth much larger than his own, Marcus grouched as he firmly held the man's eyes. "What the devil are you doing here?"

"Did Paul not tell you, I've been established as Dean at the university, Dean Alexander's replacement, but tell me Hoag, what do you think of the repair job?"

"I guess the specialist did a good job," said Marcus resignedly, trying to hide his hatred of the man.

Dean Graham changed tack and spoke of Marcus' son. "Hoag, your son has done you proud."

"My son is gifted with everything I didn't have. He's tall, a great athlete, and an exceptional sportsman."

"Yes," inflected Dean Graham. "An asset to the university," then with dripping sarcasm he added. "Unlike his father, hope to speak to you later Hoag."

Just as Dean Graham turned and walked away. Marcus said with a tinge of attitude. "It's Dr. Hoag!" He then remembered his first few years at this same university and how Graham had gradually conned then relieved the first year students of their money, and he cursed quietly under his breath.

As Dean Graham walked away from Dr. Hoag, he heard the remark regarding Marcus's doctorate qualifications, but not the offensive one. He probably wouldn't have let it worry him he knew what Marcus and a few of the lecturers thought.

Leaving the graduation hall through the refectory, the Dean turned left into the dormitory that housed the live-in tutors and lecturers, walked down the corridor to the far end, and entered the Deanery on the left; these were a set of three rooms available to the head of the university. The first room was the secretary's, and on the right wall were filing cabinets and under the window facing the cabinets, a desk with a telephone plus a computer and keyboard, then on another small desk in the left corner was housed a printer.

The next room was the Dean's personal study: this room was on the corner with one window overlooking St. Andrew's Hall, with a comfy swivel chair and a large oak desk. On the desk a writing pad, various pens, pencils and a 1930's style telephone. The room was pleasantly decorated; it also had an elaborate drinks cabinet next to the connecting bedroom door (the third room), with a floral display of Lavender set in a vase, Dean Graham's favourite bouquet, and two Victorian period chairs in front of the desk for visitors.

The Dean walked over to the telephone in his study and called an International number, the dialling codes clicked and buzzed for a few seconds and then he heard a continuous echoing ring. A woman answered, her voice was husky as if she had a cold or even worse, a 'smoker'.

"Good evening John."

"Tell him he took the bait and don't call me by name again, or you'll end up looking in the vacancy ad's."

"Huh! I'll give him your message," she grouched and added. "Why should I care, but he pays you handsomely for your work, so earn it!"

The phone clicked in his ear, ending the conversation. Dean Graham set the antique telephone handset down on its cradle in the study, just as the modern phone was being put down in the secretary's room.

"She could be a real pain in the proverbial ass," he thought aloud, but he knew she would relay the message. He looked at his watch, unaware of someone exiting the secretarial room, and thinking, I'd better get back to the presentation hall, and with that he turned and walked from the Deanery back to St. Andrew's hall.

Paul paid for the tea and walked back down the corridor towards the entrance, where he left his father talking to Dean Graham.

"What happened to the Dean," said Paul, while pulling a face. "Did you scare him away dad?"

"Sure," said Marcus. "He got boring, started lecturing me on the morals of always paying my debts."

"What debts?"

"Oh! It's a long story son, I'll tell you about it sometime," then Marcus said conspiratorially. "You know, there's something not quite right about the Dean's behaviour."

"Why do you say that?"

Marcus replied with a grin. "He was too nice to me," but thinking something else more sinister.

"The Deans ok, he's probably a little wary of parents."

"Sure son, that must be it," but Marcus wasn't as trusting as his son and could spot the telling signs of someone too interested in his business and thought; I'll have to watch myself this time.

The graduation hall was full, almost bursting at the seams as the student body sat in the front seats, with lecturers, teachers and tutors sitting on the dais. They all wore the same black gown and flat graduation hats, and the only difference was the coloured silk hoods, which distinguished the different academic degrees. Marcus sat at the back next to a small plump, but expensively dressed woman of about forty-five years, as he introduced himself to the familiar face he found she wasn't a parent, but said she was a reporter covering graduation day for a local paper and her name was Christine Greenwood, Chrissie to her friends.

He said to her with pride in his voice. "That's my son, the one with blonde hair."

The reporter, looking at the backs of all the blonde heads commented. "You and your late wife must be very proud of your son. He's a credit to you both."

Eyeing her curiously, Marcus said. "Thank you, I am, very proud."

The presentations were over and Paul had collected his degree. Printed across the top in Latin, the words CUM LAUDE (with praise), the standard formula for academic honours, Marcus' own degree had the words SUMMA CUM LAUDE Valedictorian (even higher honours with supreme praise), and the word 'Valedictorian' simply means the highest ranking student, but Marcus said nothing of this to Paul, his son was on a high, soaking up all the praise he could get from friends and colleagues.

Having shaken the hand of everyone in the hall, he went looking for his father; he knew where he'd be, in the entrance looking at the stain glass windows, a bit of a passion with him, thought Paul. There, sure enough his father was standing in front of St. Francis of Assisi, the first window nearest to the outer doors.

Paul walked up behind him and touched his shoulder saying quietly. "Dad, there's a meal set out in the refectory, we can come back later and look at the windows, there are too many to look at now, and we can view the other three upstairs later as well, if you like."

"What do you mean?" asked Marcus quickly, but quietly. "You say there are three more upstairs, not four?"

"Yes," said Paul as he pointed upwards. "They converted the two rooms upstairs to a library and a storeroom to accommodate all the new computers, and found another three windows. They were bricked up on the outside and plastered over on the inside." Paul thought his father was about to pass out, but Marcus quickly pulled himself together as his son said with concern. "Dad, dad are you ok, you look as white as a ghost."

"I'm ok, really, I'm fine, and it was just a shock to find out about the other windows. You're sure there are only three?"

"Dad what's going on? And yes just three."

"I'll tell you later, where's Dean Graham?"

"He's in the presentation room talking to some of the tutors. Why?"

Marcus was heading for the stairway to the first floor library, but Paul pulled his fathers arm saying. "We can't dad, well not just now maybe later when it's quiet."

"I've got to get up there son and have a look for myself. I've searched for those windows for years, and all the time they were upstairs, I can't believe it. Why should they reveal them now?"

"Who's revealed them? We have to talk dad, now!"

Paul and Marcus together, walked through the hall and into the refectory for something to eat and Paul asked. "What is so important about the windows upstairs and why are we whispering?"

"Keep your voice down," said Marcus quietly. "I don't want Dean Graham to overhear us," then he said. "Have you had enough to eat, come on let's go to your room where we can talk."

Paul grabbed some food off his plate and downed his cup of tea, then walked behind his father out of the refectory towards the small dormitory.

As they exited the cafeteria, Marcus almost walked straight into a small, slim woman of about twenty-three years with long beautiful dark brown hair; Marcus thought she had the look of Latin descent, with very little makeup, which gave her face a gorgeous fresh look. Paul instantly blushed at the sight of the young woman and stuttered. "He... Hello Louise."

Louise, with a deep pink hue creeping up her face at the sight of Paul Hoag standing tall in front of her replied. "Hello Paul, I hope you're enjoying your day, I see you have your degree you must have it framed." Louise looked at Paul's father. "You graduated from here didn't you sir?"

Marcus a little taken back by her beauty and thinking, Paul was infatuated with her, plus 500 other guys at the university, but she's blushing, well now the young devil.

"Oh! Um! Yes," he mumbled. "Indeed I did, pleased to meet you Louise, sorry about my sons lack of self-discipline."

"That's ok sir, I'm the Deans secretary, and I get it all the time."

Marcus and Paul with their mouths open, watched as Louise wiggled past them on her high heels. Paul began to sweat profusely and drooled. "I didn't think she would be on campus today."

Marcus shook his head and smiled as he remembered the old secretary, a fifty something matronly Miss McGregor, but said aloud. "Things have certainly changed round here." He pushed his son into the corridor, passing the ornate entrance then the Deanery and out into the small quadrangle.

"I'm housed in the large dormitory on the second floor at the front overlooking the car park."

At the mention of car park Marcus remembered he'd left his notebook in his car. "I need my notebook, but it's in the car."

With his hand stretched out, Paul said. "Give me your keys; I'll get it for you."

Marcus handed his car keys over saying he'd left it in the glove box. Paul immediately disappeared through the large dormitory and down the half circle steps and Marcus starting to feel his fifty-five years decided to sit down on one of the convenient dedication seats; the one he sat on had the plaque inscribed:

DEDICATED TO ST. BENEDICT OF NURCIA
C529 – 543AD

Marcus' mind instantly whisked him back to when he was a young scholar and the day he picked up one of the history books in this very university and read all about St. Benedict and his Regula Monachorum, a monks rule for every day life.

Montecassino Monastery, Italy C529 – 543AD

The slap, slap noise of the monk's sandals on the white stone floor, could be heard echoing along the brightly lit passageway next to the great cloister. The cloister gardens were neat and tidy with small seats where visitors or brother monks could sit and enjoy the tranquillity and seclusion of the monastery. One brother monk, Romanus was a small man of around forty-five years, with a round face and sporting the same tonsure hair cut of a monk of the era. He wore an ankle length grey cowl with a scapular over the top and a grey hood around his neck, as he passed four large doors, the monk came to the large ornate double doors at the end of the cloister passageway carrying a wooden tray, on which were a mixture of fresh baked bread, cheese, two ripe tomatoes and a goblet of wine from the winery. Romanus laid the tray on a chair, opened the double doors, picked up the tray, and entered the Abbots study. Bookcases lined the walls to the left and right of the doors, with the Abbots desk placed in front of the balcony window facing the mountains to the north, and nestling under the west window which had magnificent views of the River Liris there was a small table.

Benedict was standing next to his writing desk when the monk entered. "Master," said Romanus. "I know you didn't want to be disturbed from your writing, so I thought you would prefer to eat here."

The Abbot, a man of good stature, wearing a curly white beard, pale watery blue eyes and long slim face which always seemed to have a gentle smile, he also wore a black ankle length cowl and hood, with a black cummerbund around his waist, thought for a moment, and realising the monk was right, he could go on for another few hours writing, but decided to accept the fresh smelling food and wine his friend had brought him. "Romanus," the Abbot answered quietly. "You know me too well, thank you, and please leave it on the table by the window."

The monk did as he was bid and placed the tray on the small table; he turned and was about to remind the Abbot of the afternoon agenda of prayers, but thought better of it.

Not wanting to disturb him anymore than necessary, he turned and walked slowly out of the room closing the large doors quietly behind him.

Romanus knew the Abbot would indeed eat and drink the food and wine he had prepared, he trusted him implicitly, but it was a different story when the Abbot, at twenty years of age, finished his studies and lived in Rome for a few years. Disgusted by the degrading vice, he abandoned everything in the city and travelled to the lonely Rocks of Subiaco where he led a hermit life. Romanus had been one of the Abbot's first disciples to be converted to the Benedictine order at Subiaco, along with many other monks that were attracted to his saintly ways and when their own Abbot had died suddenly they begged Benedict to become their teacher, of course he accepted.

Eventually, a few of the young monks thinking, his strict rule too excessive, tried to poison him, some say it was the sign of the cross, made by Benedict that miraculously caused the goblet of poisoned wine to shatter and a scavenging raven that carried away the loaf of poisoned bread, which saved the life of the young Benedict.

A lot of years had passed since they left Subiaco, and travelled south with a dozen faithful monks to found the small Benedictine order at the monastery Montecassino, and left that troubled time behind.

Saint Peter's University

Paul crossed over the car park to his father's car, unlocked it and retrieved the book from the glove box, locked the car door and started to walk back to his father.

Just as he passed the rhododendron bushes, he felt the glint of sun reflecting off glass on his face, it was coming from the bell tower at the top of St. Andrew's Hall, he thought to himself, who would want to be up there on a graduation day, I thought it was locked, and most of the staff, students and families were in the refectory or touring the grounds, then another thought struck him, someone had binoculars, and they were trained on him. Without looking too conspicuous he quickly walked back to where he'd left his father sitting on the benches in the large quadrangle.

"Come on dad, my room quick, I've seen something you should know."

Intrigued, Marcus followed his son up the flight of stairs to the second floor and headed for the front of St Matilda's building. Paul's room at the end of the long corridor was the first door on the south/east facing corner. He unlocked the door, and held it open to allow his father to enter.

Marcus walked past him into the comfortable two windowed corner rooms with a single bed to the right wall, a desk, and chair under the window with a view of the car park, bookshelves and cupboards lined the left wall and a comfy old leather chair next to the second window looking out to the gymnasium and running track.

Paul handed Marcus his notebook and said with a worried voice. "Someone was watching me with binoculars dad from the old bell tower."

"Could you see who it was?"

"He was wearing a graduation cap, black hood, and gown."

Marcus peeked out of Paul's side room window and across the running track to the bell tower. "Could it have been Dean Graham?"

"I don't know dad," said Paul with a frown on his face. "It was too far away, I wouldn't have seen them if it hadn't been for the sun glinting on the lens," then added. "Why would anyone be up there with binoculars?"

"Who ever it was they're not there now. My guess is he's after my notebook." Marcus sat down in the comfy chair and looked out of the window to the car park and thought, his son deserved an explanation to what was going on.

"Ok," said Marcus slipping his glasses on and opening his book at the first page.

Paul sat in the chair next to the desk, listening to his father's explanation of why so much secrecy. Marcus showed Paul a picture of a stained glass window and a lot of scribbled writing.

1st Stain Glass Window (I)

Saint Francis of Assisi
Born 1182 Founder Franciscan Order
Baptised Giovanni-di-Bernandone
Father upset with mother & called him Francisco

Cross:	Humetty Cross/Swiss cross
Book:	Open or closed Reason for breaking Stain Glass Window
Rolls of Cloth:	Father Cloth Merchant
Stigmata:	Hands & Feet
Feather:	Not quill/Angel's Feather
Patron:	Birds and animals

"Thirty years ago I saw this window in the graduation hall, only it wasn't for graduations then, it was the old St Andrew's church, hence the name St. Andrew's Hall. The window you saw me looking at earlier on today, St. Francis of Assisi," he explained. "The red shield was a blazon, and the feather represented an angel and not as people might think a quill."

Paul at the sight of the feather remembered something his Mother had told him when he was a small boy. If ever he saw a feather floating in the breeze or resting gently on the back porch window, it was, she said, his guardian angel looking after him.

Marcus nudged Paul and said. "Are you listening to me?"

Paul brought back from his thoughts replied. "Sure, go on, feather, angels."

Marcus continued his explanation. "Or feathers from wings of birds as Francis of Assisi was the patron saint of birds and animals, but," he said quietly, as if the walls were listening. "The closed book is the important thing."

"Why? What's so special about a closed book is it because you can't read it?"

"No," said Marcus with a smile at his son's naivety. "The fact that it's closed represents a finished book."

Paul intrigued by what his father told him, questioned. "How do you know it's finished?"

"Because son! St. Francis of Assisi wasn't part of the triangle of the Benedictine."

"A triangle, I don't understand dad?"

"I'll explain all that later, but the fact is that I broke that window thirty years ago, just before I graduated, so no one would find out exactly what I knew and there was no closed book on the window then, and there shouldn't be one now. Someone is playing games with me Paul, but this time I'm going to win!" Then Marcus adeptly pushed his spectacles back on his nose and turned another page of his notebook.

CHAPTER 2

After making his excuses to the other tutors, Dean Graham slipped away from the basketball game that was in progress and exited the gymnasium, and followed the path to the car park. He walked over to his black Sedan, unlocked it and climbed in, turned the ignition key, engaged the gears and set off out of the car park. He didn't notice the small red VW pulling out at a safe distance behind him, he thought he was safe driving past the gatehouse, then on towards the village knowing what he needed and unable to get a supply on campus or in the laboratory. The village seemed the next best thing if he was to relieve Marcus Hoag of his notebook.

The only way of obtaining it was to catch him while his son Paul was called for the third basketball game, which he had arranged with the team coach and Marcus would be alone, the Dean knew exactly where he'd be and the notebook was the key.

When the Dean saw Dr. Hoag and Paul deep in conversation heading through the refectory towards Paul's room, Dean Graham left the tutors in the graduation hall and climbed the stairs, retrieving the key at the reception desk, unlocking the storeroom door and continuing up to the bell tower. He was hoping to spy on them in Paul's room with a small set of binoculars, but when he saw Marcus' son retrieve the notebook from the car, he returned downstairs and replaced the key under the library reception desk. The notebook contained almost everything Dean Graham needed to complete his last mission, and with a 100% success rate, he wasn't about to fail this one. He'd decided six months ago, that this would be his last mission, he was tired of secrecy and his plan was to finish this job and disappear to South America, and enjoy the spoils of his work, and he'd already legally acquired a 6,000 acre ranch in Argentina, and hopefully he would be there in a few weeks.

As Marcus turned the next page, Paul's interest was at an excitable high and he asked Marcus. "Which window is next dad? The cross looks like a Swiss flag on the, err, blazon."

"Patience son, patience, it's called a heraldic blazon."

"I've heard of St Francis, was he the one that hid the allies in Italy during the war?"

"How old are you son? Didn't you do history at junior school?"

"Why," replied Paul indignantly?

"St Francis of Assisi was born in 1182AD, so I hardly think he was around during the first or the Second World War. You've been watching too many movies."

Feeling a bit of a fool, Paul decided to listen and not ask any more questions.

"To answer your question about the cross, it's just a fancy of the stain glass designer, and it's called a 'humetty cross', he probably likes Swiss crosses and as you can see the surround is square, exactly like the Swiss flag. In heraldry the colour red on the blazon is classed as gules, and the scroll along the bottom displays the name of the Bearer of the Arms, but some blazon's are known as attributed arms or adopted arms."

Paul pointed out the word 'stigmata' and said. "Is that what I think it is?"

"What do you think it means Paul?"

"I guess when a person bleeds on his hands and feet, just like Jesus when he was nailed to the cross." Paul was stunned and couldn't believe what he had just said.

Marcus rescued his son's sanity and said. "It's quite common, and it happens to people all over the world, even in this day and age." Marcus changed tack to take Paul's mind off the stigmata and said. "His father was a cloth merchant and he was very unhappy with his wife, because she baptised Francis, Giovanni De Bernardon against his fathers will, so his father called him Francisco to spite her, but there are loads of little stories about Francis of Assisi."

"So why," asked Paul. "Is the heraldic blazon wrong?"

"Like I said before, the closed book on the blazon is wrong, and that tells me the people responsible for repairing this window had no idea what they were doing, either that or they wanted to bring my attention to this window, and this is their way of getting it." Marcus went quiet for a few minutes, but then said with annoyance in his voice. "Dean Graham mentioned the window being repaired thirty years ago, and me not paying the bill for it, the old bastard!"

Paul was about to ask another question, but thought better of it, but then hearing his father curse for the first time ever, made Paul a little uneasy. "Slow down dad, it's not that bad."

Marcus, realising his son was uncomfortable. "Sorry son, but the old hypocrite, he wasn't even there when I broke the window, so he couldn't know it was me, I don't understand his interest?" A thought occurred to Marcus, and he asked Paul. "Have you any idea if the window could have been repaired when they renovated the first floor."

Paul thought for a minute. "I don't know, but I know someone who will."

Marcus looked at his son knowingly, and in unison said. "Louise!" Paul, ready to go down stairs and look for the woman he dreams of every night, stopped as Marcus glanced out of the window and said. "Is her car a red VW?"

"Yes, how did you know?"

"She's driving out of the car park, now."

"Bang goes that idea, huh!"

"It only slows us down a little bit, and it's not important, if we can avoid the Dean for an hour or two we can go look at the other windows."

Marcus stood in the hallway waiting for Paul to lock his study room door, that done they both strode along the passageway and down the stairs of the large dormitory, then turned right under the small dormitory archway and left along the corridor, skirting past the Deanery and right again through the refectory.

Marcus watched as Paul grabbed a cold ham sandwich, which was starting to turn up at the corners, as he stuffed it into his mouth he almost choked as he grunted. "What? I'm hungry!"

They walked on through into St. Andrew's hallway leading to the entrance with the first three windows on their right of St Francis of Assisi, St Augustine of Hippo and St Scholastica of Plumbariola.

Marcus took the stairs one at a time, while Paul went past him taking them two at a time, but before they got to the first floor Marcus warned Paul. "Be careful son, if anyone is here, we're just looking, ok."

"Ok dad, but I think everyone's down in the gymnasium watching the basketball game, there are three exhibition games specially laid on for the visitors, and I'm playing in the third one." Paul made his way over to the left hand window and read the name across the scroll. "Saint Columbanus of Bobbio, it's beautiful, but what does it mean."

<u>4th Stain Glass Window (IV)</u>

Saint Columbanus of Bobbio
Born 543AD West Leinster Ireland
Book: Open.
Bottle: Miracle as he breathed in it (spoilt it).
Shamrock: Banished back to Ireland
Sun/Heart: Sun on his chest, holds his Rule in an Irish satchel next to his chest
Patron: Floods
Unexplained:

Marcus opened his notebook and proceeded to explain the next Saint's window.

"The shamrock is a dead giveaway, as he was Irish, and the bottle is in regards to the miracle he made when he breathed on a vat of beer being prepared for a Pagan festival, it became sour and was destroyed."

"Why did they send him back to Ireland?"

"I think it was something to do with Easter when he celebrated it and made the mistake of arguing with his superiors. He never actually returned to Ireland, because his ship hit a storm and they were driven back to shore, the captain took it as a spiritual sign and set all the monks free, but the Easter dispute continued for many years." Marcus turned another page and continued. "The cross at the top should be familiar to you."

Paul looked closer, and said with a blank expression on his face. "Enlighten me dad?"

Marcus was about to criticize his son again, but decided he'd had enough and instead he carried on with his explanations. "That cross is known in England as Saint John's Cross, or the Red Cross, Military Campaign Cross, German Iron Cross, and Regeneration Cross, there are too many to mention."

"Why Regeneration," asked Paul. "What does that mean?"

Marcus explained that the cross has eight points. "Eight symbolises regeneration for many religious ideas, and is the holistic number in Buddhism for the number of steps to end suffering. The number 8, like the symbol for infinity, is a never-ending line." Marcus then started to draw the number eight laid down, allowing Paul to understand what he meant by infinity.

"Tracing the shape of the 8 differs from the circle, square, triangle, in that the line crosses itself in the centre, this crossing symbolises death, but the line doesn't stop there, it carries on into a new life, just as the Christian Cross symbolises new life. The eight therefore represents life, death, and rebirth. In Christianity, because Christ rose from the grave eight days after entering Jerusalem, the number is associated with the rebirth of Christ and also Baptism, the spiritual rebirth of a person."

"Ok, am I right in thinking the Roman numerals have something to do with the black dots at the bottom of the window and in your notebook you have them under 'unexplained'?"

With a puzzled look and shaking his head, "I don't know son," confided Marcus. "I just don't know."

As Marcus recited all he knew to Paul, he was also writing in his notebook little facts he wanted to remember, because he could no longer rely on his memory, but his notebook would do that for him.

Paul was beginning to understand why his father was so fascinated by this heraldry thing, and he could feel himself being drawn into his world of secrecy.

"Let's take a picture of the windows," said Marcus. "I have a camera here somewhere." He promptly produced one of those inexpensive throwaways, with an inbuilt flash.

Paul said with surprise. "You came prepared."

"Of course I did." Marcus gently pushed his son out of the way. "Now move."

Paul stepped back, and taking the opportunity he walked between the other bookshelves to the next window, as he looked at the window, and read the name, his father came up quietly behind him. "The first stain glass window of the triangle, Saint Benedict of Montecassino."

Paul Commented. "The first closed book dad." Paul was about to ask his father what the heraldic blazon represented, but Marcus had walked away and was sitting down next to one of the computer tables with a faraway look on his face. Paul walked over and sat down next to him and said in sympathy. "It was that bad, eh dad?"

Marcus was remembering his time during World War II, when as a young Lieutenant standing in for his injured Captain, in charge of a platoon of soldiers not much older than himself; they were trapped at the bottom of Montecassino Hill. The allied bombs were dropping on the monastery above them and opposition sniper fire was picking them off one by one. The platoon sheltered in a small chapel with an unknown name, but it was a safe haven for a few hours, before they would eventually move up the valley and into Rome as the victors.

As Marcus' platoon climbed the hill, the last of the bombs had fallen and the Monastery was almost razed to the ground, the only things to survive were a large cross and, inset into an altar, a painting of a monk and nun sitting as if having a conversation. This was the last resting place of Saint Benedict and Saint Scholastica his twin sister. Marcus and the rest of the platoon that had survived, walked through the ruined devastation, stood and looked at the altar and couldn't help but be moved by the sheer luck that it was untouched.

Paul looking for words of comfort said to his father. "Are you ok dad, kind of lost you there for a minute?"

Marcus, hoping his son would never see such a nightmare, pulled his handkerchief out of his top pocket and quickly wiped his eyes then blew his nose and said with a tremor in his voice. "Come on son, I'll explain Saint Benedict's window and we can take a picture."

5th Stain Glass Window (V)

Saint Benedict of Montecassino
Born around 480 Norcia, Italy
Buried under Saint John the Baptist Chapel in Montecassino monastery

Book: Closed.
Cross: Plain Cross/Lily Cross
Chalice: Cracked goblet, design is designers fancy.
Book marks: Male & Female ⊕ & ⊗ Wife or Sister
Info: Twin sister Scholastica
Patron: Good Death
Unexplained:

● ●
 ●

They got up from the chairs next to the computers and walked back to the window with Saint Benedict's name on the scroll. Marcus said. "You remember I told you about open and closed books, well this is the first of the triangle of closed books. Saint Benedict finished his Regula Monachorum around C529–543AD and the book was copied that many times, the writer's were never sure what was the original book or a copy of a copy. The deacons would send copies to every corner of the uncivilised world hoping to convert all the pagans through missionaries."

Marcus flicked through the pages of his notebook and continued. "The cross on the blazon is a simple plain cross, a reflection of the Benedictine way of life, plain and simple, nothing fancy just living their daily lives quiet and peaceful."

"A bit like Yin and Yang?" said Paul.

"You're getting the idea now son, but Yin and Yang actually mean shady and sunny places."

"Like dark and light."

"Yes, you have to search your mind and try to go beyond the normal parameters." Marcus drew a picture for Paul of a full circle, one white half the other black with two small circles, also one white the other black, inserted inside each half.

"The Chinese call it the Tauitu; this symbol represents those two forces of dark, and light."

Looking at his notebook Marcus said. "If we take a look at the blazon's book marker with the plus and times symbols, the + similar to the regeneration symbol we spoke of earlier, and the x represents the cross of Saint Andrew, because it's believed that the apostle supposedly, told his executioners that he was not worthy to be crucified on the same cross style as Jesus, and persuaded them to crucify him on an altered cross."

Paul, trying to take in everything his father had explained asked. "So what do the two small circles on the blazon mean?"

"The circles represent male and female."

"I don't see it, how can two circles be male and female?"

"If you look closely on the blazon at the two circles on the ends of the book markers, they have a plus and cross symbol on them, here look I'll show you." Then Marcus drew yet another picture to help Paul understand.

"If you place a circle above the plus you have the female symbol and hand mirror of the Roman goddess Venus, now if I change the cross to an arrow, but move the arrow to the top, the circle changes to the male symbol a shield and spear of the Roman god Mars."

Paul had to sit down to try and take it all in and said. "It was so simple, I never saw it."

Marcus smiled at Paul. "That's because your mind wasn't looking for that sort of sign."

Paul pointed to the chalice in his father's notebook and said. "Ok I get it, but what about the cup?"

Marcus looked at his son with exhaustion on his face. "It's a chalice or goblet."

"Dad, a cup's a cup. Ok, a chalice, why's the chalice broken?"

"The crack occurred when Saint Benedict tried to correct the ways of a few wayward monks, as a result they made an attempt on his life with a goblet of poison, but Saint Benedict shattered the goblet with a 'miraculous' sign of the cross."

"You mean a miracle?"

"Yes, apparently there were quite a lot and they're listed in the Dialogues of Pope Gregory the Great. He was in actual fact a biographer. My personal opinion is, that it was Gregory and his personal deacons that lost the original monastic rule that Benedict wrote, and so he became his biographer to try and make amends or, to leave signs as to where he thought it could be found."

Paul wondering why he was patron of a good death said hesitantly. "I'm not sure I want to know what it means by a good death dad."

"Then I won't tell you, but I will say Benedict had a smile on his face when he passed away."

Paul heaved a sigh and continued. "Look dad, more Roman numerals and dots."

"Yes, they should be familiar to me, but I'm still not sure what they mean."

"I wonder why the windows were all blocked up, they're beautiful, and the guy who created them must have been a master craftsman. How old are they dad?"

"Well, in my time, I've seen stain glass windows date back to as early as sixth century. Now I'm not saying these windows are that old but at a guess, possibly around ninth or tenth century."

"Wow," said Paul with surprise. "You reckon they're that old?"

Marcus continued. "They were probably brought to America in the 17/18the century by the early Christian settlers who built St. Andrew's Church here in New York." Marcus pulled Paul's arm and continued. "Come on son let's have a look at the sixth window, which should be Saint Augustine of Canterbury."

They made their way round some more bookshelves, Paul walked in front of Marcus, and arriving at the next window saying with a frown. "You're wrong dad."

Marcus looked at the window and thought his heart was about to jump into his throat. "This is just superb; I always knew it would be in Latin."

"In Latin, dad I can't keep up with you."

"I'm not surprised son; I've only been doing this for 30 years."

"But you said Canterbury and the scroll reads Durovernum."

"Yes. In Roman times Durovernum was Canterbury, in actual fact its correct name was Durovernum Cantiacorum. Because of its links with Gaul, Durovernum survived in good order until the fall of the Roman Empire in Britain, and with the withdrawal of Roman troops to defend Rome against its enemies in Italy, Durovernum reverted back to Canterbury and the Saxons eventually took over that part of Kent."

<u>6th Stain Glass Window (VI)</u>

Saint Augustine of Durovernum Born 544 Rome
Book: Closed
Cross: 8 sided infinity Baptism, St Augustine Cross
Staff: Distinctive, no other like it.
Obelisk: Stands on Kent coast, footprint in clay
Chair: Or seat Latin for Cathedra (Cathedral)
Mitre: 1st Archbishop of England/Canterbury
Patron: England
Unexplained: ● ●
                ●

Paul intrigued, said to his father. "I can see the window has a closed book, so Saint Augustine must be part of the triangle."

"Yes son, he's the second Part. I already knew about Saint Augustine of Canterbury, but the Durovernum, well that's the interesting bit."

"Have you seen these windows before dad?"

Marcus opened his notebook to show Paul his sketches of the three windows they had just looked at. "I've seen illustrations of them, but nothing compares to seeing the real thing, and the illustrations are never complete, there's almost always something missing. With this window it was the name on the scroll."

Paul asked quizzically. "What about the other two we just looked at?"

Marcus flicked the pages of his notebook again and said. "Saint Columbanus, let me see."

Paul quickly pointed to the cross in the notebook. "The cross is missing."

Marcus turned the pages over until he came to Saint Benedict, and once again Paul spotted it. "The male and female circles with plus and times are missing."

Marcus with a pleased as punch smile on his face, looked at Paul. "That just proves my point son, there's no doubt you can't beat seeing the real thing."

Paul wanting to know everything yesterday asked Marcus. "Was Augustine British?"

"No son, he was born in Rome of upper class parents, he became a monk in his youth and rose to the challenge of becoming Prior of Saint Andrew on the Caelian Hill, in Rome. Gregory eventually sent him with forty other monks to Kent to establish a Christian church. You can see his unmistakable pastoral staff on the heraldic blazon."

"It look's like a wilted leek," said Paul as he narrowed his eyes.

Marcus looked closer and replied. "I can't deny, that's what it looks like, but I'm sure it's probably some type of flower."

Paul quickly quipped back. "Look dad, the cross, is that like Saint Columbanus?"

"Well yes but it's called the Saint Augustine cross. There's a wonderful story about Saint Augustine." Marcus proceeded to tell Paul about the Saint sailing by French ship to the coast of Kent. While the ship rested in the bay the small rowing boat brought him and his entourage to the beach. Augustine alighted from the boat in his bare feet, with one foot stepping on a piece of soft clay, it immediately made an imprint of his foot. The dignitaries who were waiting to meet Augustine all praised it as a great sign of impending success, and had the footprint taken to Canterbury and placed in the Cathedral for all converts to see.

Many years later a monument with a Saint Augustine cross was erected near the place where the Saint had stepped off the boat.

"Do you think the monument is still there dad?"

"Yes son Its still there, but it wasn't just the footprint that made Augustine such a success, he was also very popular with one of the Merovingian Kings, namely the pagan Ethelbert, who allowed him to settle and preach in Canterbury, and by the end of the year Augustine had converted him and his family. But more interesting is the fact that Augustine with a few more Bishops baptised 10,000 of the Kings subjects in what is now referred to as the "Miracle of Canterbury" or the Baptismal miracle of Canterbury. He was also the patron of England."

"I thought," said Paul curious. "That was St. George."

"It is St. George, but Augustine was an Archbishop and not a knight, he could do or say what he wanted in the 7th century, who was going to argue with him." Marcus turned around and walked back to the reception desk with the thought of the Saint Augustine cross in his mind and said to Paul, who had sat down at one of the tables, and about to ask his dad 'what do we do now' when Marcus said. "Can you see it?"

Paul thought Marcus had gone a little loopy in the head, as he repeated. "Can I see what? What am I looking at?"

Marcus stood on a chair next to the reception desk and spread his arms out wide towards Saint Benedict's window. "The whole room is laid out like Saint Augustine's cross. Now why would anyone do that?"

"Your right dad, I can see it now," but Paul didn't need a chair, he was tall enough to see how the bookshelves were laid out in a plus sign, with three computer tables set in each quarter of the cross. He repeated Marcus's statement. "Why would anyone do that?"

"It beats me," said Marcus as he stepped down from the chair and staring at the storeroom door, went over and tried the handle. "It's locked. Where's the key?"

"It's probably in the drawer, under the reception desk, but why would you want to go up into the storeroom, I think there's only spare tables and bookshelves up there."

Marcus quickly pointed out to Paul that someone else was up there earlier on in the day. "When we were in your room so who knows what's up there, but it's worth a look, don't you think?" Marcus then added. "How do you know there are only tables and bookshelves up there?"

"I saw the workmen when they finished the renovations, and that's where they took all the extra boxes of books."

"Look son, if we want to find the seventh window, we have to search everywhere, and it must be on Campus somewhere we can't just give up. So! Get the key and let's have a look."

Paul rummaged the reception drawer, picked up the storeroom key and also saw a letter with his father's name on it, he picked it up and closed the drawer, saying, "Dad, there's a letter addressed to you." Paul handed the letter with the key to Marcus. "I found it in the drawer."

"For me, why would anyone leave a letter in that drawer for me?"

"I think someone knew we'd be going into that drawer for the storeroom key, but get it open dad."

Marcus ripped open the envelope and read the contents:

Dr. Hoag, I must warn you not to stay on Campus too long.

Please stay away from Dean Graham; he is very dangerous and part of my investigations.

Once again Sir be very careful and try to complete your search of the seven windows quickly and quietly.

I also found a clue I don't think you have. Observe the Old Chapel statues.

A A E E U M L N N I U F D T S T R A L E U I G O P

Good Hunting Sir.

CHAPTER 3

As Louise climbed into her car, she was about to follow her assignment to the village, and hoped that Dr. Hoag would find the letter she'd left in the St. Andrew's library reception drawer next to the upper storeroom door key. Louise had waited for the Dean to exit the bell tower and quickly slipped into the library to leave the letter. She had also overheard Dean Graham's conversation earlier in the office with a young cocky female, but her assignment was to enrol as a temporary secretary and watch him. She had found out that the Dean was indeed a dangerous man to cross.

Louise had become an expert at undercover operations. When she was eighteen she enrolled at the Police Academy, her parents were not happy about it and said she wouldn't last the year out and their daughter would move on to another job. But Louise stuck it out and graduated almost top of her class. She was put on the beat with a few other rookies but almost quit because an over amorous police detective named Lou Quarry decided he wanted to put her through her paces at a police Halloween dance. He trapped her in one of the department offices then tried to fondle her breasts. She surprised herself on how easily she threw him to the ground and snapped his own handcuffs on his wrist and a radiator.

The next day she handed her badge and issue gun to the Captain, he then immediately threw them back at her, told her he couldn't afford to loose a rookie, something to do with Government and Commissioner policies and voting crap that Louise didn't understand and gave her a new beat, telling her to stay away from the offending detective and he'd have a word with him. She knew he wouldn't, but what the hell, the money was good, so she stuck it out. Eventually after a few years she made detective and, though she never saw much of the over sexed detective, she steered clear of him anyway.

After a few years under her belt as a detective, Louise went for intensive government training and was eventually spotted and allocated a place at the Federal Bureau of Investigation

(FBI) in the illegal immigration department, the work was complicated, but Louise's confidence was amazing, and she once or twice thought back to the over amorous detective Quarry, whom had retired from the force and was now a private investigator. Louise had kept a file on Quarry she liked to know where her enemies were and what they were doing, just in case of any eventualities.

This wasn't her first job in the field; she'd been very successful in catching, not the small immigrant who came into the country from over the border, but the undesirable ones. Like Dean Graham! Who came in and out of America as calm as you please on a fake passport, and each time he would use a different name, but his downfall, that was the easy part, he never changed his appearance. Now for a professional that was an arrogant mistake, especially with the new video gadgets at the airport.

If he'd only played the game and tipped the airport porter the Federal Agency would never have known of him, but each time he came through security the porter hoping that the guy would remember him and tip him extra, was always disappointed, eventually he complained to his superior who mentioned it to his superior and so on.

The tips the porters made were not part of their pay but it's an unbroken rule, that a customer always tips a good deed, even if it is part of the guy's job.

The call came through from La Guardia airport, and agent Louise Pendleton picked up the phone. She didn't think it was worth getting too excited about, so asked them to send her the tapes and she would have a look at them. After a few days the FedEx box dropped on her desk, for a moment she wondered who had sent it, and then the penny dropped. Of course, she thought, the non-tipper, oh my god what am I doing looking at these, this has got to be a wind up. Looking around the open plan office she watched her colleagues walking about, or sitting at their desks and tried to catch anyone looking at her knowingly, but they were all just getting on with their jobs, so she opened the box and peered inside, sure enough, the box was full of about fifteen tapes. Louise resealed the box and took it down to the TV/Video room and popped one of the tapes into the empty video.

After she'd had a good look at all the tapes, she wasn't sure what she had, so she decided to call the airport security and ask them to take notice of the guy's passport and record anything strange.

After a few months airport security had given her a list of five passports, the names and numbers were all different but the photo was the same on each passport and Louise had now been trailing him for six months, now there were too many players in the game and Dr. Hoag had to be gently warned about the Dean and how dangerous he is. She knew what Marcus was doing at the campus, apart from seeing his son graduate, and what he was looking for. She had picked out his file on the computer at the Bureau and decided he hadn't broken any law, and he was not in any immediate danger, so she decided to leave him an anonymous letter and sign it with a puzzle. She knew Dr. Hoag would solve it eventually. And the letter would also give him and Paul an edge to finding out all the clues he needed to keep abreast of the Dean, or whatever his name was.

As Marcus read the letter out loud to Paul, he could hear a garbled inter-com announcement. "This is Coach Farmer, will Paul Hoag please make his way to the gymnasium, he's required on the basketball team. This is Coach Farmer, Paul you're needed, the third games about to start." Paul looked at Marcus with a frown. "Oh no, I have to go dad, we'll have to do this later."

Marcus folding the letter and putting it back into the envelope, then slipping it into his pocket. "Go on, you can't keep the team waiting, I'll be ok, and in fact I might come and watch."

"You hate basketball."

"I don't hate it; I just don't like rules."

"You mean you don't understand them."

"I know what I mean, and I don't like rules, period."

Paul started laughing as he set off down the stairs and shouted. "Are you coming or staying here."

Marcus in two minds replied. "No son, I'm going down to the old chapel to have a look around."

Paul called back up the stairs, as he went down two at a time. "See you back here in about half an hour."

Marcus shouted back. "Ok son, I'll be here." Marcus went down the stairs a little slower than Paul and thinking to himself, 'So we have a triangle of players in the game.' He then entered the graduation hall, looked at the dais and thought to himself, no, you can wait until I check something out. Marcus made a detour through the refectory and left along the hall to the deanery, he wanted to use the secretary's computer.

He tried the door, it opened easily, and Marcus slipped in and closed the door quietly behind him, sat down on the swivel chair and switched the screen on. The computer beeped and the screen asked for a password. Marcus thought for a moment and entered: 'Good Hunting Sir'

The computer beeped again, and then the screen changed to a welcome page and asked the operator to enter their name:

'Dr. Marcus Hoag'. Another page came up and Marcus scanned the list and looking for a name, then said to himself. 'Ah there you are,' and read the name and contents:

GRAAM Johan:	M.ed. Master of Education
GRAHAM John:	F.H.S. Fellow of Heraldry Society
GRAM Jonah H:	Ph.D. Doctor of Philosophy
HAGHARM Jon:	M.Phil. Master of Philosophy
HOGANHAR M.J:	D.Th. Doctor of Theology

Marcus noted the second entry as he switched the printer on and pressed, "print", he thought. Who could he be working for, the Vatican maybe? No! Surely they wouldn't use someone like the Dean. Marcus turned the computer and printer off, picked up the printed sheet of paper, folded it, and slipped it into the envelope that had been left for him by agent Louise, and slipped out of the office.

When Marcus read the letter in the library, he recognised the puzzle immediately, it was the same code that Roman Generals used in the field of battle 2000 years ago to send messages back and forth between the Legions, and if the message fell into enemy hands they wouldn't be able to understand its contents. Marcus did an immediate calculation in his head and understood exactly what he had to do and the announcement sending Paul to the gymnasium was just the opportunity he needed.

He was just about to walk through into the refectory, when he heard a deep voice behind him. "Hoag, I've been looking for you."

"Ah! Dean," said Marcus a little taken by surprise, and hoping he hadn't seen him coming out of the office.

"Come through into the study; make yourself comfortable, it's a long time since we had a real chat. I must say that son of yours is a real godsend to Coach Farmer."

Marcus was about to say something, but the Dean cut him off. "It was a shame about your wife; Paul's the image of her. Don't you agree?"

Marcus, slightly taken by surprise, countered. "Of course I agree, but my wife's been dead for five years." Marcus was feeling a little uneasy and not understanding where the Dean was going with the mention of Alice.

"What is it you want Dean?"

The Dean turned to the drinks cabinet and offered Marcus a Jack Daniels Whisky, asking. "Is that with or without ice?"

Marcus looked at the whisky and thought. Just one, it won't hurt to have just one. He was just about to say 'on the rocks', when Louise walked through the office door.

"Hello Dr. Hoag, I've just seen Paul walking through the small quadrangle, I think he was looking for you. Isn't he wonderful, the campus lost the first two basketball games and then on comes Paul for the third game and they win?" Louise giggled as she put on her best act. "He's such a great all rounder, don't you think."

Marcus looked at the Dean and replied. "Thanks all the same Dean but I think I'll pass on that drink, better go see what that son of mine is up to." With that Marcus turned and gave Louise a 'thank you' wink and walked out of the Deanery.

Louise had followed Dean Graham at a distance to the village. He parked his car then entered the grocery store. She saw him walk out with something in a brown bag. Louise thought to herself, you only get alcohol in a small brown bag.

She waited until the Dean got back into his car and drove back to the university before she climbed out of her VW and walked over to the grocery store. Louise spoke to the woman behind the counter and the assistant told her that the Dean often came in, but that was the first time he had bought a bottle of Jack Daniels whisky. Louise thanked her, then bought some gum and walked back to her car, got in and drove back the way she came. When she got back to the university, Louise decided to call in at the gymnasium just as the third game was finishing. She slipped back out the rear of the gymnasium and walked along the road past the sports track. Just as she got to the Deanery window, she saw the Dean and Dr. Hoag talking. Now I know why the Dean wanted the whisky,' she thought, 'oh I hope I'm in time.

Louise Ran along the path and ducked under the rhododendron bushes, coming out at the side entrance to the lecturers hall of residence, entered the archway and skipped down the corridor and entered the deanery, just in time to see Dean Graham offer Dr. Hoag a whisky.

When Dr. Hoag had gone, the Dean's face looked like thunder, but Louise was just happy she'd stopped him getting Marcus drunk.

She sat down at her desk and was thinking of Paul and how good he looked in his shorts, when the Dean walked to the inner door and closed it. She again thought to herself. Well, at least I know where the Dean is and that should give Dr. Hoag plenty of time to do his investigating without any hindrance.

Dean Graham lifted the telephone off its cradle and dialled the same international number as he did earlier. The dialling codes clicked and buzzed again for a few seconds, but instead of a continuous echoing ring, all he got was a dull intermittent drone. Engaged, he thought then cursed. Where is the bitch?

Louise could hear laughing and people chatting; it was coming from the corridor, and then came a knock on the secretary's door. Louise called out. "Come in," and then thought, the arrival of the other students and families couldn't have been better timed if I'd arranged it myself. This would definitely keep the Dean busy. Louise got up from her chair, walked over to the Dean's inner door, knocked and walked in, then said with her shy smile. "Dean, you have visitors."

Marcus walked down the corridor and back through the refectory, then up the stairs to the library, he pulled the key out of his pocket and went straight to the storeroom door, unlocked it and climbed the stairs slowly, unsure what to expect.

Paul showered and changed in quick time, and walked out of the changing rooms. His friends called him back, but he wanted to catch up with his father and said he would see them later. As he walked away, Paul punched the air shouting, "losers!" His friends chased him to the rear door of the gymnasium all laughing, but no further then just waved to him, Paul waved back and carried on down the road past the running track, then diverted under the rhododendron bushes; the very same track Louise had taken earlier, but instead of following the left path under the archway, Paul turned right and entered Saint Andrew's Hall, passed the three stain glass windows and thought, I must ask dad about these other two windows, with a quick bound he jumped the stairs two at a time.

Marcus heard the noise on the stairs and expecting to see Paul bound up the next stairway, gave an unexpected sigh, and said. "Well hello there, what brings you up here?"

"This is my old alma mater as well you know, you don't have a monopoly."

Marcus looked at the reporter. "What year?"

Christine said. "A lady never divulges her age," but then she quickly said. "1950."

"See that was easy."

"It must be that silver tongue of yours Dr. Hoag."

"Marcus, please."

"Ok Marcus, but please my friends..."

Marcus interrupted her. "Your friends call you Chrissie, see I remember," and then he added suspiciously. "When were you planning on telling me how you knew my wife?"

"I'm sorry Dr. Hoag, I mean Marcus. I didn't mean to upset you, I would have told you earlier but the presentations went on a bit longer than I thought, and I had to get through interviewing a lot of students and heads of faculties." Chrissie then proceeded to explain that she and Alice had been roommates and all Alice talked about was this really great guy she had met. Marcus began to smile, thinking it was him she meant, but Chrissie said his name was John, John something.

"I don't believe it," she pondered with her hand across her forehead and feigning forgetfulness. "I can't remember his second name."

Marcus' face paled. "It wouldn't happen to be Graham would it?"

"Now you come to mention it, yes, it was."

Marcus sat down heavily on the crate of books. "Dean John Graham."

"His name is Graham," replied Chrissie. "But I didn't realise he was the Dean of this university, I thought it was Dean John Alexander."

"Then how come Dean Graham is here?"

Chrissie never got to answer Marcus' question; Paul came up the stairs and overheard their conversation. "She's right dad, Dean Graham is only standing in for a few days for Dean Alexander, I thought you knew that and you were both acquainted."

Chrissie quipped. "Old adversaries if you ask me Paul."

Paul looked at Chrissie with a far away recollection in his eyes. "I'm sorry but who are you again?"

Marcus introduced them both, and then said on a lighter note. "I heard you won your game?"

Paul looked at him strangely and Marcus winked. "I met Louise again earlier and she told me. I think she has a thing for you son." He then punched Paul on the shoulder and immediately regretted it when Paul blushed crimson.

"Dad, please you're embarrassing me."

Marcus glanced at Chrissie, but she had walked over to the back wall and deep in thought. He walked over to her and said softly. "You were telling me about Alice and John Graham."

Chrissie turned round and said just as softly. "What's John Graham doing here Marcus, it can't just be coincidence that Dean John Alexander's not here, and we three are."

Paul walked over and sat down on one of the crates and proceeded to tell them both how Dean Alexander had got himself run over by a hit and run driver, and was in hospital with a broken leg badly bruised ribs and a slight concussion. "That's why they called Dr. Graham to stand in, something to do with etiquette or token of respect."

Marcus prompted the correct address. "You mean deferential esteem Paul."

"It sounds too convenient Marcus."

"Yes, I agree." Marcus looked at Chrissie then hesitated. "You're not really a reporter are you?"

Chrissie was just about to vindicate herself when Paul quipped. "I'll vouch for her dad."

Marcus, with a curious look at his son allowed Paul to continue. "I think I saw you once or twice with mom when I was younger. I know you were her friend, because she spoke about you and I think you both went on holiday together.'

Chrissie a little hesitant at what she could or should reveal, simply replied. "That's right." She then looked at Marcus. "It was before you were married and had Paul."

Marcus, still curious and wanting an answer; "Paul said he saw you when he was younger, and you didn't answer me when I asked about Alice and John Graham."

Chrissie could sense the slight hostility in Marcus's voice, and decided to come clean about the real reason she was here, and to clear the air regards John Graham. "Dr. Hoag, Paul, you're probably not going to like what your about to hear, but here goes."

Paul and Marcus intrigued sat on the boxes again and listened while Chrissie walked back and forward, saying. "You remember I told you Alice and I were room mates, we graduated together, and she was seeing a John Graham, although I never met him I remember her telling me that she'd ended their relationship because she didn't trust him and he was always borrowing money from her. Six years later she met you Marcus and married, then she was pregnant, that's when she retired from her government job and wanted to bring up Paul and look after a husband she adored."

Marcus interrupted and asked. "What government job?" Chrissie replied, "Alice and I were investigators in an agency within the government, a bit like Internal Affairs, but we specialised in uncovering undesirables secrets and imputing them to a database, its all computerised now, but back then it was all leg work. That's why Paul thought she went on holiday, we were actually on assignments. When you got married we did the odd couple of days, usually in the area where we lived. That's why you didn't know about it and she couldn't divulge any information."

Marcus looking at Paul, but directing his question at Chrissie, asked. "How and why did she die?"

"That's why I'm here Marcus, I think she just got too close to John Graham's secrets and disappeared."

Marcus looked disdainfully at Chrissie, but then glanced at his son's pained expression. "I'm sorry Paul, but Chrissie's right, your Mother – she disappeared."

"I knew there was something not right," reflected Paul. "The funeral just felt all wrong, and the memorial it all happened too quickly."

Chrissie with sadness in her eyes said. "We had to make it look that way Paul, just in case she was still alive, for her safety."

"So you're saying mom could be alive, somewhere."

"Yes, we hope so."

Marcus said what Paul was thinking. "You hope so!"

"We don't know. She just disappeared without a trace. Marcus it's taken us a long time to pick Graham's trail and he is certainly an undesirable character." Chrissie began pacing up and down again, saying; "Louise and I are partners and we're trying to work out exactly what his next move will be. After Alice died sorry, presumed missing, I was assigned to a new agent just out of training college and Louise is a really good agent. I won't go into details of how we picked up his trail, just trust me we did, and if he tries to leave the country on his false passports, he will be picked up this time."

Marcus unable to believe his wife was alive, not after five years and no contact said calmly. "So what of Alice, how was she involved?"

"Alice was working on an assignment in the Boston public library, and she saw a guy she recognised, afterwards she told me it was John Graham, and went over to speak to him. She said he acted strange and told her she'd got the wrong person and then he just walked out of the library, leaving the antiques catalogue he was looking at on the table. Well Alice picked it up and she couldn't believe her eyes. John Graham had left a bookmarker in the page he was looking at, and the antique crown on that page was her assignment. You see three months before Alice disappeared, the same crown, a 6th Century Saxon Diadem headpiece had gone missing from the Verulam museum repair workshop in London. The crown reappeared two days later back in the repair workshop, as if nothing had happened. No one knew where or what happened in between the headpiece going missing, but the museum was just happy it turned up. British Intelligence curious, asked Interpol and of course American agencies to put some agents on the case."

"Was it checked for authenticity when they found the crown," asked Paul.

"Well, yes, that's what they can't understand. Why steal something, to put it straight back There's no logic."

"Hmm," Marcus sighed and then said. "But why was Alice involved?"

"Because Alice lived in the area that John Graham had been seen in, and he's kept his head down, until now! That's why Alice was in the library, she was observing the catalogues, and if anyone paid too much attention to them, she called me."

"So," said Paul. "Let me get this right."

"You and mom were investigating for the government.

Mom investigating alone, a Diadem missing.

Diadem possible fake.

Mom rings you when she saw John Graham.

She disappears.

John Graham disappears.

You and Louise working together as investigators."

Looking at Chrissie, Marcus said inquisitively. "No son you got the last one wrong. Louise is an F.B.I. agent, but Chrissie here is only an investigator. Am I right?"

"Yes Marcus, well done! But how did you know?"

Marcus fished in his pockets for the envelope Louise had left him, opened it and gave it to Chrissie, saying. "Louise left this downstairs in the reception drawer, and this!" Marcus gave her the printed sheet. "I got this off her computer in the office."

Paul questioned, while looking at the letter in Chrissie's hand. "I'd forgotten about that letter, the code at the bottom what's it mean dad?"

Chrissie unsure about the code either, waited for Marcus to explain.

"I guessed only a good F.B.I. agent would know and understand such codes. It's a 5 x 5 code. Look, I'll show you." Marcus wrote on the back of the letter. "The letters read five across and five deep."

```
A  A E E U
M  L N N I
U  F D T S
T  R A L E
U  I G O P
```

Paul intimated it was meaningless and said so. "It makes no sense."

Marcus turned to his son with exasperation across his face. "What did I tell you before about opening your mind?"

Paul tried to concentrate and after a few minutes, smiled and said. "I got it! If I read down the first column A MUTU and then the second column AL FRI third next END LO. Paul decided to read the complete message A MUTUAL FRIEND AGENT LOUISE P." Paul looked at Chrissie. "What does P stand for?"

"Pendleton, Louise Pendleton."

Paul looked at Marcus and said. "How did you know the password was 'Good Hunting Sir'?"

"That was an educated guess son."

Paul asked Chrissie. "What's on the rest of the sheet of paper?" Chrissie looked at the printed sheet and Marcus interrupted her again. "They're all aliases of John Graham."

Paul added. "Dad they're also all anagrams."

Chrissie said mockingly. "He's getting good, this son of yours. As I was saying, Louise and I were both assigned to find out the connection, if there was one between all three situations, the Diadem headpiece, Alice's disappearance, and John Graham's aliases."

Marcus didn't want to ask the question, but knew he had to. "When did she last contact you?"

Chrissie hesitated at the unexpected question, and said quietly. "She called me when she recognised John Graham in the Boston library."

Paul quickly working it out said. "Five years and three months."

Marcus instantly feeling subdued leaned on one of the bookcases, but glanced up at Chrissie and bemoaned. "Alice didn't just disappear, Chrissie, she's dead because our relationship had already begun to disintegrate and if she didn't want to contact me; she would have contacted you or Paul." As Marcus spoke the bookcases suddenly slipped forward, then the whole pile of them came falling forward and Marcus shouted. "Look out!"

Chrissie and Paul jumped back and just escaped serious injury, while Marcus was looking at the door that had been revealed by the falling bookcases. All three just looked at the door, wide eyed and mouths gaping open when Paul said. "Where on earth did that door come from?"

Marcus turned the door handle. "It's locked!"

"Try the key dad."

"I left it in the door downstairs."

"Ok, I'll get it." Paul quickly made his way around the fallen bookshelves and hurried downstairs to retrieve the key.

Marcus looked at Chrissie and said with a frown. "Five years, she can't possibly be still alive?"

"Part of me hopes she's alive, but I try to be realistic. What worries me most is she's made no contact in all that time. I have a feeling it's all connected to you and the seven windows you're looking for."

Marcus looked at her a little sheepish and said. "There aren't seven windows."

"But I thought that was what you were looking for?" Chrissie made a slip of the tongue and revealed. "Your profile said you've been searching for seven stain glass windows for years." Looking guilty, Chrissie realised she'd unwittingly given vital government information away.

Marcus admonished her as he quickly picking up on her mistake. "Well, well! If I were a British secret agent I'd have to shoot you for giving vital information away."

Chrissie instantly blushed and countered. "So shoot me."

"Shoot who?" asked Paul as he returned with the key.

"Just a figure of speech son, try the key."

Paul climbed over the bookcases again, inserted the key, and turned it. *Clunk*! The door opened, revealing a small dark room with a bookcase across the doorway and more cases of books stacked three high. "It's just a small storeroom dad."

To the right of the door Paul noticed a light switch, clicked it up and down. "The light bulb's blown."

Marcus quickly asked if anyone had a torch and Chrissie rummaged in her shoulder bag and produced a small penlight. "Will this do?"

Marcus said with narrowed eyes. "I bet you were a great girl guide?"

Chrissie pleased she was almost forgiven for the earlier revelation quipped back. "I'm always prepared for eventualities."

Marcus tried to move further into the small storeroom and said to Paul. "You could be right; I think there are only crates of books here. Give me a hand with this bookcase."

They both pushed it to the sidewall, and Chrissie asked. "Why are there no windows?"

Paul and Marcus looked at each other and both begun to lift the boxes down and place them on the other side of the door, giving Marcus room to walk along the opposite wall.

Marcus started tapping the wall from the left corner working his way along and only getting a dull sound. He got half way and the dull sound changed to a hollow sound. "Bingo!" Marcus shouted and then asked. "Give me something sharp, a pen, or a nail file, anything."

Chrissie took the penlight from Marcus and twisted it, revealing a small solid pointed knife. She gave it back to Marcus and he said. "Your full of surprises, aren't you?"

"It's for emergencies, standard issue."

Marcus took the knife and with help from Paul they managed to strip away most of the rough plaster to reveal another stain glass window, but this one was bricked up on the outside.

Marcus stepped back to get a better view and almost fell over onto one of the crates, but Paul and Chrissie reached out and caught him. All three looked at the window and Chrissie said with annoyance in her voice. "I thought you said there were only six windows?"

"No. I didn't."

"Yes. I distinctly remember you saying 'there aren't seven windows'."

Marcus with a smile on his face looked at the window and said. "There aren't seven windows. There are eight."

"Wow! Dad this one has got to be the best, it's fabulous, and the colour is just amazing. Why wasn't this window opened up, like the others?"

"My guess is they didn't know it was here son."

"And that's why your here Marcus to solve the mystery of these windows," quipped Chrissie, but then glanced up at Paul, "And also to see this young man graduate."

Marcus, half listening to Chrissie, was retrieving his notebook from his pocket, opened it and started writing furiously, handed Paul the small camera and said. "Take a picture son."

Just as Paul took a picture of the seventh window, he could hear a feint buzz, coming from Chrissie's shoulder bag. Chrissie opened her bag and extracted a small cell pager, read the message. "It's from Louise."

'Unable to contain Dean JG for much longer LP'

"Marcus we must get out of here, hurry!" With those words of wisdom, all three quickly restacked the crates, exited the small storeroom, locked the door, and started to restack the bookcases to almost the position they were in and hurried down the stairway. Marcus locked the door, but instead of replacing the key in the reception drawer, slipped it into his jacket pocket.

They all managed to arrive at the downstairs entrance to St Andrew's Hall, as Louise came running through the archway and into the entrance. Flustered, she called Chrissie to her. "Did you get my message?"

"Yes. Where's Dean Graham?"

"He left the deanery after the students and their family left and then went down to the science block library. But I know he'll make his way up here eventually." Then Louise's tone changed and she looked at Marcus. "Dr. Hoag, if John Graham doesn't get what he knows you're looking for, you know how dangerous he can be?"

Marcus looked around and said conspiratorially. "Come on, this way."

They all headed into the graduation hall and followed Marcus up on to and across the dais to the back wall. Marcus dropped down behind the raised platform and whispered. "Be careful when you climb down it's a bit of a squeeze." Marcus happily assisted Chrissie down from the dais and Paul was blissfully aware of Louise's curves as he lifted her down. Within a few minutes they were all behind the platform and hidden from view. Marcus with a quick tap of his knuckles released the mechanism, which allowed the low dais panelling to slide back.

Dean Graham sat making small talk and thinking, I'm only here for a few days, and I hate having to be nice to the boring students and their families. The Dean felt it was an absolute waste of time, he hated the pretence, but if he wanted to complete his last mission he'd just have to comply with his employer's instructions.

Mr Fulton, one of the students father stood up and shook the Deans hand saying with sincerity. "We've enjoyed the visit immensely; thank you Dean and a cheque will be in the post to help with the renovations for the new sports hall."

The Dean stood up and walked to the inner door, opened it and held it open for the visitors saying in a pleasant voice. "I've an appointment in the science library; I'll walk down with you as far as the car park."

As they all filed past Louise, she said goodbye, but before the Dean followed them out he turned and said. "If you want Louise, you can go home now; I don't think the campus will need you again today."

Louise replied. "Thank you Dean, It was a pleasure to meet you."

After the outer door closed behind the Dean, Louise quickly sent Chrissie a message on her small pager, then stood up from her chair and checked to see if anyone was still loitering in the hallway, all clear.

Her telephone had rung twice, and knowing whom it was from, she pressed the mute button and kept it on hold then waited until the visitors and the Dean had gone before she answered it.

"Hello."

"Louise, this is Jack McClellan, I have the information you wanted. The call came through around noon."

"Hi Jack, ok I'm ready."

"She's supposedly in London somewhere and we also received a wedding ring with an inscription inside: *'Alice & Marcus'* and the ransom are the lost Saint Benedict's Monastic Regula Monachorum. I haven't a clue what that is, but the clock is ticking and they want it within three days. Good luck Louise."

"Thanks Jack, I owe you one." Louise put the phone down, got up from her swivel chair, and grabbed her bag, closing the door behind her she ran down the corridor, under the archway and across the gravel path into St. Andrew's hall.

CHAPTER 4

Underground tunnel

Marcus followed by Chrissie led the way through the narrow secret panelling under the dais, then Louise entered and bringing up the rear, Paul. As Marcus' son came through last he closed the secret panelling and plunged everyone into eerie darkness. Chrissie had changed the penknife back to a torch and handed it to Marcus who switched it on and began to descend.

As the water dripped from the ceiling making the steep stone steps extremely precarious, it took almost five minutes to reach the bottom of the underground tunnel. Marcus started swinging the torch back and forward, as if looking for something on the stone floor.

"Ah! There they are." He knelt down and reached into a small recess and lifted out two lamps full of oil. Marcus reached in his trouser pocket and pulled out a strip of matches, tore one off and struck it on the abrasive strip and lit the oil lamp, then handed one to his son.

"Why do I keep getting the feeling you've been here before dad?"

"That's because I have son, I found this tunnel on my first semester here, and if you remember I told you the graduation hall used to be a church, well the dais was transformed from an altar. I'm not sure how old this tunnel is but I reckon it could be well over a century old, it was probably used for smuggling contraband, and such like."

Paul was amazed at Marcus's knowledge and thought, I'm his son, but I don't know if I'll ever be as adventurous as him.

Marcus tapped Paul on his arm as if he could read his thoughts and said. "Don't worry son, it takes years of training to do what I do, and be successful. You'll learn eventually. I came here just under a year ago, when I dropped you off at the start of the semester, and came down here and left the lamps and a few other items, just in case I found the windows."

Chrissie said with a shiver. "Well I'm sure glad you did, but it's a pity you didn't leave a few warm jackets down here, I'm frozen."

Marcus edged a few feet further up the tunnel and reached into another recess and pulled out a canvas bag, unzipped it and pulled out a couple of jumpers and said. "They might be a little bit musty but they should keep you warm." Then he handed Louise and Chrissie a jumper each.

"Where does this tunnel lead to?" asked Paul.

Marcus, Chrissie, and Louise, as if in a Barber Quartet, together, said in unison. "The old chapel," they looked at each other and began to laugh, but realised the seriousness of the situation and staid their mirth. Marcus lifted both his arms and spread his fingers wide and whispered. "Shh! Quiet! Let's get moving."

The tunnel walls were smooth and the ceiling was just high enough to allow Paul not to stoop. The floor was giving Louise a few problems because of the high heels she was wearing but Paul said. "Lean on me and I'll balance you."

Louise put her right arm around his waist, and Paul could feel her breast next to his ribs, but for the first time since he'd known her, he didn't blush or feel inadequate, it just felt good and then they moved on and followed Marcus and Chrissie along the tunnel, until they came to a right turning. Marcus said as he turned and addressed his followers. "Be careful there's a small rock fall, but we should be able to climb over if we go steady and there might be a drop of water." They walked on until they came to a crossroad.

"Marcus, which way?" asked Chrissie.

"We go left here. Straight on and right only lead to more steps, but no exit." They turned left and carried on until coming to another right turn. Marcus a little concerned said. "The walls have been constricted and it'll be a tight squeeze, but we should be able to wriggle through, just watch where you step, there's a lot of rubble strewn about that wasn't here before."

Marcus went through first, but Chrissie was beginning to feel the pangs of fear and her breathing began to quicken. All of a sudden she started to choke and squealed. "I can't breathe, Marcus I can't breathe."

"Come on Chrissie, calm down keep calm." Marcus put his arms around Chrissie and pulled her away from the enclosed space. "Listen to me, keep calm your ok, I'm here." For the first time in years, Marcus had put his arms around a woman and it felt good.

Paul and Louise came through the constricted area unscathed, and with concern in her voice Louise appealed to Marcus. "We have to get her out of here sir, this always happens when we're in these situations."

"Are you ok now Chrissie?" Chrissie a little worse for wear just nodded and held Marcus's hand.

The foursome moved on to another left hand turning, but when they arrived, they all stood and looked at the water lapping the edges of the passageway. Paul griped good-humouredly. "Come on I can carry you all through, one at a time."

He slipped his trainers and socks off and handed them to Marcus. While Marcus held them at arms length and tweaked his nose with his thumb and forefinger Paul rolled his trousers up to the knees, then picked Louise up in a vice like grip and carried her through the knee deep water. Louise clung to him with her arms around his neck, and thought to herself; oh this feels wonderful, just to be close to him.

Paul waded through the water and round the left bend; he carried on until the water got shallow and back on dry stone. Paul put Louise down and gave her the Lamp saying. "I won't be long." Squeezed her hand then waded back into the water. He then crouched down and gave Chrissie a piggyback ride through the water and deposited her onto the dry stone floor. "You ok now Chrissie?"

"I'm fine now, I just don't like confined spaces lad."

Paul went back for Marcus, but when he got there his father was using his hanky and wiping his eyes. "The fumes from the oil lamp were affecting my eyes."

"Come on dad, let's get out of here." Paul squatted down to let Marcus climb onto his back, stood up and waded back through the water. "Is the exit much further?"

"No son, just around the next right bend."

Louise and Chrissie had walked on towards the next right hand corner, but couldn't go any further and waited for the others.

Marcus and Paul came up behind the two women and looked at the rockslide. "Come on Paul," said Marcus. "Let's shift some of the smaller rocks, they're not too heavy, and then we can climb over the rest." They set to and after ten minutes they had cleared a small path next to the wall, just enough room for them to walk single file following each other.

Marcus taking Chrissie's hand and Paul taking Louise's, they arrived at the bottom of another set of steps and began to climb upwards.

Dean Graham left the visitors in the car park and entered the science library thinking aloud. "There is no way I'm going to get Hoag's notebook the easy way so it'll have to be the hard way, and I guess I need a little help." The Dean walked over to the many cupboards on the far wall, unlocked one with a key that was fastened to his car keys, opened it and lifted out a small leather holdall, unzipped it and pulled out a Nagant M1895 revolver wrapped in wax paper, plus a silencer and a box of 7.5mm calibre bullets. He attached the tiny silencer to the gun and slipped it into his deep inside jacket pocket, then placed the bullets into each of his side pockets, pushed the wax paper back into the holdall and replaced the bag, locked the cupboard then walked out of the building, crossed the car park and headed for the graduation hall.

Along the road past the sports ground he saw more students and their families heading back from another part of the university, and decided to go straight up the steps and on through the large archway, past the memorial seats and enter the deanery from the quadrangle. Dean Graham walked through the secretary's office and into his temporary office, picked up the telephone, and dialled the number again. This time he got through.

Gabby answered the telephone, and knowing whom it was, said. "He's been waiting for your call." She then passed it to the man standing next to her.

"Where have you been, we've already issued our ultimatum. Have you got the notebook?"

Dean Graham feeling agitated and annoyed with himself said. "It's not that easy, there are too many people on Campus, I can't go up to him and ask nicely for it."

"We're on a time limit here. Do you think he knows about the ransom and his wife yet?"

"Its hard to say, she's had plenty of time to tell him, and I'm sure he thinks Alice is dead, but to find out she could be alive, he'll move quickly. They've seen the other windows and once he's solved the puzzle he'll probably leave the States and head for England and I'll be right behind him."

"Remember three days, and there's a bonus for this, provided I'm not involved." The phone went dead.

John Graham remembering what happened just over thirty years ago stood stony faced, he would like to say that he'd hated Alice Connor, but he didn't, when she told him she didn't want to see him again after finding out about all his lies and wouldn't give him any more money. After all, it wasn't as if she couldn't afford it, her family were rich, her father was a millionaire twenty times over and her mother came from a well to do family, so what was her problem, she wouldn't miss a few thousand dollars. But Alice had her principles and said 'no more money'. He could see her now, five years ago, standing in the Boston library convinced he was who she thought he was. He just walked away from her but didn't realise she had picked up the catalogue he was reading until ten minutes later, when he remembered he'd left it open on the table, decided to return, and that's when he saw her in a phone booth with the catalogue in one hand and the telephone in the other. He thought he'd have to do something. When Alice replaced the receiver, John Graham was standing in front of her. He could see she was nervous and didn't expect to see him again, he told her he did remember her and asked if she would like to have lunch. To his amazement, she accepted. He thought he would have to cajole or flatter her, but it was easy, she probably thought she could get some information out of me. "Huh dumb beautiful broad!"

He took her to lunch and knowing she couldn't hold her alcohol, slipped a few gins into each glass of red wine, then they returned to his apartment in town. Alice made her excuses and asked where the bathroom was, as she entered he followed her and closed the door, pulling her to him he held her hands behind her back then forced a smothering kiss, it was rather nice, he arrogantly thought. She tried to push him away but he grabbed her neck with his free hand, and his other hand held both her small slim hands tight behind her back. Unable to breathe she kicked and tried to resist, but eventually her last breath was taken from her and she went limp. John Graham cradled her dead body in his arms and thought, why did it have to be this way, why couldn't you have just loved me Alice.

The same evening no one saw him wheeling a large suitcase by its extendable handle out to the car park, it was too simple. He buried her somewhere in a forest under an outcrop of rocks, miles away from civilisation.

Dean Graham, with a pained frown, replaced the receiver on its cradle, turned and walked out of the Deanery, muttering. "Where the devil have they gone?" Just then Paul's friends from the gymnasium came round the corner. "Good afternoon sir."

"I'm looking for young Hoag."

"He went to meet his father upstairs in the new library sir."

The Dean walked past them without another word, and entered St. Andrew's hall from the archway, then headed up the stairs. Finding only one or two students with their parents in the library he went over to the reception desk to retrieve the storeroom key. He rummaged in the drawer, but finding no key, went over and tried the door just in case they were actually up there now. The door was locked. Dean Graham descended the stairs then headed left out of the graduation hall and under the bushes, then left again to search the rest of the campus.

Old Chapel University Grounds

The stone steps were slippery, if it hadn't been for the fact that Marcus had a firm grip of Chrissie's hand she would have ended up at the bottom of the steps with a few broken bones, she knew she was a little over weight and tried to shed a few pounds by various diets, but try as she did it wouldn't budge, she felt she wasn't meant to be thin and gave up.

They eventually arrived at the top and Marcus put his finger to his lips then mouthed silently. "Keep still and quiet." He went on ahead until he couldn't go any further, doused the oil lamp, and set it down on the stone floor. With this trap door Marcus had to crouch down and crawl on hands and knees for about two metres because the ceiling dropped to waist height. Once he was facing the panel above him he quietly released the catch and the wood floor panel slid back.

Marcus waited and listened for movement or voices, hearing neither he pulled up and looked over the top of the chapel altar; again there wasn't a sight or sound of anyone. He dropped back down and whispered an audible order. "Quickly, come on Paul; let's get Louise and Chrissie out first."

Once they were all out of the tunnel and beyond the brass altar barrier Louise and Chrissie both slipped the jumpers off and gave them to Marcus, he quickly threw them down into the tunnel, but left the wood panel open. If Marcus closed the panel he wouldn't be able to open it again, it was a one-way catch and could only be opened from the tunnel side, feeling sure nobody would be getting that close to the altar, he decided to leave it open. Marcus looking at Louise and thought, in her note she said to observe the statues.

"Louise," said Marcus. "Your note, what did you mean, about the statues?"

"I read a little bit about Saint Augustine up in the new library, and he had a closed book on his window but on the statue this book has letters on it. I don't know what the connection is, but I thought it might help you."

Marcus thought for a minute, then reached for his notebook, opened it up at Saint Benedict's page, but couldn't find the reference he wanted, turned a few more pages and came to Saint Paulinus of Eboracum's page and said. "Yes here it is, C.S.P.B. its Latin: Crux s. Patris Benedicti (The Cross of our holy Father Benedict)."

"What about the other letters, are they Latin also?"

"Yes Louise, the C.S.S.M.L.N.D.S.M.D., is actually what is called a rhythmic Latin prayer: Crux sacra sit midi lux! Nunquam Draco sits midi dux!"

Paul hearing the word 'Draco' expressed concern, "'Draco' as in Dracula?"

"No Paul, Draco in Latin doesn't mean Dracula the translation reads. May the holy cross be my light! May the dragon never be my guide?" Paul with relief in his voice said. "Don't do that to me dad, its bad enough having to trail through a dark and dank tunnel but vampires, no thanks."

Marcus looked at his son quizzically. "Dracula, Vampires?"

Chrissie quickly quipped. "Ooh my!"

Marcus started to laugh at Chrissie. "Don't you start, will someone please explain to my son who Bram Stoker is."

Louise volunteered, taking Paul's hand and pulling him past the confessional box and up the stairs to the bell tower saying. "We'll keep a look out for Dean Graham."

"Good idea Louise," said Marcus.

As Paul and Louise disappeared up the stairway Chrissie intimated. "She's smitten with him Marcus."

"Yes, He needs a good woman with brains. He's just graduated, but still in nappies."

Now it was Chrissie's turn to smile and she said. "If the situation wasn't so serious, I'd want to laugh at the both of you."

"I haven't seen that much of him since Alice, you know, but it's not that I didn't want to. I just felt it would be easier for him if I weren't around. Always telling him what to do, not allowing him to grow up and make his own mistakes in life."

"I understand, but he's your son Marcus not someone else's."

"Come on Chrissie lets investigate the back rooms." He opened the left hand door next to the bell tower stairway and held it open for Chrissie to go through first.

As they walked into a small hallway Marcus explained the left backroom door was a changing room for priest's that were taking the church service and confessional. Marcus followed Chrissie into the changing room, and had a look around, they even tried tapping the walls, but there was nothing out of place in this room, so they moved to the next door, which was the second or middle bell room door. Chrissie said with surprise. "I forgot they used bell ropes, It's quaint, but there's not much room, is there!"

"You can say that again," said Marcus with a frown. "Once you and I get in here there's no room for anyone else."

Chrissie pushed Marcus out of the way with her finger, and about to walk out of the tiny room but quickly quipped. "Well! You're a cheeky old devil!"

Marcus grabbed her hand and pulled her back into the room. "I could sue you for assault on my person and defamation of character."

Just as Marcus touched her Chrissie almost blushed, but pulled herself together and again quipped. "I'll counter sue, that's my hand you're squeezing."

Marcus let go her hand. "Let's have a look at the last room which is the changing room for the choir." Both made their way to the third door.

"Marcus, the only thing different in this room is the wood panelling."

Marcus walked around the room, tapping the walls and again finding nothing out of place, suggested they have a look at the statues again. Chrissie hung back. "I'll be with you in a minute, I want to check something."

Marcus walked through into the church from the small hallway then made his way over to the statue in the corner next to the altar, but all he could see was the Saint standing on a white marble cross of Saint Andrew, then checking the scroll and finding nothing else walked over to one of the pews and sat down. Once more Marcus' mind returned to the book he'd read as a young student.

Monastery Montecassino C524 – 543AD

The old Abbot finished eating and swallowed the last of his goblet of wine, turned around and walked back to his writing desk, sat down and picked up his quill, dipped it into the ink but paused a moment and thought, this is the last few words I write before Romanus and I leave for Rome. With a weary look on his face, he finished writing the dedication for his Regula

Monachorum. The writings were to change the thinking and teachings of the future western monastic world.

The ringing of a bell sounded in the monastery, and the same monk who served Benedict his noon lunch answered the bell. At the gate he could see three elderly nuns all dressed in grey cowls drawn in at the waist by cords of cloth, and dark grey wimples, he immediately recognised one as the Abbot's twin sister.

Where Benedict was tall, the nun was small and petite, but she had the same long slim face, long slender fingers and her eyes were the same watery blue as the Abbots.

The monk new she was coming, but usually visited the second week of April and this was only February. Scholastica came to the monastery once a year and always in the same spring week, so he wondered what had brought her so early.

"Scholastica," Romanus said with a smile. "What a pleasant surprise, I trust you had an uneventful journey."

"I wish to see my brother," she said softly. "I have something special to tell him."

Romanus thought for a moment, he had a dilemma. His master would not want to be disturbed from his writings and prayers again so soon, but then again, she was his sister and she had travelled a long way. He made a decision.

"Please come through, you can wait in the cloister."

She followed him up the steep path and into a high cloister with small marble seats, the cloister was where Benedict had made a few modifications to the great entrance, it was cool in the heat of the day and warm in the balmy evenings, and allowed visitors to rest after their long walk up the steep incline to the monastery.

As they walked, the priest told her of the Abbots impending visit to Rome. "He is so not looking forward to going, but of course you know he doesn't like to travel too far from the monastery and his writings."

"To Rome!" she said with surprise. "Why to Rome? Has the grand master called him? Is there something wrong? Is he to leave the monastery?"

"No, no," Romanus said quickly, trying to calm her down. "The master will tell you all about it when he comes out of prayers, please, make yourself comfortable, he shouldn't be too long, and I'll bring you some refreshments while you wait."

"Thank you Romanus," she pointed to her sister nuns and said. "We've had a long trek from the convent."

At the mention of prayers the nun seemed happy to sit and wait for Romanus to fetch her brother. She bowed her head as if saying her own prayers, and knowing she could never show her excitement to the monk, but in reality, she could hardly contain herself to tell her brother the wonderful news.

She had been ordained the Abbess of Plumbariola. The very first Benedictine convent, the same convent Benedict lived at the bottom of the Rocks of Subiaco, and of course to grill him about why he was going to Rome.

Old Chapel University Grounds

Paul allowed himself to be led up the bell tower steps by Louise and had to keep his thoughts and emotions in check, there was a big difference between helping Louise in the tunnel and her wiggling her bottom in front of him while she preceded him up the stairway. As they reached the top and entered the bell tower through the tiny doorway, Louise said innocently. "Come here and I'll tell you about Bram Stoker."

Paul feeling brave replied. "Never mind Bram what's his name," and promptly threw his arms around her tiny frame and pulled her to him, and of course she responded by putting her arms around his neck kissing him lightly, but Paul was having none of it. Holding her tight he pressed his mouth harder kissing her soft lips, and Louise didn't pull away.

They were still embracing when Chrissie, shouted up through the holes in the ceiling where the ropes came through. "How much room have you two got up there?"

Paul called back softly. "We've all the room in the world."

"I'm coming up." Shouted Chrissie again, as she walked through from the hallway into the church and asked Marcus to go back into the room with the bell ropes and she would explain when she got upstairs.

Chrissie climbed the stairway and entered the bell tower. Ignoring both Louise and Paul, and seeing what she wanted to see shouted down to Marcus. "There's plenty of room for the both of us up here Marcus."

Louise and Paul thinking, she's gone crazy. Puzzled, Louise replied. "It's her age."

Paul smiled but wanting to know what Chrissie really meant. "Ok, so there's plenty of room up here!"

Marcus sounding excited shouted up. "Get down here all of you, Chrissie is on to something."

Once they were all downstairs and standing in the small room with the bell ropes dangling next to them, Paul said as he put his arm around Louise. "It's a bit of a squeeze?"

Louise snuggled up to Paul. "It suits me fine."

"Exactly!" said Chrissie. "There's loads of room up in the bell Tower but down here it's a tight squeeze, something's not right?"

Marcus nodding in agreement turned and quickly exited the small room. "Come on let's check out the Priest's changing room again." They all turned right and trooped into the room next door, but again finding nothing paraded out and along the hallway into the other changing room, searching for something different.

It was Paul who spotted it first. "The wood panelling, there's none in the other room. That must be it."

Marcus going straight over to the panelled wall, started tapping from left to right, but finding nothing amiss, stepped back and studied the wall saying. "Chrissie and me, we checked this room earlier, but there has to be a reason why one room is panelled and the other isn't."

Paul stood back and scanned his green eyes upwards. "This is the choir changing room, right, well choir boys are usually small and boisterous, and if we are looking for a possible secret door or sliding panel it would have to be high up." Paul began tapping the panels higher than Marcus could reach.

"That one sounded a bit hollow dad."

"It certainly did Son, hit it a bit harder."

Paul used his fist and the wood panelling disappeared inside the secret cupboard. Paul felt around inside and finding a catch, released it and the lower panel swung inwards.

"Well done lad," said Marcus proudly. As he entered the tiny space he stretching his hand out to Paul saying. "The camera, give me the camera."

While Marcus was busy scribbling in his notebook, Paul finding the camera climbed into the tiny room and took a photo of the last stain glass window, speechless at its beauty he stepped out of the tiny room and walked out of the changing room with Louise following behind, he was utterly moved at what he had seen.

Marcus swung the top panel shut and closed the lower panel door, hearing it click into place he stepped back once again and said to Chrissie. "It's beautiful, perfectly beautiful!"

Chrissie pulling Marcus' arm said quickly. "Come on Marcus I think we should get out of here."

Marcus nodded in agreement and they both walked out of the room and into the church, and seeing Paul running back from the front entrance, whispering loudly. "Dean Graham is walking this way; he'll be here in a few minutes."

"Come on everyone," whispered Marcus. "Get back into the tunnel." They all hurried past the statue of Saint Augustine and down the middle of the aisle passing the wooden pews with small cushions placed at intervals, climbing over the brass barrier and disappearing behind the high altar. Paul went first then Louise and next came Chrissie, but not too happy at her skirt being pulled up around her thighs. Marcus brought up the rear, but couldn't help bobbing his head back up just to see Dean Graham's face and knowing he was way ahead of him.

CHAPTER 5

Old Chapel

Dean Graham walked through the ancient church doorway; puzzled and angry at not finding Hoag anywhere on campus, thought this had to be the last place he could be, decided on a different tactic and pulled the revolver and silencer out of his jacket pocket, shouted loud and threatening. "Hoag, I know you're in here, there's nowhere you can hide." Just then Dean Graham made the worst mistake of his sad life and called out menacingly. "Her last breath tasted wonderful Hoag."

Marcus, from behind the alter, jumped up and about to confront Dean Graham, but the Dean saw him out the corner of his eye, spun round, and fired the revolver twice. *Crack! Crack!* The bullets just missed Marcus as he dived over the brass barrier sliding behind the marble statue of Saint Andrew, landing in a heap in the corner. Dean Graham fired another three times, but the shots pinged of the statue. Marcus unsure about what to do next, saw Chrissie's head bob up and shouted at her to, get down, just as Dean Graham fired another shot, but not at him. Chrissie was the Dean's target.

Marcus scrambled to his feet, ducked out from behind the statue, and like a man possessed by a demon ran straight at the Dean, then with all his might, jumped up, clenched his fist and punched him full in the face. The Dean completely taken by surprise at how swiftly Marcus moved, crumpled and fell unconscious to the ground, his nose splattered with blood. Marcus quickly turned and ran to Chrissie fearful of what he would find.

He needn't have worried she could look after herself. She saw the Dean aiming the old gun at her and ducked just in time, but decided to let Marcus fuss over her for a few seconds.

With compassion and anger he grouched at her. "You silly woman, I told you to keep down." Unthinking, Marcus put his arms around Chrissie for the second time in one day.

They all traversed back down the tunnel, but instead of going all the way back to the dais in the graduation hall Marcus led them back to the last rock fall and pushing a gateway on the right, carried on along a different route.

As they climbing another set of stone steps, the four emerged at a manhole between the science block and science library, and then walked quickly to the car park. Paul climbed in with Louise in her car while Chrissie jumped into Marcus's car and both cars in convoy pulled out of the car park and left Saint Peter's University campus.

Dean Graham eased himself up from the dusty chapel floor, and wondered where he was. Did Marcus Hoag just punch him in the face or did he dream it. The warm blood oozing out of his nose and down his shirt and suit quickly brought him back to reality, he pulled out a hanky from his top pocket and held it to his nose, while his head felt like hell he drunkenly picked himself up, retrieved the gun and put it back in his pocket, thinking, the lucky little bastard must have been hiding behind the altar, but wait a minute how come there was a woman with him He unsteadily made his way down the aisle and climbed over the barrier, looked behind the altar but couldn't see the trap door he was standing on. Puzzled and a little fuzzy he staggered back to the entrance, as he held his nose with the hanky he hurried back to the deanery.

Once he was back in the Office he made straight for the bedroom, looked at his face in the mirror over the basin and thought, It's not that bad, I can put a plaster pad over it. With that done John Graham removed his blood stained clothes and washed himself, but before he changed into his spare clothes, he lay down on top of the bed and instantly went to sleep.

The Village

Leaving the campus ahead of Paul and Louise, Marcus said to Chrissie. "She's dead Chrissie, Alice is dead, Dean Graham confessed just before he shot at me."

"I guessed as much but we, well we all lived in hope and this just confirms our suspicions. How do you feel Marcus?"

"I don't feel anything, I lost Alice five years ago, and I got over it and moved on."

"Moved on to Jack Daniels whisky, sounds like your still grieving."

"Seeing Paul has made me realise, its not just about me any more, I want to be part of his life again and seeing him with Louise, well I feel different inside I don't feel the need for a drink anymore."

"How long have you been trying to keep dry?"

"Oh Jesus Chrissie, is it that obvious?"

Chrissie changing the conversation said with worry across her face. "Did you realise there were seven bullets in that gun?"

Marcus glanced at Chrissie wide eyed and said with surprise. "I'd no idea, it all happened so quickly. He was aiming at you and when I thought he'd shot you I just saw red."

Chrissie with affection intimated while hugging his arm. "Marcus Hoag, my hero."

Marcus's head told him to keep on driving, but his heart was starting to beat faster. Wanting to change the subject he said to Chrissie. "Do you know if the village has a store that'll print the photos?"

With a glint in her eye and knowing Marcus was changing the subject. "Sure, it shouldn't be too expensive either."

The two cars arrived at the village store and after a quick conversation with Paul, Marcus said. "Paul and Louise will get them printed and we can get a meal over the road at the café."

"Great," said Chrissie. "I'm starving."

Marcus and Chrissie walked into the large café, sat down at a roomy booth, and a middle-aged waitress walked over asking if they both wanted coffee. "Can we have four coffees please?" asked Marcus. The waitress walked away, then returned with four cups in one hand and a coffee pot in the other, proceeded to pour.

Paul with Louise following behind walked in with a smile on his face saying. "We can pick the prints up in a couple of hours. I'm starving, what's on the menu?"

After they had all eaten and the waitress had cleared the plates away and refilled their coffee cups. Paul said. "What about the other two windows dad, you forgot to tell us about them."

Marcus reached into his jacket pocket and brought out his notebook for the umpteenth time, saying. "At this rate I'm going to need a new notebook." He laid it open on the table in front of him, far enough away to allow Paul and Louise opposite to see the pages and close enough for Chrissie to read from it. "Ok, Saint Augustine of Hippo Doctor of Grace"

<u>2nd Stain Glass Window (II)</u>

Saint Augustine of Hippo
Real name, Aurelius Augustinus (Doctor of Grace)
Born 354AD
Book: Open
Cross: Fleurie Cross Flory/Florets or Fleuronny
          Faith, Wisdom & Chivalry in Heraldry
Son: Adeotadus (The Gift of God)
Heart: Heart of Jesus
Caritas: Charity
Tippet: Bishops Stole
Patron: Brewers
Unexplained:
●
●
●

"The window," questioned Paul. "It depicts an open book."

"That's right Son, he's not part of the triangle. The Tippet or Stole on the window shows he was very well liked. The red heart shape is regarded as the Heart of Jesus."

"Caritas," Louise said. "Inside the heart of Jesus, is that what it means Marcus?"

Paul interrupted and said softly. "No Louise, it means selfless love, love of God and love of man."

"Well done Paul," as Marcus wrote that down in his notebook he said. "I must have forgotten to put it in."

Chrissie looked at the Cross and asked. "Is that a Fleur-de-Lis? Its French isn't it?"

"Yes," said Marcus. "Lis is French for Lily, but this is a Fleurie Cross, the name given to the Co'te Fleurie (Flowering Coast) in Normandy northern France. It's a great tourist attraction because of the D-Day landing beaches. There are a few other spellings and I've marked them down, it's very similar to the Fleur-de-lis and represents faith, wisdom, and chivalry, but only in heraldry. He must have been an exceptional cleric to be included in the stain glass windows."

Chrissie asked with a puzzled look. "How come he had a son, I thought priests and monks never got married?"

"Hmm, apparently he must have done, to have a son." Marcus flicked forward through his notebook and spotted another Saint that had a wife. "I thought as much, Saint Benedict was married as well. In that era it probably wasn't frowned upon to have relationships. You must remember the early Romans were a frisky lot, but the name Adeotacus (Gift of God) tells me he was already preparing to be a priest."

"Yes, sounds very saintly." Said Chrissie with wide eyes as she looked up and trying to believe Marcus.

"What about number three," asked Louise? "This one looks to have a heart as well."

"Ah! Saint Scholastica of Plumbariola, there's not very much we know of this lady except she was the twin sister of Saint Benedict."

<u>3rd Stain Glass Window (III)</u>

Saint	Scholastica of Plumbariola twin sister to Saint Benedict of Montecassino
Born	480 Nurcia Italy
Book:	Open
Heart:	Heart of Jesus
Cross:	8 sided/Infinity loop (Baptism) ∞
Gemini:	The Twins (Benedict)
Patron:	Storms
Unexplained:	● ● ●

"The cross is the same as Benedict's plain and simple and another reference to the number eight and infinity loop. The heart is probably the love she had for her brother Benedict as they were supposed to be very close and on the same wavelength."

"What do you mean, 'Same wave-length', dad?"

Marcus looked at Paul and said with a little bit of annoyance in his voice. "They were clerics; they were twins, brother, and sister. Sometimes I wonder about you son." Marcus looked at his watch. "I wonder if the photos have been developed yet."

"Louise and I will go; you two stay here and have another coffee." As Paul and Louise got up and walked towards the door, Paul with a hint of sarcasm called back. "You might have cooled down by the time we get back!"

"Take your time," answered Marcus. "I want to talk to Chrissie, alone."

"Alone!" quipped Chrissie tentatively. "Hmm, I'm not sure I like the sound of that."

Marcus, ignoring Chrissie's coyness, asked. "How much can we trust Louise?"

Chrissie brought back down to earth, sat back in her seat, and looked at Marcus. "Bearing in mind she's in love with your son Marcus, and Louise was the one that first spotted John Graham's activities, and I've told you, she's smart Marcus exceptionally smart, but can you trust her. No!"

"You're kidding me." Marcus couldn't believe what Chrissie had just said. "What do you mean; No?"

"She's a federal agent Marcus; she works with other agents, not just with me. She has to report everything that happens on an assignment, if she doesn't, her job is on the line."

Just then Paul and Louise walked in with the photos and handed them to Marcus.

"Never mind the photos," said Marcus. "Sit down, both of you we need to talk." Marcus waited for them to settle, hailed the waitress to fill the cups again before he said. "Louise, you've been pretty quiet up to now, I want to know what you couldn't tell us in the graduation hall and why you're not observing John Graham anymore?"

Louise looked at Marcus and smiled saying. "There's no fooling you is there Marcus. Ok! I got a call at the deanery from a colleague at the Bureau, and he informed me, we have three days to find The Regula Monachorum or you would never see your wife Alice again. They made out that she was alive. We were pretty sure John Graham had murdered and disposed of her body, but..." Louise was about to reveal something else, but Marcus stopped.

"You said, but! Come on tell the rest Louise."

Louise a little taken by surprise thought, oh what the hell and immediately said. "But they gave us proof of her kidnapping."

"What proof?" asked Marcus.

Louise took a deep breath and continued. "Marcus they sent us a wedding ring with you and your wife's name inscribed inside."

Marcus sat back, but looked across at Paul, and said with resignation. "Paul your mother is not alive, I don't care what anyone says, or what proof Louise has because Dean Graham was serious when he admitted his involvement with her death."

Paul lowered his head and Louise instinctively placed her arms around him, but spoke softly to Marcus. "We have other agents watching John Graham, and I'm assigned to you to watch your backs in England. You are going to England, are you not Marcus?"

Marcus held back, feeling that Louise hadn't told him everything. "I'll give you this Louise your good just like Chrissie here said, 'you're smart'. But my dear, you're not as smart as me; I know there's something you're holding back, even if I have to go to England to find out what it is. I'll go."

Louise was unsure about Marcus, so she smiled and reached across the table, placed her hand on his and said. "Marcus you don't fool me, your chasing dreams but all your dreams are right here in front of you."

"And that little speech Louise," said Marcus with a soft smile. "Just proves my point. Come on let's book four business class flight tickets, my treat." They all got up from the booth. Marcus paid for the meals and left a generous tip then walked out of the warm family run café.

True to her word Louise had made sure she had backup now that things were moving along swiftly, and while Paul was busy getting the photos printed she thought it only prudent to call in another couple of agents. They would ensure that John Graham wouldn't follow them or even get out of the country without the agents knowing about of it. If he tried, they should apprehend him. She couldn't afford another slip like Marcus and Chrissie almost being shot.

Eight hours later John Graham woke up with an almighty headache, looked in the mirror, and hardly recognised himself. His face, especially around the nose and both eyes were black with a slight swelling to his forehead, where Marcus's knuckles had connected and laid him out. 'Cold water', thought the Dean, that's what I need a cold water compress. He held a wet towel over his head while he dialled the International number.

"Hello," said Gabby. "Why didn't you call earlier? You're late."

Graham, not in the mood for her fishing, said. "Put him on."

"He's not here, he had to go out, and he expected you to call earlier."

"Book me on a flight to England and I'll pick the tickets up at JFK airport."

"Yes sir, right away, sir!" Arrogant swine, she silently cursed to herself, and then added. "What name, 'sir'?"

"Gabriella, just do it."

"Ok! Ok! It's done."

The Dean replaced the receiver and sat down on the bed, still a little woozy and seeing double, picked the phone up again and dialled for a cab to come pick him up. That done he stood up and put on his change of clothes, retrieved the revolver from his jacket pocket and place it at the bottom of his holdall, picked up his passport, looked at it and thought, yes, this one will do. Slipped it into his inside jacket pocket, picked up his holdall and walked unsteadily out of the deanery, through the quadrangle, passing under the ancient archway and down the half circle steps to the cab waiting for him in the car park, climbed in and said to the cab driver. "Take me to JFK airport, pronto."

The driver looked at him in his mirror but saying nothing, carried on down the driveway and away from St. Peter's University.

CHAPTER 6

Flight from J.F.K. USA
To Heathrow, London
11th June

Marcus gathered his group and made sure all passports, tickets and boarding passes were in order before passing through passport security and on into the flight lounge. It was just after 3am at JFK, but when they arrive in England they will have lost five hours and that would make it approximately 3:00pm when they land.

Marcus sat down on one of the rows of seats. "Let's get some sleep before they call us for the flight."

Chrissie sat next to him and said softly. "How long do you think it'll be?"

"I guess at half an hour."

"I think I'll pass and try to sleep on the plane."

There was no need to tell Paul or Louise to get some sleep, they were already snuggled up together asleep on the spare seats. Marcus looked at his son and thinking, he wished he had his relaxed way of grasping life, it all looked so easy for him, or maybe I'm just getting old.

"Where do we go when we get to London Marcus?"

"I've arranged for a hire car to be waiting for us at the airport. When we get there I just hope I can remember which side of the road to drive on. I thought we could book into a bed and breakfast on the way to Canterbury and do a bit of Cathedral exploring."

"Sounds exciting," whispered Chrissie as she rolled her eyes. "Whoopee, Cathedral exploring, you need to get out more Marcus."

Just as Marcus with a smile on his face closed his eyes, the garbled announcement for their flight came over the intercom. Marcus thought, so much for thirty minutes sleep.

The aeroplane was a lot more comfortable than the flight lounge seats. As the flight took to the air, Paul and Louise went back to sleep, but Marcus and Chrissie were still wide-awake.

Chrissie made a confession to Marcus. "I'm terrified of flying, always have been, my stomach starts to turn over and my head spins, it's just awful."

Marcus pressed one of the buttons on his reclining chair, and a Stewardess came forward. "Is it possible to have a glass of water and a flight sickness pill for my friend?"

In an English accent, the stewardess replied. "No problem sir would you like anything else?"

"No thanks, just the pill and water."

The stewardess returned and within half an hour Chrissie was feeling a lot better and started to nod off to sleep, while Marcus' head was full of questions, symbols and Saints and used the time to update his notebook, but eventually through sleep deprived exhaustion he finally drifted off into a dream filled sleep of Saint Benedict and his spirited sister Scholastica.

Monastery Montecassino C524 – 543AD

As the Abbess waited in the cloister for her brother to make an appearance from prayers, Scholastica and her two sister nuns enjoyed the late lunch Romanus had prepared, she wondered why Benedict would want to go all the way to Rome, and he never leaves his beloved monastery. A thought occurred to her, of course how stupid of me, the Monachorum, he must have finished it, if brother Benedict had completed his writing, and, if that was the reason he was travelling to Rome. As Scholastica looked up at the afternoon sky a plan was manufacturing itself inside her head, he might, and just might possibly allow her and her nuns to travel to the city.

As she sat contemplating these things she heard a door open, it came from the side of the cloister she was sitting in. Scholastica turned her head and there, standing to the side of her was her brother the Abbot.

Scholastica stood up, looked at her brother. "Benedict, I'm so happy to see you, it's been another year now, and I must tell you my good news," then with a rush of words she told him of her new position as Abbess at the convent in Subiaco, she had so many different feelings and emotions inside her, but as she looked at the Abbot he didn't seem to be listening to her, but preoccupied and withdrawn, even tired looking. With sisterly love in her voice she spoke with affection. "Brother, you look so tired, all that writing you do, and it's making you ill."

Benedict was listening to his sister and was genuinely happy for all her achievements, but he couldn't bring himself to concentrate on her words, he was remembering the painful memory of his time at Subiaco and the treachery of the monk's he left there.

"I'm well enough sister, but I also have news. I travel to Rome tomorrow."

Scholastica looked at her brother and with surprise in her voice pressed. "'Tomorrow' must it be so soon?"

"Yes. I have finished my writings, and the Holy See wishes me to hand it to him personally."

"That's a great honour. May the sister's and I stay overnight in the monastery and travel to the city with you tomorrow, and possibly meet the Holy Father again?"

Not thinking what he was saying, Benedict turned to his twin sister, and in a harsh tone, asked. "Why would you wish to travel to Rome again? It's a very long way. I also don't think it appropriate sister, for you to stay overnight in the monastery."

Scholastica thought her brother could be very cold in the things he said and promptly started to weep.

The Abbot was a little surprised at his sister's reaction to his question, undaunted by her tears, as he had seen them before when they were small children growing up in Nurcia. He asked the question again, which only made the nun cry louder and the Abbot could only think she wanted her own way and this was her way of getting it. So he turned and walked out of the cloister and through the oratory door.

Romanus, who had been watching the proceedings from the cloister doorway, followed the Abbot out, but couldn't help but feel sorry for Scholastica, she was so happy about her news. But now the Abbot had been, he thought, a little insensitive.

Scholastica stood at the entrance to the cloister with the sun on her tear stained face, when a sudden gust of wind blew up from the valley, the bright sunlight and blue skies clouded over and with a thunderous noise and a downpour of heavy rain, the lightening ferociously streaking across the sky lighting up the whole monastery. As the Abbess stood in the rain, her tears mingling with the heavy droplets, placed both hands together in front of her and thanked the Lord for hearing her plea. She wanted to spend what time she had left with Benedict, and this she knew would be her last visit.

The Abbot and monk heard the commotion and both walked briskly back out through the cloister to sister Scholastica. Benedict lifted up his hands to the assumed miracle of the rain filled clouds and begged her forgiveness and with compassion in his voice, he said. "I'm such a foolish brother, forgive me sister."

In between her tears and the rain across her flushed face, she said. "You're forgiven brother," and made the sign of the cross.

Brother and sister sat in the cloister with their friends talking and praying well into the evening until it was time for the Abbess and her nun's to leave the monastery. The rain had ceased by this time and saying her goodbyes, Scholastica exited the cloister with her faithful nuns following close behind.

They walked down the incline away from the monastery, and as she got to the large gates with pax (peace) written across the top, her blue eyes twinkling and clarity in her voice, she turned and looked straight at her brother and said. "My sisters and I will lodge in the village at the bottom of the mountain and also at the convent close to St Peter's Basilica; I look forward to seeing you tomorrow in Rome, brother!"

Romanus watched the perplexity on the Abbot's face as the nun's walked away, and a smile crossed over his own face. Early in the afternoon the Abbot hadn't seen the storm clouds start to build up on the east side of the monastery, but Romanus knew who had, and he whispered to himself. "Aah how the wiles of a nun, no an Abbess, confound me."

Heathrow London to Canterbury

Alighting from the huge aeroplane, Marcus led the way to passport control and on past the exit sign, collected their light luggage from the carousel, then passed through customs to the hire car reception desk, collected the keys and documents and headed outside to the new hire car waiting for them in the car park.

Marcus opened the car boot and they all deposited their small luggage into the spacious compartment. Marcus climbed in behind the wheel with Paul in the passenger seat and a map on his lap. Chrissie and Louise slid in the back and giving the usual backseat driver instructions, until Marcus said. "Have you two ladies ever driven on the left before?"

Chrissie and Louise looked at each other and hunched their shoulders in agreement and both said together. "Carry on, you're driving."

"I take that as a 'no', thank you ladies." Little did they know but Marcus had lived in Britain for six months before he married Alice and he visited back and forth quite often.

"Ok son what road numbers do we want for Canterbury?"

Trying to fathom the map, Paul unsure, said. "I think we want the M25 and follow that route all the way to Sevenoaks, Maidstone and then on to Canterbury."

They wound their way out of the airport complex and were soon on their way southeast, passing the English countryside with unbelievable speed.

Loving every minute of the adventure, Paul oblivious of the dangers that lay ahead looked over his shoulder at Louise. He was thinking back to the café and how his father had confronted her. He thought I mustn't let my heart rule my head, but oh! She has got everything in the right places; he then winked at her and was totally enraptured by her huge smile.

Chrissie, sitting quietly in the back of the car watching Paul and Louise's new love ritual, cast her mind back to the time when she first met Marcus Hoag, of course he didn't remember her, he was too wrapped up in Alice at the time, but she wasn't the angel he thought she was and Chrissie couldn't tell him anything, she was sworn to secrecy by Agnes Connor, Alice's mother but life had a tendency to kick you in the teeth when you least expected it, and that's exactly what happened to Alice.

Before she met Marcus, Alice toyed with the then young John Graham's affections, he'd fallen madly in love with her, and at that time he had two jobs, one as a waiter in the evenings and working during the day in her fathers company as a mailman. God! It must have been difficult for him trying to pay his student fees, but he managed it. She could see him now, a tall handsome guy with a great personality. But he also had an arrogant ambitious side to him and of course his plan to impress her father was his second priority, Alice being his first. I think he must have thought Alice's father could supply him with the knowledge and money to take him all the way to the top, but Alice had grown bored of John's infatuation with her and her family, she wanted to end their relationship. Chrissie remembered Alice had found someone else and she and John Graham had this almighty row that went on all day with Alice throwing things at him and the names she called him weren't in Chrissie's vocabulary.

He eventually walked away hurt and broken. She never saw him again he was out of her life for good, or so she thought. Alice had made a mistake, she humiliated him, and that's what eventually came back to haunt her.

Marcus and John Graham were ignorant of the young men Alice had dallied with. Why! Because her daddy had bailed her out of jail that many times and covered it up so nobody knew of it. Chrissie had lost count of the times she'd been woken up during the night, Alice sneaking around well after midnight trying the key in the lock, cursing because she was so drunk and could hardly stand up, Chrissie remembering the countless times she'd put her to bed.

When Alice's father died suddenly, her Mother thought she could control her, but she was wrong her half sister always looking so glamorous knew exactly what a man wanted and went out to get it, just because she knew she could. The turning point in Alice's wild life was sitting in front of her. He was also the man that Chrissie had fallen in love with all those years ago.

Chrissie was brought back to the present by Marcus asking; "We're about two miles from Canterbury, what about this bed and breakfast coming up. Shall we book in for the night and then go on to Canterbury and have an evening meal?" They were all in agreement so Marcus pulled into the B&B car park, booked them into two twin bedrooms, grabbed a tourist map, and set off again into Canterbury.

They had made really good time. Landing at Heathrow around 3:30 pm half an hour in the airport, two hours motorway travelling to Canterbury and the time now was almost six pm. Just time for a good meal and back to the B&B for a nightcap and sleep.

The meal was delicious and the wine went down far too easy, although Marcus didn't have any as he was driving, but he enjoyed the evening with Paul recounting his exploits on the various team games and his fellow athletes, and how some of his friends managed to escape the clutches of coach Farmer. Louise looked to be enjoying herself and letting her hair down with her own tales of how she could handle herself in tight situations. The only one that didn't seem to be fully enjoying the evening was Chrissie; she was talkative but only out of politeness and seemed not to want to spoil the happy atmosphere. The group sat in the restaurant longer than expected, no-one wanting to get up first to leave, but eventually they returned to the B&B.

Marcus collected the two bedroom keys, kept one and handed the other to Chrissie, saying. "I think Paul and I need our beauty sleep we'll see you both in the morning."

Paul gazed at Louise and giving her a gentle hug, said. "Goodnight Louise."

Marcus watching his son's awkwardness, said with exasperation. "For God sake give the girl goodnights kiss and let's get to bed." Which he duly did, but Chrissie simply said goodnight and walked down the corridor, while Louise slowly followed behind.

Marcus and Paul changed into their pyjamas and climbed into bed, within a few minutes Paul was sound asleep. But Marcus had something on his mind and it wasn't John Graham or any thing to do with the stain glass windows of St. Peter's University. His thoughts were of Chrissie. Chrissie, Chrissie, he repeated her name in his head over and over again. What was wrong with her tonight, something spooked her, but what could it be.

She didn't feel well on the flight.

She might not travel very well in a car.

Was she concerned for John Graham? No! That can't be it.

Unable to sleep Marcus climbed out of bed, slipped his complementary dressing gown and slippers on and quietly opened the bedroom door, then just as quietly closed it behind him; he headed down the stairs to the lounge where a tea and coffee trolley had been laid out for such eventualities as insomnia. He poured himself a cup of hot tea and was about to sit down in one of the comfy chairs when a familiar voice whispered.

"Can't you sleep either?"

Instantly Marcus' cup almost toppled over in its saucer. "Oh! Bloody hell Chrissie, you gave me a fright, I didn't see you there. Why aren't you asleep?"

"For the same reason your not."

Marcus shuffled over to the sofa in his one size too big slippers, sat down on the double sofa next to Chrissie and said gently. "What reason would that be then?"

"I wanted a cup of tea."

"No other reason?"

Chrissie not wanting to reveal too much of her feelings said. "I guess I just needed time to get over the flight and possibly too much wine."

"No you didn't."

Not quite understanding what Marcus meant, she hedged. "What do you mean 'no I didn't', I don't understand."

"You've been quiet all evening and it's nothing to do with the flight, carsickness or wine. Come on Chrissie what's wrong and why are you sitting down here on your own?"

Chrissie unable to stop herself from lying anymore told him everything she had thought about on the flight and travel down in the car, everything except how she felt about him and exactly who she was.

Marcus looked at her for what seemed to Chrissie an eternity and eventually said. 'I knew all about it, everything, Alice's past history with men, only she didn't know that I knew, by the time I'd discovered her past liaisons she was pregnant with Paul. Chrissie, I couldn't risk confronting her, so I just carried on as if nothing had happened. At first I felt sorry for John Graham, but when I dug a little deeper into his past. I realised that he probably would have ended up in jail anyway.'

Chrissie couldn't believe what she was hearing, he knew all the time, he knew. "What do you mean he would have ended up in jail?"

"John Graham was stealing from the restaurants customers. As the customers came in he would take their coats out back and just before he hung them up, he would go through the pockets and take anything of value he found, put the items in an empty trash can then collect it later after his shift. He would pack the job in and move on to another restaurant and do the same thing over and over again. He was a small time thief with big ambitions and over the years he went on to bigger things."

"What do you mean bigger things?"

"You should know, you're the undesirables investigator or is that just a cover for something else Chrissie?"

"I'll be honest Marcus, I haven't done any of that kind of work since Alice went missing, and I still work in the same department but not in the field. Louise asked me as a favour, and when I found out you were involved, I...I, well I....I wanted to see you again."

Marcus took Chrissie's cup and his own and set them both down on the glass coffee table. He clasped both Chrissie's hands in his and said in a soft but slightly shaky voice. "I was wondering how long it was going to be before you were going to tell me you remembered me. You see I thought you weren't interested, I'll admit the name Greenwood threw me a bit at first, but I guessed you'd either got married or just changed your name."

Chrissie with tears in her eyes, said. "I never married; it's my Grandmother Connor's maiden name. I used it to make sure John Graham didn't recognise me, not that he would anyway because we never met, but just in case."

"When I started seeing Alice I remember you were always in the background. I could never understand why Alice never spoke about you much and you never visited, not even to see Paul."

Chrissie looked at him with soft sincere eyes. "Oh but I did Marcus, when we covered a few assignments together, you were never there, but Alice and Paul seemed really happy."

Marcus stood up and pulled Chrissie up from the sofa, as they both walked through the lounge and begun to climb the stairs, Marcus confided in her a past that he never thought he would ever reveal to anyone. "Chrissie, I love my son with a passion, and I did love Alice. She was a beautiful woman, and for the first year we were married it was wonderful, I remember the times we had were just so perfect, but I soon realised I'd made a mistake and she didn't really want me. I have no idea what happened. It was like she just decided that she didn't want me anymore." Marcus snapped his fingers. "Just like that, it was uncanny, and I worried about Paul, if she could do that to me then would she possibly do it to her own son, but of course she didn't, she worshipped him."

They reached the top of the stairs and walked to their separate rooms; Marcus looked at Chrissie and said. "Why did she do that to me?"

"She was a complicated woman Marcus; I think her love was all or nothing, no grey in between."

Marcus walked down the corridor to where Chrissie stood about to open her room door and looked deep into her moist eyes and whispered. "Don't leave me Chrissie?"

"I'm still here Marcus, and I'm not going anywhere."

Marcus pulled her close to him, cupping her face in his hands he kissed her on the cheek, then slowly nuzzled his way round to her tear stained lips and gently kissed her full on the mouth.

2nd Flight from JFK USA to Heathrow, London
11th June

The cab driver pulled up outside JFK flight departures, and waited for his passenger to pay his fare. John Graham paid the cabbie exactly what he owed for the fare, without giving the driver the usual tip, just walked off, and entered the airport building. The cabbie looked at his money then slipped it into his top pocket. Pulled out a hand held mobile phone and spoke into it. "Tony! He's on his way through to the collection desk." But his partner Tony was in the restroom getting rid of the beer and greasy curry he'd eaten the day before and his mobile was in his jacket pocket and that was hanging in the empty security office.

"Tony, come on answer me 'dammit'."

"Excuse me sir," said the transport officer with a booking pad and pen in his hand. "If you don't move your cab to the correct taxi rank and wait your turn for customers I've no option but to give you a ticket."

Jack just looked at him and thought, great, just great! Louise will have my balls for this, 'dammit'! The agent pulled from his inside jacket pocket an FBI badge, climbed from the taxi, and hurried over to the row of International telephones.

Dean Graham walked over to the collection desk and picked up his travel documents, then crossed over to the check-in counter and handed his passport over. The check-in clerk looked at him oddly then took his light luggage and placed it on the conveyor belt sending it down to the appropriate flight gate. He handed the passport and documents back and said. "Have a nice flight sir."

John Graham with his documents walked towards passport security, handed his passport over and collected his boarding pass then walked through the security gate and headed for the flight lounge.

No one recognised him with the huge padding across his nose, and he had used his real passport. Written in black ink across the top was simply Msr. JHH Morgaan. It felt strange using his own name, but because of Louise he was certain the Federal agents were closing in on him, they already knew all his aliases and Paul was right, they were all anagrams of his real name, and airport security weren't looking for a guy with a great big plaster on his nose. Hearing his flight called and after boarding the aeroplane, he settled down and waited for take-off.

As John Graham alighted from the aeroplane in London, he was oblivious to the strange looks from the other passengers, some especially the elderly ladies felt sorry for him and wondered if he'd been in some kind of accident, if only they knew the only accident the Dean had was being born on the wrong side of a rich Family. He walked out of Heathrow arrivals building and climbed into his hire car, slipped the clutch and put the car into gear then accelerated away from the airport network, taking care to stay in the left hand lane; he headed for the M25 and on to Canterbury.

CHAPTER 7

Canterbury, Kent
12th June

Sitting at the breakfast table, Marcus and Chrissie looked at each other slowly eating breakfast, not saying a word, but savouring last night's revelations. They could feel a great weight had been lifted from their shoulders, and both had also given away their feelings for each other. Paul and Louise were in their own world, and chatted constantly and gulped their food down as if it was their last meal.

As Paul finished off his glass of orange juice he asked Marcus. "What are we doing today, are we going down to Ebb fleet to have a look at that monument, St. Augustine cross?"

"No son," answered Marcus. "I already have all the information on the cross."

"When, how?"

"Do you remember about ten years ago I was asked to do a talk in London on symbolism?' Marcus reached into his pocket, removed his notebook and opened it up near the back and started to show them a drawing of a monument with strange wording. 'Well! I drove down there and copied the full inscription and drew a picture, because you know what my memories like."

Chrissie couldn't make the words out and Louise's Latin wasn't wonderful, so Paul began to read, a little unsteady at first but quickening the pace read it again, and then translated it.

Augustinus
Ad Rutupinalittola in insula Thaneti
Post tot terrae marisque labores
Tandem adveetus
Hoe in loco cum Ethelberto rege congressus,
Primam apud nostrates coneionem habuit
ET fidem christianam
Quae per totam Angliam mira celeritate diffusa EST,
Filiciter inauguravit

A.D. DXCVI.

Augustine

At length, they were brought to Ebbs Fleet in the Isle of Thanet and after so much labour on land, and at sea.

At a conference with King Ethelbert on this spot, delivered his first discourse to OUR' people, and auspiciously founded the Christian faith,

This was diffused with wonderful rapidity throughout the whole of England

A.D.596

Marcus suitably impressed looked at his son, and as they all gave Paul a little applause, he stood up and took a bow, saying. "Ah, it was nothing, just a little thing I love to do, you know, translations come easy to me and the A.D. 596." Paul thinking that was how old the monument was, continued. "Now that is awesome dad."

Marcus, with a cheeky smile across his face grinned at his son. "If you think that is so – awesome, translate the inscription on the opposite side of the monument, on the next page."

Paul once more began to read and his voice dropped to a whisper. "No way, no way!"

Marcus stood up and walked away laughing at his sons gullibility. Chrissie and Louise dumfounded by Marcus' happy attitude said in unison. "Read the translation Paul?"

Reluctantly, he read on.

Quarum Rerum
Ut apud Anglos servetur memoria,
Hoe monumentum ponendum curavit
G.G.L.G. Comes Granville, Portuum Custos,

A.D. DCCCLXXXIV.

English Translation
In order that the memory of these events may be preserved among the English people,
Granville George Leveson-Gower, Earl Granville,
Lord Warden of the CinquePorts has caused this Monument to be erected.

A.D. 1884'

Louise and Chrissie looked at Paul and then they all began to laugh and shouting. "1884!"

Paul watched his father laughing as he walked out of the room, and thinking, its good to hear him laugh again, and then they all trooped out of the breakfast room following Marcus to the waiting hire car.

Marcus drove the car expertly along Wincheap, passing an Industrial estate of the same name, taking a right at the roundabout then up Pin hill towards Rhodaus Town, which was connected to Bridge Street and eventually pulled into the car park at the back of the magnificent Canterbury Cathedral.

The foursome stepped out of the car and walked around by Burgate, which opened out to the front of the Cathedral, and were amazed at how huge it was, Paul asked quizzically. "Is Augustine buried here?"

"No son," Marcus didn't need his notebook to answer Paul's question; he knew the exact resting spot of Augustine. "He was buried in a grave that was dug by the side of a Roman road, which ran from Deal to Canterbury, over St. Martins Hill and near the unfinished church, which he started in honour of Saint Peter and Paul and afterwards dedicated to his memory. When the church was completed his relics were transferred to a tomb in the north porch, a hospital is said to have been built over the site of his last resting place."

Chrissie asked. "So he's not buried in the Cathedral?"

Marcus shook his head. "No!" then went on to say. "Augustine was given a church at St. Martin's, named after St. Martin of Tours, by King Ethelbert and his Queen who was a French princess and a Christian, it still stands today and it's the oldest church in England."

Chrissie quipped. "Shouldn't we be heading over there, instead of being here?"

"No, because in Latin Seat means Cathedra (Cathedral) and on the heraldic blazon in the 6th stain glass window Saint Augustine of Durovernum, there's a chair or a seat on top of the second triangle closed book."

Louise and Chrissie stood looking in amazement as Paul and Marcus walked in through the large southwest door and entered the nave. Both women quickly followed them and passed through the same entrance to be amazed yet again at the beauty and grandeur of such high vaulted arches and gilt roof bosses. Catching up with Marcus and Paul, the foursome carried on up the central aisle and on into the martyr.

Marcus knowledgably said. "This is where Thomas Becket was murdered. The best known event in the Cathedrals history, the murder of Archbishop Thomas Becket, and his shrine was part of the pilgrim route to Rome for thousands and the word cantor came from the pace of the pilgrim's horses as they rode to Canterbury."

Paul curious, asked. "Why would anyone want to murder an Archbishop, I thought the church would protect him?"

"When he was made Archbishop," interrupted Chrissie. "King Henry VIII expected him to support his cause, but he changed his allegiance to the Pope and the church. This pissed the King off and he shouted, 'Who will rid me of this meddlesome priest,' well, four Knights overheard him and took the King seriously. They killed the Archbishop on these very steps with two ragged steel swords, a broken sword point snapped off on these very steps as he fell."

Marcus intrigued, asked. "How'd you know all this Chrissie?"

"The famous actor Richard Burton played Thomas Becket in the film. Oh, what was the name?" Chrissie looked up having a problem trying to remember the exact film and just for a minute she could have sworn she saw the Dean.

"Louise, Louise, I think I've just seen John Graham standing by the Bossanyi stained glass windows in the southeast transept, I don't think he's seen us yet."

"You can't have, he's still back in the States and right now should be under arrest if he tried to leave the country."

Marcus quickly ushered them out of site of the Dean. "Come on hurry let's find a window that has a reference to birth or baptism."

Paul was about to ask another question, but Marcus stopped him and said. "Don't ask questions, I'll explain later. Take Louise and look on the trinity chapel walls and windows." Marcus waved his hands at Paul and Louise. "Go, go hurry up."

Marcus turned to Chrissie and taking her hand hurried into the chapter house and said. "Are you sure you saw him?"

"Yes, his eyes looked terrible, all black with a plaster or something over his nose. Marcus, it makes him look ugly and evil. I have this feeling he knows about Louise and he's played along with her to ensure you got the message about Alice."

"Well, that little trick," said Marcus, as he pulled Chrissie through into the great cloister. "Back fired, didn't it."

Chrissie was starting to feel nervous, and intimated. "I don't think we're going to find anything in here, let's try the west window, we missed it as we came in." They both walked back through the martyry and turned right which brought them back into the nave. Conscious of their feet making a clip clop sound on the polished stone floor they kept to the side of the pews to dull the noise.

Marcus arrived at the west window first and saw what he was looking for before Chrissie got there. "Look," he said. "It's Adam digging in the Garden of Eden, and the black dots next to his name. It has to be a clue." Marcus quickly pulled his notebook out and furiously scribbled what he'd seen in the window, turned to Chrissie, and whispered. "Run Chrissie, for god's sake run."

John Graham was strolling down the south side of the quire and again hadn't seen them and Marcus once more hurried Chrissie along. "Come on let's go outside and round the west window and back track through the northwest door to warn Paul and Louise."

That's exactly what they did, but instead of coming back into the nave they ran up the steps entering the great cloister and again passing the columns, ran through the martyry again, then walked quickly up the quire and into trinity chapel. Marcus would have loved to stay and study the corona, which was built as a separate shrine for a part of Becket's skull, but finding Paul and Louise was more important and John Graham was walking back up through the nave at this very minute.

"Where are they?" he said to Chrissie. "I told them to look up here." Just then Marcus saw John Graham coming up the quire steps and reach into his right side pocket; obviously not wanting visitors or priests to see the revolver he'd kept his hand buried on.

"Dad, dad this way," Paul with Louise next to him whispered loud enough for Marcus to hear, and standing on the north steps of the quire out of view of the Dean. "Quickly dad, Chrissie, come on we can escape out through the northeast door."

Marcus pulled Chrissie by the arm and in their haste they knocked over a thick shield and cross swords that were placed on a stand near the steps. Paul helped Chrissie up the last of the steps and ran as quickly as they could, bypassed the north side of the chapter house and the entrance to the crypt then turning right to the northeast door. As Marcus tucked in his shirt, which had come loose in the fall, into his trousers and Paul whispered. "The door, it's locked."

"Quickly," said Marcus. "Down into the crypt."

Louise reached the bottom of the narrow steps first and entered the 11th century crypt. She crossed over to the south side and hid behind one of the decorated columns.

Paul and Marcus followed Chrissie down the steps, but slower, and reaching the bottom a good 30 seconds behind Louise. They turned left and hid behind the high recess next to St. Gabriel's Chapel. Paul immediately asked. "Where's Louise?"

"She must have crossed over to the south recess," replied Chrissie. "Oh Paul, I'm sorry but I thought she would take the first hiding place, which was here."

"She knows what she's doing," said Marcus. "Louise is drawing John Graham away from us."

Paul ashen faced whispered. "You mean like a decoy?"

"Yes, but don't worry about her she can look after herself." Just as Marcus spoke, he thought he could smell the scent of Lavender and heard someone coming down the narrow steps into the crypt.

John Graham decided to approach the Cathedral from the north, parked his car on Palace Street and entered Mint Yard Gate, then walked the rest of the way down towards the northwest door and carried on into the nave. The beauty and architecture of the high columns and stain glass windows were lost on

Graham, his only concern and aim was Marcus's notebook, and he meant to have it today. Time was running out, he needed to finish this job and of course pocket the $1.5 million he would receive for completion.

He crossed over the nave and entered the southwest transept, walked down the steps and into the south quire, stood looking at the Bossanyi stained glass window for a few minutes. Bored, he retraced his steps back to the southwest transept, but instead of returning back through the nave, he turned left into the Warriors Chapel and thinking to himself. Where are they? Canterbury Cathedral has to be their first stop in England, according to the window of Saint Augustine in the new library back at St. Peter's University.

John Graham walked out of the small chapel and slowly strolled back down the nave, that's when Marcus and Chrissie saw him for the second time and ran quickly out the west entrance. Graham never saw them until he turned around and started to walk towards the Trinity Chapel. When he eventually made his way through the quire and down the trinity steps they had disappeared. He saw the sign for the crypt and the northeast exit, he followed the passageway to the exit, and also finding it locked, returned to the crypt entrance deciding this was the only place they could have possibly gone. He steadily descended the narrow steps into the crypt.

Dean Graham walked into the crypt and crossed over to the central aisle and stood in eerie silence, waiting and listening.

Marcus looked at Chrissie and Paul then put his fingers to his lips and mouthed. "Quiet! Keep quiet."

The silence was overwhelming and Louise was trying to hold her breath but at the same time her mind was racing. Yes, she thought, I have to make my move now before he realises where the others are. Just then she stepped out from behind the column and in her most innocent, but surprised voice, said. "Dean Graham! What on earth are you doing here? I didn't know you were a Cathedral buff."

Marcus could hear Louise waffling and motioned for the other's to follow him out of the exit doorway.

John Graham with a sly grin pulled the revolver with a silencer attached out of his pocket and grabbed Louise's arm, twisting it up behind her back forcing her to go down on her knees. She was powerless and couldn't believe how strong he was and the gun was pointing at her head. With extreme malice in his voice he shouted loudly for Marcus to hear. "The notebook, give it to me now!"

The loud words echoed around the chamber taking Chrissie and Paul by surprise and Marcus stared at Paul as he whispered. "Don't leave Chrissie, what ever happens, don't leave her."

Paul simply nodded while Marcus turned around and walked into the central chamber and confronted John Graham. "Let Louise go." As he waved the notebook in his right hand his voice also echoed around the ancient crypt. "She has nothing to do with this..."

With a painful squeal, Louise interrupted him. "Marcus, no your life's work, no don't give it to him."

Graham pushed the gun further into Louise's head and said angrily. "I won't miss this time, throw it over here."

Marcus threw the notebook and it landed at John Graham's left foot. He immediately released Louise, pushing her to the right, away from the notebook and picking it up.

Marcus edged slowly over to Louise and helped her to her feet asking if she was ok. "I'm fine, but your notebook sir."

"Let him have it, it's not worth anyone getting killed over."

"How right you are 'Hoag'," said Dean Graham. As he pointed the guns silencer at Marcus, he squeezed the trigger, shooting Marcus in the chest. Before the others could respond Dean Graham retreated up the stone crypt steps.

Chrissie instantly screamed while Paul simply gasped, they both ran towards Marcus, but he had slumped to the stone floor.

Canterbury/Lincoln

The hire car skidded out of the parking space and careered down Palace Street, turning left into St. Radigund Street heading for Canterbury West train station. John Graham patted his inside breast pocket making sure he had the precious notebook and spoke aloud. "It was so easy, dumb bitch! Thought she could fool me with her little miss perfect secretary routine, I need to get to a phone." He pulled into the train station long stay car park and dropped the car keys into an overnight deposit box, ready for an employee of the hire car company to pick them up, walked up the ramp and crossed over to the ticket window, opened Marcus's notebook and turned to the back pages of the book, scanned the drawings and returned it to his inside jacket pocket.

The Dean purchased a one-way ticket to London and asked where the nearest telephone box was located. The ticket operator pointed out of the window behind Graham and said. "You're change Mr." He pushed his hand under the window and received a couple of pound coins and some change.

John Graham lifted the telephone receiver and fed the machine with the small coins, dialled the London number with more ease than in the states and waited. The call went through instantly. A voice other than Gabby's answered. "This had better be good."

"Have I ever let you down, anyway I have the notebook and I'm travelling up to Lincoln now and after that I'm headed for Durham."

"But why, what's at Lincoln and Durham?"

"What do you think? My one and a half million dollars, that's why."

"The auction starts tomorrow at 4pm. Don't be late."

Graham put the phone down as his train entered the station. He picked up his holdall and climbed into the first class carriage. As the train pulled out of the station he pulled the notebook from his pocket and opened it up at the relevant page and settled back to try and work out why Hoag gave it up so easily.

7th Stain Glass Window/Dean Grahams Notebook

Saint Mary of LinduM Colonia
Book: Closed
Stn. Glass: Sower (Special Significance)
              Windows (SS)
              Bishops eye
              Teaching eye
              DeAn's eye

Chair:	King, (SS) Seat, Latin for Cathedra (Cathedral)
Font:	Baptism, Tournai Font, Black maRble
Cross:	Plain and simple
Imp:	LinColn imp (SS) sits high up in the Angel choir
	Angel (SS) Choir

Tournai 4 corner Font sits in the nave, near south aisle sides carved with grotesqUes and lions with foliate tails, possibly to repreSent the original sin which baptism removes.

"Hoag certainly did his homework, I'll give him that," ingratiated Graham, as his train headed for London's St. Pancras Station.

The Crypt/B&B Canterbury

Marcus lay on the stone floor clutching his chest and Louise unsure what to do, simply knelt down next to him. Chrissie ran over to Marcus and threw herself to the floor, with tears in her eyes and shouting. "Why did he shoot Marcus, he had the notebook?"

"He's crazy," said Louise sadly. "But someone else is pulling his strings."

Paul knelt down and crushing Marcus's head in his hands and said. "Oh dad, what has that maniac done?"

"Paul, you're choking me," stifled Marcus. "And your right Louise, someone is certainly pulling his strings."

"Dad your ok, you're not dead."

Chrissie immediately passed out and slumped to the floor, but Louise caught her before she hurt herself. "Marcus you're ok, but how? He shot you at almost point blank range."

Marcus opened his shirt to reveal a small metal shield and pulled it away from his chest, then massaged the bruise on his right pectoral muscle where the bullet hit the metal and made a dent. Marcus refastened his shirt saying. "I fell over the shield at the bottom of the Trinity steps, so I picked it up thinking it might come in handy."

Paul with a wave of his finger and a seriously angry voice cried out. "Dad, don't ever do that again! Poor Chrissie, I don't think she can take any more surprises."

"Sorry son, but the illusion was necessary to make sure we got out of here alive."

Louise was picking Chrissie up off the floor as Marcus stumbled over to her and putting his arms out pulled her to him and simply said. "I'm sorry Chrissie love, that was stupid of me, but I'll explain it all when we get back to the B&B."

They walked back towards the car park and climbed into the car, Marcus throwing the keys to Louise, saying. "You drive."

Louise about to throw them back said. "I'm not insured."

"Sure you are. I got joint insurance at JFK Airport." Louise just smiled and reversed the hire car out of the parking space and turned left, back the way they came, and passing the industrial estate then heading back towards the bed and breakfast.

Louise said to anyone who was listening. "How did he do it? How did he get into England? I'll have Jack McClellan and Tony Ford doing the kindergarten runs for not detaining him. This was not supposed to happen!"

Louise pulled into the B&B car park, turned the ignition off and jumped out of the car and walked away from the trio that was left dawdling. She went straight to reception and asked if any calls had come through for her. The Manager informed her that there had been two calls from the same person, and he'd taken a message. He reached over to the small pigeonhole with their room numbers over the top and pulled out an envelope and handed it to her. "That was very good of you, thank you sir."

"You're welcome my lovely," he replied, in his best Kentish accent. She smiled and walked into the lounge, just as Paul and Chrissie walked in and sat down close to her. Marcus went over to the complementary tea trolley and made four cups of coffee. That done he passed them round and said to Chrissie. "This should make you feel a bit better."

Chrissie quickly glanced up at Marcus and with affection he hugged her shoulders and said to Louise. "Read the letter Louise."

Louise opened the envelope and pulled the letter out, unfolded it and started to read.

"The idiots," she said angrily. "They lost him at the airport. They're supposed to be professionals, and they lost him, and he's been making calls to a London auction house."

Louise,

Sorry we lost subject at the Airport, we don't know how it happened. He was under surveillance, and then disappeared.

We did some checking and he made a few phone calls to England. We are fairly sure it was to an auction house. We'll try and keep you informed of anything else that crops up.

Jack McClellan

"An auction house," said Marcus, and then he began to understand the involvement of all the players in the game. "Are we all sitting comfortable, because I'm about to enlighten you all again regarding a certain, private auction house in London."

They all sat back and gave Marcus the floor. "You remember Alice saw the catalogue, displaying a 6th century Diadem headpiece. Well I remember the same thing happening just over a year ago to a 6th Century mosaic from Ravenna. Jesus is portrayed as a Greek-Roman Priest and King, with the 8-point sun cross halo behind his head. It disappeared and a few weeks later it turned up back in Ravenna in perfect condition, no damage, as if it had never been missing, exactly the same as the Diadem headpiece. It didn't register with me until Louise mentioned auction house."

Paul asked. "Have you been to this auction house?"

"No son, but a friend of mine was invited there to authenticate the mosaic, it was the genuine thing and as soon as the auction ended, it disappeared with the highest bidder, until it turned up again in Ravenna. It was a complete mystery."

"What's so important about the mosaic?" asked Paul.

"Anything to do with Jesus and artefacts from the 6th Century is important son. Let me ask you all a question? How old would each of you say Jesus was when he was crucified?"

Louise immediately griped as she was still smarting after reading her colleagues note. "I guess approximately thirty eight!"

89

Paul placed his hand on Louise's shoulder trying to soothe her. "I don't know, around forty maybe."

Chrissie agreed with Louise. "I guess thirty eight too."

Marcus picked up his pen and started to write figures on a sheet of paper. "You remember I told you about + well those symbols come into play here."

```
Saint Augustine of Hippo born      354
Saint Scholastica of Plumbariola   480
Saint Columbanus of Bobbio       + 543
                                  1377
```

```
Saint Benedict of Montecassino born  480
Saint Augustine of Durovernum        542
Saint Paulinus of Eboracum         + 573
                                    1595
```

He then added. "Without Saint Francis of Assisi, add the births of all the other saints on the stain glass windows and you get":

$$1 + 3 + 7 + 7 = 18$$
$$1 + 5 + 9 + 5 = 20$$
$$38$$

"The result is, the supposed age of Jesus of Nazareth, more commonly known as Jesus Christ when crucified on the cross."

"I thought," asked Paul. "Your memory was so bad you couldn't remember anything without your notebook?"

Marcus reached into his inside jacket pocket and pulled out his notebook and said. "You mean this notebook?"

They all looked at Marcus as if he had two heads and looking at the notebook, they were struck dumb. Marcus explained. "I bought another one at the airport and thought it might come in handy."

"What about all the information and windows?" quipped Chrissie.

"I copied as much information as possible and added two new windows, but omitting the 7th window Saint Paulinus and the 8th window plus a few other bits of nonsense that he will never understand anyway."

"But what are the new windows?"

"Well Chrissie love, right now John Graham will be well on his way to Lindum Colonia, and when he finds nothing there, he'll make his way to Dunermum."

Louise repeated the names and Paul began to laugh and said. "That's brilliant dad. Lincoln, Durham, and you're still ahead of the game. How do you do it?"

"Simply experience son, experience and timing."

"Ok Dad, what does your experience tell you about the 7th stain glass window, Saint Paulinus?"

Marcus flicked through his notebook and laid it open at the appropriate page; he then glanced up at Paul and said. "This Saint was such an 'awesome guy'." Before Marcus could say any more, Paul interrupted. "The photo's, we have a picture of the window, but it's in our room."

"Go fetch them son, it makes it easier for Chrissie and Louise to understand."

Paul got up from the sofa and looked at Louise.

"No said Louise, I'm not coming with you, you're too much of a distraction for me, and we'd never find them."

Paul bounded up the stairs. While he was gone Louise asked Marcus. "Why did you ask us to look for anything to do with births or baptisms on the windows earlier?"

"On the seven stain glass windows there's a reference to every Saint's birth or baptism in a special way."

"Special way?" asked Chrissie. "There's only one way, you're born and baptised at a font in a church or chapel."

"You misunderstand Chrissie when I say birth, I don't mean as children are born. I mean as in the birth of creation, Genesis or the Garden of Eden, being baptised a second time with a different name. A font, certainly but..." Marcus was about to say something else, when Paul returned with the photographs and with a scowl on his face, he said. "The pictures aren't very good, only three have developed properly."

With panic in his voice Marcus grizzled. "Three? But which three pictures?"

Paul flicked through them and said. "I can't find them, where are they? They were here in the envelope with the negatives."

Marcus took the pack from Paul and placed each hazy picture on the coffee table in front of them, and there hidden behind the fourth last picture were the three photographs of the stain glass windows. Marcus about to give his son a mouthful of abuse again, changed his mind, decided he'd been through enough today and it was an easy mistake to make, even for Paul.

"Keep your hair on son it's not your fault your in love." Then Marcus looked at Chrissie and gave her a loving wink.

Louise and Chrissie both looked at each other and Chrissie trying to cover her blushes said. "What's on the menu today? I'm starved."

At the mention of food Paul's face lit up. "Good idea Chrissie, come on Louise it must be time for lunch." The three of them got up from the sofas and walked through into the B&B dining room leaving Marcus behind to pick up the photos, as he got to the last three he looked at them and said to himself, well, well I thought that was where you were hidden. Once more Marcus' thoughts returned to the pages of the book from the university library, which were so vivid in his memory of St. Benedict and his faithful Monk Romanus, and their journey from the top of the mountain at Montecassino Monastery, travelling up the valley and on towards the eternal City of Rome.

Monastery Montecassino/Rome C524 – 543AD

"We've a long journey in front of us Romanus," the Abbot said with a heavy frown.

"Yes master," answered Romanus.

"Did you wrap the book well, and secure it firmly to the donkey?"

The monk for the second time checked the donkey and answered the Abbott. "Master, we must make a start, or it will be dark before we get to Rome."

"I'm well aware of the time Romanus."

"Yes master," the monk said wearily. He had been trying all morning to hurry the Abbot along, knowing full well that he didn't want to leave his beloved monastery, but this journey to Rome, was very important. You don't ignore an audience with the Papal See.

Romanus checked the saddlebags for the third time and they eventually set off on their long journey up the valley towards Rome and hoping to arrive in the late evening at the Holy residence close to the great Basilica of St. Peters where Benedict's twin sister Scholastica and her two nuns were staying.

After a long ride up the valley the sun was already a deep orange glow just above the horizon, they eventually arrived at the outskirts of Rome and followed the Via Labicana road; it wasn't long before they rode past the Coliseum, the great arena, where the slaves turned gladiators used to fight for their lives, but no more. Benedict and Romanus made the sign of the cross, both assuming the same thought, a nightmare of a place.

The sun had set behind the Roman buildings and Romanus asked the Abbot if he would you prefer to bathe at the Trajan baths or go further on into the city. "Let's press on," said the Abbot. "We only have to cross the city to the Tiber River and we're almost at the great Basilica, we can bathe at Agrippa's spa, and rest overnight at one of the monasteries nearby."

Romanus had never been to Rome, but had listened to countless stories from the Abbot and his fellow Monks. He marvelled at the variety of the temples and the great Palace of Domitian and to the south side of the Palace, the Circus Maximus, where the great chariot races were held.

Benedict and Romanus slowly ambled on through the unkempt streets, winding their way past the various Forums. In the distance they could see the magnificent Forum of the great Julius Caesar. As they passed through the now darkened streets and hay-strewn alleyways, they eventually emerged at the baths of Agrippa surrounded by the magnificent Pantheon, relieved the donkeys of their burden at the monastery, and making sure the beasts were properly stabled and rested ready for the return journey. The Abbot and monk eventually retired for the evening.

CHAPTER 8

Canterbury/Lincoln
12th June

Stepping out of the train carriage Dean Graham walked towards the London taxi rank, told the driver his destination. "Take me to Kings Cross station." As the Dean sat back in the taxi his thoughts returned to how he'd dealt a blow to his adversary, the north of England, and ahead of Hoag. The Dean wasn't sure if Hoag knew of his past demeanours but he couldn't take any chances of him following. The bullet he gave him should slow him down, but he knew it wouldn't kill him he had as many lives as a cat and he was remembering a year ago when they almost crossed swords. A mosaic Hoag was supposed to authenticate, but the company he worked for at the time asked his opinion and he decided against Hoag, as he was too controversial and wouldn't be easily swayed by a bribe, so they appointed a friend of his, Daniel Firth and paid him handsomely for his silence, and if it became public knowledge they'd know exactly where the information came from, Graham new that Firth had passed all his information on to Hoag and subsequently Hoag was watching him, and had always been one step ahead, but not this time, thought Graham.

The taxi pulled up outside Kings Cross station; he paid the fare and again walked away without tipping, offered his money to the machine and receiving a ticket to Lincoln. Dean Graham walked through the turnstile and punched the ticket out at the opposite end. He then progressed down the steps to the awaiting northbound train at the platform ready for the passengers to fill its carriages.

The train, also known as The Flying Scotsman and Mallard Line was the London to Edinburgh route that travelled all the way up the East coast of Britain, stopping at Lincoln, York, and Durham. The Mallard was designed by Sir Nigel Gresley and built in Doncaster and still holds the world speed record for steam locomotives.

At one time the journey would have taken about 10 ½ hours stopping at York for a half hour lunch. At the turn of the century (1900) the train was dramatically modernised, adding corridors, heating and dining cars and the journey was reduced to 8 ½ hours and a 15 minute stop at York.

It wasn't until 1924 the North Eastern railway officially renamed the Special Express as the Flying Scotsman, a name under which it had unofficially been known since the 1870s.

As the Flying Scotsman locomotive design developed, the train got faster and the journey eventually decreased to 7 hours.

The Dean settled down yet again into the first class carriage hoping that his journey would be fruitful. With a wry smile on his face Dean Graham lapsed into a light sleep and instantly he became swept away by his thoughts of money.

Canterbury to York

Marcus paid the Manager of the bed and breakfast Inn and eventually all four were secured into the hire car seatbelts and on their journey travelling northwards. Reaching the outskirts and eventually passing through London's famous Squares, unmistakable statues of admirals and former statesmen, the Houses of Parliament, the Mall, exquisite Buckingham Palace, and Hyde Park. Marcus would have loved to stop and show off all he knew about London, but the clock was ticking and he needed to know how this triangle of events would end. So on they travelled up the corridor of Shires, passing through Bedford, Lincoln, and Nottingham. Both Marcus and Louise took their turn at driving with a couple of stops for coffee, sandwiches and a comfort break. Eventually by early evening they arrived at the capital of Yorkshire, York itself and headed for yet another B&B. Marcus's knowledge of York was limited and they pulled into the first overnight hotel they found.

"Very nice," said Chrissie. "We're going up in the world, a B&B to a B&B Hotel."

Marcus ignored Chrissie's comments and accepted the northern City brochure with maps and particular opening times of all the events that happen in the city from the proprietor.

Paul was hungry as usual so they all trooped into the nearest restaurant and ordered their individual meals. While they ate dinner Paul still curious regarding why Marcus had broken the 1st stain glass window, and with his mouth full of food he asked. "I still don't understand why you broke the 1st window dad, there doesn't seem to be any connection to any of the other windows except the age of Jesus?"

Marcus allowed Paul to waffle on and just sat quietly eating his steak pie, peas, and French fries. Paul continued. "You say there's no book on the window, nothing significant about Saint Francis and…," Paul lifted his finger and pointed it at Marcus saying. "There are no black dots, so come on dad. Why did you break it?"

Marcus slowly laid his knife and fork on his empty plate and wiped his mouth with his paper napkin and slowly admonished Paul. "Don't speak with your mouth full and don't point, its rude, especially in a public place."

Chrissie and Louise looked at Marcus and laughed nervously, but Paul was having none of it and stared his father down, saying. "Your stalling, so come on, tell us, why?"

Marcus stood up, scraped his chair away from the table, and started to walk away from them, but Paul pulled his arm back and made Marcus turn and face him saying. "Why?"

Marcus with a smile on his face said. "You've already answered your own question." He then walked over to the waitress, paid the bill of fare and they all followed behind him and walked out of the restaurant.

Chrissie walked with Marcus but not touching or linking her arm she said. "Don't be too hard on him Marcus, he's still young."

"Your wrong Chrissie, Paul's old enough to understand manners and use his education to better himself."

"Marcus Hoag you're an old fraud."

Marcus with 'guilty' written all over his face smiled. "Are you referring to me?"

"Yes you. I heard all – about those times you disobeyed your tutors and went swimming in the lake at the university, even when they told you it had a dangerous undercurrent coming in from the mountain rivers, you took no notice, and about the time when..."

Marcus held up his hands and said. "Guilty as charged, Ok I'll ease up on him, anyone would think he was your son Chrissie."

"Marcus! Don't be so cruel."

Chrissie waived her hands in the air and walked off shouting. "Just because I didn't marry, it didn't mean I couldn't have children."

Marcus stood and watched as Chrissie walked away and he spoke aloud, "Did I hit a nerve or what?" He shook his head and followed her along Blossom Street, passing under Micklegate Bar Museum and up onto the beautifully preserved York City wall which surround the busy city.

Paul and Louise were following fifty yards behind, although they couldn't quite hear Chrissie and Marcus's conversation, Paul guessed it was about him and felt pangs of frustration. He had wanted to please his father, but he sure made it difficult when he got it wrong. He resolved to try harder and also to please the young lady that had a grip of his hand like a vice. He pulled her hand up to his lips and kissed her soft fingers saying. "I'll try very hard, to make you proud of me."

Louise, unsure what Paul meant, smiled and on tiptoe reached up and kissed his cheek, saying. "I love you just as you are." They both followed Marcus and Chrissie up on to the ancient city wall and followed it round to the left passing the York railway station and on towards the War memorial gardens.

Marcus eventually caught up with Chrissie and he placed his left hand in hers as they walked, then in his most humble voice he whispered. "Our first quarrel, am I forgiven?"

Chrissie looked at him coyly and with a twinkle in her eyes she said. "You were forgiven the moment you held my hand."

"Women," said Marcus. "I will never understand women!"

They both strolled along the high wall; following the steps down to Lendal Bridge and crossing the famous flood high River Ouse. As they passed over the bridge they waited for Paul and Louise to catch up.

The foursome walked down Museum Street towards the largest gothic Cathedral in Northern Europe. Marcus drawled.

"I think it's too late to go inside the Cathedral so how about we take a walk down High Petergate and on towards Stonegate, we can call in at an English pub and maybe try one of the beers on sale." All three glanced at Marcus with a knowing look, but said nothing.

"Ok," said Marcus. "Have you three got a better idea, because my feet are starting to ache and Chrissie's knees are going to collapse underneath her? It's been a long day, so I thought we earned the right to relax for an hour."

Paul quickly said. "Come on into the pub, I'll pay."

Marcus looked quizzically at Paul. "Have you any English money?"

"Lend me some money dad."

They all exploded into laughter as they pushed Paul into the pub first and sat down in the comfy leather seats in a corner facing the bar. Marcus ordered four half-pint glasses and the foursome settled down to sip the frothy light beer. Louise looked at Marcus and was about to mention his notebook, but Marcus had anticipated what she was about to ask, he produced the notebook and laid it out on the highly polished pub table. He flattened it out with his thumb and started reading to his captive audience of three.

7th Stain Glass Window (VII)

Saint Paulinus of Eboracum/York/Rochester
Born 573 Probably Rome

Book:	Closed
Chess Piece:	Pawn
Cross:	Cross & Crown/Crown of Thorns/ Crown of Glory Cross
Coin:	St. Benedict Coins (Font and black)
Sack:	Fonaby Stone, Stone Sack, or Sack Stone Famously rode to Caistor on an Ass
Patron:	Small Church's

Famous for Baptising a King (Edwin in 627AD) returned from York to Rochester. At Rochester when he received the Pallium of Archbishop of York.

Unexplained:

"Saint Paulinus of Eboracum, the old Roman name for York."

Paul asked. "Is there a Roman name for Yorkshire?"

"The Anglo-Saxon name is Deira, but north of Catterick (Catraeth) and the River Tees was called Bernicia, personally I think they are beautiful names and it's a shame they changed, but that's progress." Marcus took a sip of his small beer, wiped his mouth, and carried on with his monologue.

"Anyhow back to Roman York and Eboracum's Saint Paulinus, the third and last closed book of the triangle. If you remember I said he was a special monk, rising to the rank of alleged first Archbishop of York and Rochester, Kent."

Marcus began his explanation. "Paulinus was tall, with a slight stoop, black hair, a thin slender aquiline nose to fit a long face and awe-inspiring in appearance. A monk from St. Andrew's monastery in Rome when Pope Gregory The Great, you remember I spoke of him earlier, well he sent Paulinus to Canterbury and ordered him to travel to York because Gregory wanted York to be the metropolitan See in England, the second to the Vatican.

In the year 627AD he accompanied the Christian princess Ethelburga of Kent when she came north to marry King Edwin. Paulinus eventually persuaded Edwin to convert to Christianity and baptised hundreds of his followers. He built a church of timber in York for the Baptismal occasion and the church was classed as the first York Minster.

The timber church didn't last long, but with the support of Edwin's followers, Paulinus built another church of stone and dedicated it to Saint Peter. The church itself was rebuilt again by Saint Wilfred, but it was Egbert the first recognised Archbishop of York who made the Cathedral school and library the envy of Europe."

Paul quickly said. "I thought Paulinus was the first Archbishop of York?"

"He should have been, but before his Pallium for York had reached Britain, King Edwin had been defeated and killed in battle in 633AD. Paulinus feeling the Royal family were in danger decided to return to Kent with Queen Ethelburga and her children. He spent the rest of his days as the Archbishop of Rochester/York."

Chrissie asked. "What's a Pallium?"

As the Barman rung the bell for last orders, Marcus said to Paul. "Here's some money, go to the bar for another four halves of beer."

Paul hurried over to the Bar and just as quickly returned and settled down again to listen to his father.

"Where was I?"

Three voices echoed in unison. "We were discussing the Pallium!"

"Ah yes. It's a Vestmented ornamentation of white wool presented by the Pope to Archbishops on their appointment, and the sign of a Papal confirmation."

Louise asked. "How old was he when he was appointed."

"Well," said Marcus. "He would have to be over 60 to be presented with Papal Confirmation, so I guess that makes him..."

Paul quickly piped up. "He would be sixty years old. He was born in 573AD the Pallium arrived when King Edwin died in 633AD, voila, sixty years old!"

Louise had already worked, it out but allowed Paul to have the praise from his father. She felt he deserved it.

"Well done son," said Marcus. As he quickly glanced at Louise knowingly, he said. "I guess he's a chip of the old block! Do we have time for any more or are we too tired?" Marcus was about to turn another page of his notebook when a second bell rung.

The Barman shouted. "Time Ladies and Gentlemen please."

Marcus closed his book and eased himself out of the leather seats, turned and helped Chrissie to her feet. Paul and Louise were already up and ready to leave the warm pub. Once outside in the evening June air they could smell the fresh bouquet of the pendulous flower baskets that dangled at intervals along the path from their street lamp chains. The group set off retracing their steps back to the hotel, but instead of returning by way off the Cathedral they turned left and walked down Helens Square, turning right back to Lendal Bridge. Marcus and Chrissie stood on the bridge admiring the lights of the riverside by night.

As Marcus put his hands around her plump waist and squeezed her she said softly. "What a wonderful evening, I'd forgotten how lovely the summer evenings could be."

"Come on Chrissie lets catch up with Louise and Paul."

"If I didn't know you better," Chrissie said as she linked Marcus's arm. "I'd think you were afraid to be alone with me."

Marcus started to laugh, and said. "I think the beer is starting to kick in and yes I am afraid of you." Marcus shaped his right hand like a claw and said. "You're a she-devil in disguise. Grrr..!" They both started to laugh and hurried over the bridge and back past the memorial gardens and train station, then following the path down Blossom Street towards their hotel and a good night's sleep.

Lincoln/Durham

The Modern equivalent of the Flying Scotsman pulled into Lincoln railway station, with a slight jolt and feint rumble came to a dead stop. The second leg of Dean Graham's journey was over and feeling pleased with himself for being abreast of Hoag, he strutted out of the station and into a waiting taxi. Before the taxi driver could inquire where his exceptionally tall and bulky fare wanted to go, Graham arrogantly grouched. "Lincoln Cathedral, I don't need the sightseeing detour or the tourist talk, just get me there, a.s.a.p."

The taxi driver set off without saying a word but thinking plenty, arrogant old bastard, who does he think he is, I'll show him what no tour means, and he'll have to pay for it. Charlie Lister's wife had kicked him out of their home that same morning for being lazy, and accusing him of loving his job more than her. So he had a bee in his bonnet now, and the guy in the back had transformed into his wife, and he would try to hit every red traffic light he could possibly think of. The taxi driver wasn't sure if his fare knew Lincoln or not, but he was going to risk taking him the long route, just because of his arrogant demeanour. Normally he would take the quickest route which was to spin his taxi round in St.Mary's Street and head for Broadgate leading to Lindum Road and down Pottergate to the Cathedral, but not today, no, not today.

Dean Graham sat in the back of the taxi, blissfully unaware of how he had upset every taxi and cab driver he had ever met, he just didn't care, as long as he got from A to B with no hassle, and watched as the thin, tired looking driver swung the taxi up and down the Lincoln streets to deposit his passenger outside the large imposing Cathedral. The driver shouted the fare and arrogantly held out his hand, and as quickly as Graham paid double the normal fare, Charlie pushed the money into his money pouch and accelerated off, screeching his tyres as he went.

Dean Graham thought. Huh! What's his problem?

Walking up Minster yard, Graham was on the south side of the Cathedral and entered the early English Galilee porch turning left into the great transept, then right down through the choir and angel choir. Dean Graham pulled the notebook from his inside jacket pocket and flicked through it, unsure of what he was looking for.

On finding the page with the bishop's, teaching and dean's eye windows he was completely at a loss as to where to find them, quickly retraced his steps back through the choir. Just as he turned he glanced up at the angel choir and started turning the pages of his notebook again and thought. Ah, the Lincoln Imp. He looked up again to see high at the top of one of the columns, the stone carving of a mischievous laughing imp. The image was made famous by the legend that when let out to play by the devil this little imp was blown to Lincoln by the wind. After causing mayhem in the Cathedral, he sat at the top of the column and surveyed his bad deeds. While he laughed he was turned to stone by an angel.

"Well," said Graham. "If there's a clue here I just can't see it." He turned, walked down the north little transept entering the chapter house on the right, now even the Dean who normally hated church trawling couldn't help but be slightly overwhelmed by the vaulted ceiling, windows and oak Royal Chair, the arms of which are carved with the leopards of England and lilies of

France, it was used by Edward I when he invested his son the first English Prince of Wales (eventually becoming Edward II). Graham just stood and looked amazed for nearly ten minutes, a record for the architecturally uneducated Dean. So much history thought Graham, but no leads to what I'm looking for; he turned and walked out of the historic chapter house oblivious of the special acoustics it held.

Bypassing the library cloister, which holds one of only four copies of the Magna Carta and turning right into the north aisle of the nave and crossing over between the high columns to the black Tournai Font? The font material came from near Tournai in France and was shipped over to Boston, Lincolnshire and transported in kit form up the River Witham to Lincoln and there assembled in the Cathedral.

Dean Graham looked all around the font, looking for clues as to why he was here, decided to sit down in one of the empty pews to gather his thoughts on Marcus's notebook. He wrote down some notes but kept coming up with the same conclusion.

Special Significance (SS): Sower, Window, King, Lincoln Imp, Angel

The Dean unable to fathom or comprehend what he'd written, whispered to himself. "Hoag's notebook must be missing some vital information this can't be it. I will have to go to Durham and try to work it out from there."

Graham stood up and walked out of the Cathedral the way he came in, through the south transept and Galilee porch. He crossed over the grass verge and hailed a taxi from the kerb, climbed in and settled into the back seat. The driver asked him where he was headed and Dean Graham just stared at the driver confused. "Didn't you drop me off here just under an hour ago?"

The driver replied. "That would be my brother, he never stops talking, rambles on and on, it's a wonder you got here at all. I bet he took the long way round, through all the traffic lights? Did he charge you the earth?"

Dean Graham tried to tell the driver to take him to the station but he wouldn't stop talking. "How much did he charge you?"

Graham in a harsh tone replied. "I don't care how much he charged me. Just take me to the station, I don't need the sightseeing detour or the tourist talk, just get me there will you."

The taxi driver pulled away from the kerb and headed for Pottergate, turning right onto Lindum Road and all the way down Broadgate crossing the river Witham and turning right down St. Mary's Street, but instead of turning left into the train station, Michael Lister turned right and deposited his passenger at the bus station.

Dean Graham paid the driver his fare, and didn't realise where he was until he alighted from the taxi, but by then Michael Lister was driving away and with a wave of his hand, he disparagingly shouted. "Have a nice day Sir."

The Dean with a shocked expression on his face spoke aloud. "Where's the God-damn train station?"

An elderly woman passing-by looked at him with pensioners wise eyes and said in a wonderfully colourful slow Lincolnshire accent. "Na then ma duck, nae need tae look mardy, thou's at bus station, if thou wants train station its over't main road, but, if thou'll tack ma advice, thou'll travel be bus, much safer n' cheaper. Tara ma duck!" The elderly lady walked away chuntering to herself and leaving Dean Graham to try and understand exactly what she'd said.

He watched her walk away and an unfamiliar smile crossed his face, as the only words he understood were 'much safer and cheaper'. There didn't seem much else to do but take the old lady's advice, so he turned and walked to the bus station ticket office.

CHAPTER 9

York
13TH June

Marcus was first down for breakfast and enjoyed his full English breakfast of fried egg, bacon, sausage tomato and two slices of toast. As he drank his second cup of tea, Louise and Chrissie put in an appearance, and ordered two continental breakfasts consisting of two rolls, butter and lots of jam.

"Where's that son of mine, if he doesn't hurry up there'll be no bacon left for him?"

Just as Marcus spoke, Paul walked into the country style breakfast/dining room and sat down. Marcus about to give his son a telling off for being late down looked at him patting his tummy and saying. "Must look after my physique, I'm not a big eater in the morning dad, you shouldn't be either," Paul lectured as he winked at Louise. "It's not good for you all that grease and fat."

Marcus glanced at Chrissie and Louise and said. "When did he start being so concerned about his diet?"

Louise said laughing. "Oh! About 30 seconds ago."

Chrissie and Marcus stared in disbelief, then started to laugh when the waiter entered the room with a huge plate of double egg, bacon, sausages, baked beans, tomatoes, fried bread and a huge mound of toast, and placed it in front of Paul. "Enjoy sir."

Paul looked at the waiter and asked. "Can I have some hash browns as well please?"

"They're coming right up sir!"

"Son, where, do you put it all?" said Marcus as he gapped at his son's mound of food.

Paul with his mouth full tapped his legs and answered. "You were right dad, hollow legs."

While Louise sat watching Paul wolf down his breakfast she sipped her tea and said. "He's a growing boy Marcus."

Chrissie and Marcus shook their heads, made their excuses, and went upstairs to freshen up before walking back to the city centre.

Chrissie curious at Marcus's next plans said. "How long will your bluff keep Dean Graham at Lincoln and Durham and what do you hope to find at St. Peter's Cathedral?"

Marcus finished brushing his teeth then packed his toiletries into a small personal bag and zipped it up, then whispered to Chrissie as he pulled her close. "Don't worry about Dean Graham I've given him plenty of dumb clues to keep him busy for a while and York Minster will reveal her secrets when we get there."

Chrissie tried to gently push him away. "Louise will be up in a minute."

"Never mind Louise, come here wench."

Chrissie feeling like a young girl again and thinking back, all those lonely years I had given up of ever winning over the debonair widow Marcus Hoag. It had taken Chrissie a long time to realise that she could never love anyone else, she also admired his passion for history and wanting to discover and understand new things, but most of all she was happy for Marcus because of his love for his son, Paul. She wondered how they would both feel if they knew she was Alice's half sister. I'll tell him as soon as this job is over. Or should I tell him now. No, it's best to wait.

Her father had divorced her mother when she was two years old, but Daniel Connor never stopped loving his first-born child. Her mother would deposit her on his doorstep and say. You look after her for a weekend or for the whole week depending on how much money she had left. Her mother wasn't a saint but she wasn't a bad mom either and allowed her to stay with her father as long as she wanted. That's how it was and continued after he remarried. Daniel Connor fell in love with a beautiful socialite, Agnes Kenwright a millionaire's daughter. When her parents died suddenly in a car accident, Agnes married Daniel and that was the start of her fathers rise to the top. Alice was born during the Christmas holidays of 1930 but Chrissie hardly ever saw her younger half-sister, nannies made sure of that and her happy visits became less frequent, but her love for her father never ceased, even when she was a teenager she was never allowed to stay for long at the family home and continued to lived with her mother, until Chrissie at

22 years and Alice two years her junior, on the insistence of her father both then entered St. Peter's University together.

By this time her father was making his fortune with a little help from Agnes Kenwright's inheritance. During the war in the Pacific and Europe he was selling and distributing marine engineering merchandise to the Government. Her father had a natural enterprising ability and knew exactly when and where to buy even after the war years ended he expanded his business beyond the States and into Europe.

"Chrissie," Marcus whispered. "You're miles away, when we're married you'll have to give me your undivided attention and obey my every wish."

"What did you say?" Chrissie was all ears now. "Was that a proposal?"

Marcus looked at her for a full minute then pushed her gently down onto the two single beds that had been pushed together, kissing her fingers then used the old fashioned way of working his way up her right arm to her neck and whispering. "Aah Chrissie, if you'll have me my darling."

Chrissie pulled him round to face her and said. "Only if you always love me like this."

"That is a promise I intend to keep Chrissie." Marcus kissed his love full on the mouth.

Louise, without thinking or knocking walked into the bedroom, but just as quickly about turned and walked out again, saying to Paul. "You don't want to see what I've just seen."

Paul feeling a little melancholy said. "I could see something was happening between them, and I know Chrissie's good for him."

"Yes I agree your aunt is a lovely woman." Just as Louise said it, she knew she had made a mistake.

"What do you mean, aunt? I don't understand! How can Chrissie be my aunt?"

"Would it make a difference Paul, if she was?"

"Not to me, but it might to my father."

"Let's go freshen up and I'll tell you all about it."

Marcus came down stairs without Chrissie, on the pretence that he wanted to pay the bill for the hotel, but he walked straight over to a telephone booth that was in a small recess near the entrance door. He pulled out his notebook opened it up, picked up the phone and dialled the numbers.

The phone was immediately answered by a young English spoken boy of about 10 years old. "Hello! Who wants my dad?"

"Simon! It's your Uncle Marcus here." Marcus wasn't Simon's proper uncle, but from an early age young Simon had always called him uncle, and he kind of liked the sound of it. He could hear the 10 year old giggle and he asked. "Why aren't you at school today?"

"Uncle Marcus, I've got a cold, and the doctor said I must stay in bed for a full week, but I'm allowed to get up and play, as long as I stay in my bedroom."

"And are you in your bedroom Simon?"

"Well! No, but I have my pyjamas on."

Marcus smiled and thought to himself, Simon sounded just like Paul when he was the same age, always ready with a defensive answer, and he replied. "Where's you're daddy?"

"He's here now. Bye Uncle Marcus, I love you."

"Bye Simon, I love you too." Marcus could hear his friend scolding Simon in his Mancunian accent and sending him straight to his bedroom.

Danny Firth's wife had developed leukaemia six months after Simon was born, and she eventually lost her battle with the drugs when the boy was two years old, just at the time when children need their mothers the most. Simon seemed to grow up very quickly and always gave the impression he was a lot older. Marcus tried to get Danny to go out more but his excuse was always the same, he had to look after his son's best interests first.

"Hey mate, how you doin', haven't heard from you for ages. You do know you've just made Sy's day, I won't be able to do nowt' with him all week now."

"Danny, I need you to do something for me kinda hush, hush." Marcus explained what he wanted.

"You'll be cutting it a bit fine mate, but consider it done. Speak to you soon."

Marcus put the telephone down and walked out of the booth, as Louise, Paul and Chrissie came down the stairs Marcus took Chrissie's hand as he shouted. "Are we all ready, come on lets go hunting."

As Paul and Louise walked out the hotel door Louise nipped back in saying, "I've left my comb in the bedroom, I won't be long, and I'll catch you up."

She stepped into the telephone booth hoping the line that Marcus had rung would still be registered with the exchange. It was! She extracted the number and recognised it immediately and thought, you old fox Marcus, exactly what I would have done, and it's nice to have back up. Louise tottering in her high heels as she caught up with Paul, locked arms and whispered. "You won't say anything to Marcus about, you know what?"

Paul knew exactly what she meant and he thought, it didn't bother him in the least, but when his father finds out Chrissie's secret, he wasn't sure how he would react. He didn't like deceit and he replied. "He'll find out himself in his own good time Louise, don't worry."

Marcus and Chrissie hand in hand walked slowly through the elaborately adorned west door of York Minster, with Paul and Louise bring up the rear they traversed down the north side of the nave and glanced into St. John's Chapel, they followed the wall round to the Five Sisters window and about to enter the Chapter House, but there was a sign across the entrance with, 'Closed. Bishops in session' written across it.   Marcus said "That's a shame because the Chapter House has a beautiful cloister ceiling.'"

"Are there some clues in there we need dad."

"No Paul, but it has some wonderful acoustics, not as special as Lincoln but pretty good." They walked on past the Astro and Hindley clocks turning into the north quire and passing several chapels then walking towards the great east window and the high altar. Marcus turned and walked down the central quire heading back through the quire screen and stood next to the central tower surveying the nave and scribbling in his notebook. Instantly as Marcus took in the grandeur of St. Peter's York Minster, a spiritual sense of peace and quiet descended on him and his thoughts once more returned to the Abbott and another grand spiritual place, the architectural brilliance of Saint Peter's Basilica in Rome.

Saint Peters Basilica Rome C524 – 543AD

The following morning both Abbot and monk, washed and refreshed, exited the monastery and crossed over the fast flowing Tiber River, to the impressive Hadrian's Mausoleum, more formally known today as Castel Sant'Angelo.

"One day Romanus," said Benedict. "The walls of this Great Basilica of St. Peter will eventually encompass the whole of this area."

Romanus was suitably impressed with the Abbot's forward thinking knowledge and wanted to ask how he knew all these facts, but could only nod his head taking in all of these new surroundings, he also couldn't understand why the Abbot would want to leave a wondrous place such as Rome.

Benedict walked on up the long tree lined avenue with the monk following close behind him, he could see Romanus was indeed impressed by his knowledge, but his thoughts for his twin sister Scholastica was starting to take precedence the closer he got to their destination.

They pressed on and eventually arrived at the entrance to the Basilica. Romanus taking in the grandeur of the buildings, and with his finger touching the marble colonnades, said. "It looks so peaceful and serene, do you think the Abbess is in good health master."

"Scholastica," the Abbot replied with a forced smile, "is very old and painfully fragile Romanus.'

Romanus smiled and almost reminded his master that he was the same age as his twin sister, but decided against it and simply said. "Master, look over there, under the cloister, it's her two companion nuns."

"Good! Go speak with them Romanus, while I inform Deacon Pelagius of our arrival."

The monk walked over to the cloister and spoke to the nuns while the Abbot carried on up the steps and entered the Basilica.

Benedict spoke with the Deacon and was asked to wait for a few minutes, then he saw Romanus quickly climbing the steps hurrying towards him and he related the nun's story.

"Master," he said with a rush of words. "It seems she had an audience with the Holy See, but wished to return to her convent and nothing they said would stop her. They said it was most unlike the Abbess and thought there was something ailing her."

The Abbot without speaking turned and walked up the grand stairway to the Papal quarters wondering how he should best approach the Papal See regarding sister Scholastica.

The Deacon, with a curl of his finger, beckoned the Abbot to enter the Papal apartments. Benedict responded and entered the sanctity of the Papal See.

The Abbot couldn't help but marvel at the long galleries and wonderful architecture, the beauty of the wood panelling and how the light penetrated through the clerestory windows, almost like silver spears.

He was still looking up when Pope Vigilius entered the room.

"Benedict," he said with a broad smile. "I trust you had a good journey? Have you had any refreshments yet?"

Benedict ignored Pope Vigilius' niceties, and immediately inquired of his sister.

"I spoke to her," said Vigilius as he sat down behind his opulent writing desk. "And she was indeed unwell, so I sent her back to the convent at Subiaco with a Papal escort."

Before Benedict could reply, Vigilius said. "I see you've brought the monastic rule with you, please, may I see it."

The Abbot removed the book from his satchel and handed it to the Papal See. Vigilius flicked through the pages and said without looking up. "I'll have my monks and deacons make copies and issue them to every monastery under Papal guidance. Your Regula Monachorum will be known and practiced throughout the missionary lands."

Pope Vigilius without warning stood up, proffered his hand to the Abbot, and expecting Benedict to kiss the papal ring, but the old Abbot simply bowed his head, touched the ring with his long bony fingers and feeling inwardly pleased his work had been accepted, stepped back, and took his leave of Vigilius. Benedict slowly removed himself from the papal quarters and went in search of Romanus.

Meanwhile, Romanus, while waiting for the Abbot, felt he had neglected his prayers and seated himself close to the holy shrine read the inscription:

SAINT PETER THE CHIEF APOSTLE
WAS BURIED HERE IN 64AD

As he waited for Benedict to finish his business upstairs his mind became curious and he spoke aloud his feelings. "I wonder what it would be like to live within the walls of the great Basilica; maybe someday I will come back."

Little did Romanus realise, but this was only one of two visits he would make to Rome, the second visit would be permanent.

As the Abbott and his monk made their way down the steps towards the River, but unknown to them they were being watched from high up on his balcony window, Pope Vigilius stood surveying them. He then glanced down at his Papal ring and remembered when Benedict's sister had made her leave of him. She also refused to kiss his Papal ring, but bowed her head and touched the ring with her slender fingers. The Pope became annoyed and dismissed her, as he did her brother a few moments ago. Immediately he called for Deacon Pelagius.

The deacon entered his master's apartment and bowed his head. "Master you wished something?"

Vigilius turned fully round, picked up the monastic rule and handed it to the Deacon and ordered him to place it in the vaults. "The Abbot's work will have to wait its turn before being copied. Remove it now Pelagius and place it in the vaults."

St Peter's York

"Where's dad?" enquired Paul.

Chrissie turned, thinking Marcus was next to her, and finding he wasn't, had the feeling he'd abandoned her, she said. "He was here just a minute ago, where is he?"

"Look," said Paul. "He's through there in the central part of the Minster. Come on, let's find somewhere to sit down and ask him about St. Paulinus." All three followed Marcus's footsteps down through the quire. Marcus' brought out of his thoughts turned around and saw Chrissie's hurt look on her face, walked up to her and before she could say anything he said. "I thought you were behind me, I tend to get carried away when I enter these places, so don't fret if I wonder off again."

"I'd prefer it if you'd tell me first," she said unhappily.

Marcus gave Chrissie a peck on the cheek and whispered. "Sorry love!" They all sat down in a group on the available small chairs in the nave, and Paul wanting his father to finish off telling them about St. Paulinus, asked. "Come on dad, Paulinus, you didn't finish telling us about him."

"Oh yes, I'd forgotten about him," said Marcus as he skimmed through his notebook. "He was part of the triangle of closed books, baptised a King, Pallium of York/Rochester and Chair of York."

"We know all about them," said Louise. "You told us last night."

Chrissie and Paul nodded in agreement and Marcus said. "Did I tell you about Fonaby Stone?" No one spoke. "Ok! As Paulinus rode along a track to Caistor south of the Humber River on an ass, he met a man sowing corn. Paulinus asked for some grain to feed his ass; the man replied that he had none. Paulinus spotting a sack in the field asked what it contained. 'That is not a sack; the man lied, but only a stone.' Paulinus replied. 'Then stone it shall be.' The stone is now known as Fonaby Stone, also Sack Stone or Stone Sack and sits upon Fonaby Top, and any attempt to remove it or damage it, results in dreadful misfortune for the person or persons responsible."

Paul and Louise begun to laughing and Paul began to ridicule his father. "He's having a laugh, 'dreadful misfortune.' Crap! You don't believe all that do you dad?"

Marcus looked at Paul and said seriously. "If you knew the story behind the same stone, if you came across it, would you move it?"

Paul just shook his head and Marcus said. "I thought not."

Chrissie pointed to the small bookmarkers and said. "One looks like a coin and the other a chess piece. What's the connection?"

"The coin is Saint Benedict's coin. On the front is Benedict with a book in his left hand and a cross in his right, on the table is the cracked chalice and a Raven."

Paul was about to say something, but Marcus grouched. "I know you think it's a cup, but to me it's a chalice ok!"

That wasn't what Paul was looking at but something else he had noticed, and thinking his father had made another mistake in his notebook, kept quiet for now and just listened as his father carried on.

"You remember I told you the story in the new library at the university, about the letters on the front around the coin are in Latin, Eius in obitu nostro praesentia muniamur (May we be strengthened by his presence in the hour of our death)?"

Chrissie curiously asked. "What does it mean in the hour of our death?"

"Benedictines always regarded Saint Benedict as a special patron of a happy death, he himself died in a chapel at Montecassino while assisted by two of his faithful monks. He stood with his arms raised-up to heaven, smiling and then passed away. On the reverse side of the coin, we've already seen this at the old chapel, C.S.P.B."

"Crux Sancti Patris Benedicti," said Paul.

"The cross of our Holy Father Benedict," Marcus continued with a smile. "Give us the rhythmic plainsong prayer Paul?"

Paul began to recite the prayer, but in a musical intone. "Crux sacra sit mi-hi lux! Nunquam Draco sit mi-hi dux!" and then tried to recite the plainsong musically in English but not quite sounding the same and drawing some curious looks from other visitors he carried on. "May the holy cross be my li-g-ht? May the Dragon never be my gu-i-de?"

Marcus quickly said. "That was terrible; remind me Chrissie, not to ask him to sing again"

The group tried but unsuccessfully muffled their laughter, and Marcus about to carry on with his explanations of the next bookmark was interrupted by Paul, as he could hardly contain himself any longer, pointed out to his father that he had made a mistake in the notebook. "The chess piece, you think it's a pawn, but I think it's a christening font."

Marcus, taken aback by his son's observation, said. "You could be on to something son, but what makes you think that?"

"Look at the words opposite the coin. You've written font and black, instead of front and back and I just thought it does look like a font rather than a pawn on a chess board, but I don't understand the black."

"Black, back of the coin son," and Marcus started to scribble once again in his notebook and said. "I think you're right, I'll alter it."

"What happened to the picture you took," asked Chrissie, "Remember Marcus in the old chapel?"

Marcus pulled the photos out of his jacket pocket and thumbed through them saying. "Only three developed properly, so we can throw away the rest." He began to put them back into the envelope, except the three last pictures of Saints Augustine, Paulinus, and the 8th window, which had no name along the bottom, and placed all but the 8th window into his notebook, he gave the envelope with the spoilt pictures to Paul and said. "Just throw them away, they're of no use to us now, and I've enough rubbish in my pockets."

Paul dropped them into a waste bin next to his chair and urging his father, said. "Come on dad read it; I thought we were on a time limit?"

Marcus said casually. "Not any more we're not."

Paul red faced, as he remembered his mother was not alive and Dean Graham was out of the race, hesitated, and mumbled an apology. "Sorry dad, I – I didn't mean..."

As Marcus winked a knowing wink he said. "Its ok son, forget it, I know what you meant."

Chrissie affectionately patted Paul's hand and quietly whispered. "We all miss her Paul, probably more than you will know."

Paul simply nodded, keeping his eyes averted from Chrissie's as Marcus continued to show what he knew of the 8th window to all he regarded now, as his family.

"The 8th window," said Marcus. "A closed book, but not part of the triangle, and this window only highlights the important points of the other windows and keeps bringing us back to the number eight, infinity, birth, and baptism. The chain above the font is used to lift the font cover when christenings were booked."

<u>8th Stain Glass Window (VIII)</u>

No Scroll with a Saints name?
A mere summing up of the triangle of S.G.W's

Book:	Closed (not part of the triangle)
Font:	Baptism. <u>Saint Paulinus</u>
Chalice:	Cracked. <u>Saint Benedict</u>
Staff: ⳨	Canterbury Cross <u>Saint Augustine</u>
Chain:	Used to lift the font cover
Cross:	Upside down. Saint Peter Alpha & Omega/Beginning & End 8 infinity loop
Blazon:	Colour Tawney not red Gule
	Symbolic Joy
	Gemstone Jacinth
	Heraldic Tenney
	Astro.Assoc. DH
Unexplained:	● ● ●

Paul pointed to the upside down cross and unable to understand the significance, until Chrissie interrupted both Paul and Marcus and said. "An inverted cross is sometimes known as Satan's cross because it points downwards to Hell, but this is a misnomer; Satan was never crucified on a cross, because it's believed he fell to his death. For some the inverted cross is a pagan image and resembles the Nordic hammer of Thor. Saint Peter believed to have been crucified upside down at his request, did not feel worthy, just like Saint Andrew and the Latin cross, to die the same way as Jesus. Therefore many Christian sects use this cross as a symbol of humility." Chrissie pleased with her little recitation began to smile. "And here endeth the lesson,"

As the others gazed at her in stunned amusement, she sat back in embarrassment. "So! I went to Sunday school."

Marcus said with a grin across his face. "What Sunday school?"

Louise, normally quiet while Marcus has his notebook out, asked. "Why the Greek letters alpha & omega?"

Marcus, pleased that Louise was starting to join in the window discussions, said. "Looking at that form Louise, it looks like we're nearing the end of our search, the beginning, and the end. Going back to Jesus, this is a cornerstone of Christianity, that Jesus Christ, as part of the Godhead (second Person of the Trinity), and has existed since before the creation. Jesus called himself 'the alpha and the omega, beginning and end'. I find it fascinating where all this detail on the windows emerges from."

"Let's have a look at the photo dad?"

Marcus pulled out the photo and placed it on a seat in between them, and Paul picked it up. "The colour of the blazon is wrong; I thought you said they were always red gules, but this one is more orange. Why?"

"The colour," Marcus explained. "Was tawny (Light brown and a tinge of yellow or orange) and not meant to be part of the seven stain glass windows but a guide, hence the different colour."

Paul still confused, asked. "What do the rest of the symbols mean, especially the last one, Astro Assoc. DH?'

Marcus looked at Paul without reading his notebook and said. "Astrological Association and DH, stands for Dragon Head."

"Dragon Head," said Paul puzzled. "Where have we heard that word before?"

Chrissie quipped. "He's right Marcus. You mentioned it in the old chapel on the scroll and Paul sang it just now, the rhythmic Latin prayer."

Paul was about to sing the Latin prayer again, but Marcus held up his hand and said. "No, no not again please not again, once was enough."

"But, she's right dad." Paul got up and wondered over to the reception desk next to the south entrance looking for a pamphlet that might help, and Marcus said to Chrissie he wanted to have a look down the south nave and wouldn't be long.

Chrissie and Louise sat quiet and tried to absorb their tranquil surroundings and Louise took the opportunity to enlighten Chrissie of her mistake in revealing her connection to Alice.

"Don't worry about it Louise, I'll tell Marcus when I'm ready, that is if he doesn't already know, you know what he's like with secrets, timing is everything with him."

Paul collected a free leaflet and crossed over to one of the large columns on the north side of the nave and stood looking up. Unable to believe his eyes, he searched for his Father, on seeing him on the south nave whispered loudly. "Look at this dad!"

Chrissie and Louise turned around and gazed at Paul as he stood pointing upwards and whispered with a softer undertone. "Look dad!"

Both women began to laugh in spasms as Paul, leaning on the pillar and gesticulating his finger upwards called again to his father, but Marcus didn't hear him, or simply ignored what was under his very nose, he was too wrapped up in finding the window he would love to investigate, 'The Jesse Tree', but Marcus simply scribbled as much information as he could before being dragged along by Louise and Chrissie to the central nave where Paul was still standing, but not pointing anymore, just looking up at the huge Dragon Head which was attached to one of the nave's high column.

Lincoln/Durham
12th/13th June

The look of surprise on the face of the Dean as he alighted from the taxi, and not knowing where he was, would have made Marcus Hoag suitably pleased. The Dean took the advice of the old lady and walked over to the Lincoln bus station office, booked a ticket to Durham and thought to himself, I can probably get something to eat and catch up on some sleep.

The Dean had no idea that the railway station was only 500yards away across the main road, and after waiting half an hour he stepped on to the long distance bus with his holdall stowed away in the huge compartment underneath. He sat down exhausted by jetlag and promptly drifted into a dream filled sleep, his next stop, Durham and the shrine of Saint Cuthbert dubbed, "The Wonder Worker of Britain."

Dean Graham stepped off the overnight bus, retrieved his holdall, and walked over to the large lockers on display, deposited his baggage and locked the metal door, placing the key into his trouser pocket. He almost raised his hand to hail a taxi, but thought better of it and saw a bus with Durham Cathedral written across the front; he hopped on and paid the miniscule fair. The local bus eventually arrived at the bottom of the hill at the Cathedral. The driver, especially for tourists had called out the stops and indicated a few of the 630 conservation properties and listed buildings (569 of which are within the city centre) all the way from the bus station, and was much appreciated by his passengers, especially Dean Graham. He alighted from the bus and trekked his way up the long incline towards what he hoped would be his inevitable goal.

The Dean walked through the ancient south entrance, emerging into the cloisters and passing through the south transept, walked up the quire and on to St Cuthbert's shrine in front of the chapel of the Nine Altars, built to accommodate the vast numbers of pilgrims visiting the shrine which also features the second Great Rose window, the first is in York Minster and classed as a work of historic art. Dean Graham sat down next to the shrine and pulled out what he thought was Marcus's notebook and studied the heraldic blazon in front of him, but try as he might he still couldn't fathom the connection between the two great cities. As he stood up about to turn and retrace his steps back down the quire towards the nave and Galilee Chapel (Lady Chapel) which held the venerable Bede's tomb, he bumped into one of the young priests who had appeared from the south quire aisle, and his notebook suddenly dropped from his grasp.

The young cleric bent down and picked up the book and handing it back to the Dean, said. "My apologies sir, your notebook I presume."

Dean Graham took the book and opened it at the 8th decoy window, and although it galled him, he asked the young man what he thought the page in the notebook could possibly mean.

8th Stain Glass Window/Dean Graham's Notebook

Saint Cuthbert of Dunermum/Durham
Born 634AD Dunbar NortHumberland (Scotland)
Book: Closed
Windows: Prince BishOps
Flag: Durham trAditional flag
Durham: From old EnGlish Dunholm (Hill-Island)
Legend: Founding of Durham. Monks led by a milkmaid whom had lost her dun cow that was found resting on this spot.
Mint: Minted own coins, separate from Westminster Mint.

<u>Treasures of Saint Cuthbert</u>   8 coins
                                    8 saints
                                    8 jewels on Book
                                    + 8 points, Infinity

The young cleric studied the page of the notebook. "I can agree with everything that is written in your notebook, but the treasures of our saint are not coins, saints, or jewels on a book but are the relics of our Saint Cuthbert and they are certainly not for viewing."

"Indeed," said Dean Graham.

He decided to ask his advice about the 7th decoy window and turned the pages, passing the notebook back to the priest.

"I have to agree also with what you have written down for Lincoln, but..."

Dean Graham about to take the notebook from him, said. "What do you mean, 'but'?"

"Have you noticed sir, how some of the letters in your notebook are raised up as in capital letters incorporated inside the words, and I also noted you've written Special Significance: Sower, Window, King, Lincoln Imp, Angel."

"What of it, it doesn't mean anything?"

"Ah! But it does in the North of England." The young cleric pulled a pen from his pocket and scribbled in the Deans notebook, then handed it back. "I think someone is pulling your leg sir, but good luck anyway." He then walked away smiling to himself and thinking, tourists, always treasure hunting.

Letters rearranged as follows, would be written on the back of a sealed love letter:

Special Significance:

Sower	S = *Sealed*
Window	W = *With*
Angel	A = *A*
Lincoln	L = *Loving*
King	K = *Kiss*

Raised capital letters inside words translate a childish code:

7th *Window*	M A R C U S
8th *Window*	H O A G

Dean Graham had to sit down as he looked at the scribbled letters on what he thought was Marcus Hoag's original notebook and cursed under his breath as he realised he had been duped yet again, and this was going to cost him dearly. He looked again at the notebook with disbelief at what was written.

The rage resounding in Dean Graham's head almost overpowered his senses when he read, 'childish code', and Marcus Hoag's name in capital letters across the page. If he could he would have burnt it with the fierce anger he was feeling inside. Instead he stormed out of the Cathedral and threw the notebook into the nearest bin, thinking, ok Hoag! So where can you be.

Dean Graham walked back down the pathway towards the bus stop, knowing that a tour bus stopped every ten minutes and suddenly he couldn't believe his luck. Sprawled across a billboard in front of him was an advertisement for York railway museum, and the train he travelled up in was the famous modern Flying Scotsman, which passes through York on its way to the north and Edinburgh. The billboard announced one of the original steam trains is housed in the York museum. Graham thought to himself, what can I lose by going to York, absolutely nothing, but I just might be able to pick up Marcus Hoag's trail, and if I don't then I lose a million and a half bucks.

His determination got him thinking all the time as he hopped onto the next bus and was transported back to the bus station to collect his holdall from the locker. He telephoned the hire car company which he'd used at Heathrow airport and they had a car waiting for him at Durham railway station, he only needed to walk the ten minute journey down Station Approach and within two hours he was in York, and walking past the War memorial gardens and eventually crossing Lendal Bridge.

He'd parked the hire car in one of the small car parks along the swollen River. As he walked he thought to himself. I will find him, but first I must find the Cathedral, and there, straight in front of him was the magnificent York Minster, with its imposing twin towers and gigantic single tower that can be seen from twenty miles along the vale of York and beyond.

Graham passed through the west door and sauntered up the south side of the nave passing the Jesse tree window, which had held Marcus's interest only fifteen minutes ago. Dean Graham looked around him and thought of asking the receptionist some questions but instead decided to sit down to think about his next move. As he sat down he glanced to his left and saw a small photograph on one of the seats along from where he was sitting, he recognised it immediately, he had never seen the picture before but it was unmistakably the eighth stain glass window from the university. The Dean picked it up and looked at the front and back. What a stroke of luck, he thought as he looked at it and could see no reason why Hoag would leave it there. He must have thought I was out of the running and forgot about it, he read what Marcus Hoag had written on the back.

Slipping it into his pocket, he hurried out the south facing doorway and under the splendid Rose window (named the Heart of Yorkshire) and wound his way back to the car park and his hire car. With a sigh of relief and thinking, at last I know exactly where I'm going, and once again, the dollar sign's started to flutter inside Dean Graham's head.

York/Bridlington
13th June

Paul, Louise and Chrissie gazed up at the huge upturned shape of the Dragon Head and gasped in amazement, until Marcus brought them all down to earth with his laughter; he looked at his three companions and said. "I'd already seen it and knew it was connected to the eighth window and a font, thanks to Paul's sharp eyes. I told you the window has a chain, which lifts the font lid or cover by the Dragon Head pulley system, but they obviously stopped using it for some reason."

Paul turned his attention to the floor beneath the Dragon Head pulley system and questioned. "What happened to the font?"

"Paul," said Marcus. "Go ask the receptionist for a brochure about where we can find the third font?"

Louise and Chrissie listened, fascinated as Paul walked towards the information desk while Marcus explained that there should be three fonts in York Minster and the most important one was missing.

Paul reached the desk, enquired about the third font and why it was missing. The young twenty-year old female student informed him that the font had indeed been moved during the Civil War and now resides in St. John's Church, Bridlington. She went on to inform Paul that there are two more fonts in the Cathedral, a permanent one in the eastern crypt and a second movable one in the nave. Paul thanked her and she handed him the appropriate leaflet with her phone number written on it. Paul turned beetroot red and said. "No thanks, I have a friend with me," and he passed the information leaflet back to her, replacing it with one without her phone number on and walked back to the group.

Louise watched as Paul returned with a full blush on his face. "What was all that about? You look like you've been in the sun too long."

Paul put his arm around Louise and kissed her forehead and said. "Nothing, nothing for you to worry about, come on I've got the leaflet about the font."

Marcus and Chrissie were also watching the scene with the receptionist and couldn't help having a little chuckle between them and Marcus said. "He's going to have to be careful not to hurt Louise's feelings, if ever they part; I'm not sure which one will be hurt the most by it."

Chrissie said nothing; she just nodded her head and thought to herself. The same could be said about us if ever we part Marcus my love.

Marcus said to Paul and Louise. "You two find the crypt and have a look at the font."

Paul backed up and said with a frown. "Oh no, I'm not going down a crypt, not after what happened last time."

"Don't be a baby Paul," said Marcus, a little louder than he meant. "Just have a look and come straight back here while Chrissie and I have a look at this other movable font. Go get out of my sight."

"Ok, ok, we're going." And with hurried steps Louise and Paul disappeared past the information desk and into the treasury and crypt while Chrissie and Marcus walked over and sat down for a well-earned rest on the seats to the left of the small font. Marcus fished in his pockets and pulled out his notebook and began to look at the last three photographs again. As he looked at them he realised he didn't have the third picture and said to Chrissie in a hurried voice. "Where's the third and last photograph Chrissie?"

"Paul asked for it and you put it on one of the visitor chairs, but I don't know if he actually picked it up."

"Damn! Where were we sitting?"

Chrissie looked up, then leaned forward and pointed round the font at the other side of the nave and suddenly drew back her hand, quickly cupped her mouth with both hands and stared in front of her. As she drew in sharp breaths in between whispers she quickly said to Marcus. "John Graham! – Dean Graham! – Marcus he's here! Over there!"

Marcus quickly put his arm around Chrissie and held her tight as he gently calmed her down and said. "Just try to breath easy. I just hope Paul and Louise stay down in the crypt."

As Dean Graham walked out of the Minster, Marcus soothed Chrissie again saying. "Aah! It looks like he's going out the south entrance and we can relax now, but that was a close one."

"How did he get here so soon Marcus?"

"That's what I'd like to know. Are you sure we can trust Louise? I remember a conversation we had not so long ago and you said we couldn't trust her."

"That's not what I meant and you know it. I meant she couldn't be trusted not to get in contact with her department."

"I know, I know," he said and gave Chrissie another hug. "I'm just thinking out loud that's all."

"Look Marcus, Paul, and Louise are coming out of the crypt, we have to warn them."

Marcus and Chrissie got up from the seats and hurried over to the crypt entrance. "Let's get out of here son and take a walk back through the precinct to the hotel. We've just seen Dean Graham and I'm not prepared for a confrontation, come on, let's go."

Paul, about to ask why and how, but Marcus hurried on ahead holding on firmly to Chrissie's hand and gesticulating to Paul and Louise saying quietly. "Come on! Move it or he'll see us."

While they hurriedly walked through York, Marcus quickly read the brochure and found that the font had indeed been moved to Saint John's Methodist Church to protect it during the Civil War. Saint John was the Prior of Bridlington in 1362 or Burlington as it was then called, and he was made a saint in 1401.

Marcus heaved a sigh of relief as they arrived safely back at the hotel, paid the Bill and his party, sitting in the hire car with seat belts on, set off for the east coast of Yorkshire. Paul map reading again said, "God! I am so hungry."

Louise tapped him on the head and said. "Don't worry Paul I feel peckish as well, what about you Chrissie?"

Chrissie nodded her head and gave Marcus a gentle nudge on his shoulder and said. "We could do with some gasoline Marcus, why don't we find a place where we can get lunch as well?"

"First place we come to," said Marcus. "And it's called petrol in Britain, not gasoline."

"I knew that," said Chrissie. "You're just showing off."

CHAPTER 10

Bridlington, East Yorkshire
13th June

An hour later Marcus and his party arrived at the seaside resort of Bridlington. They drove down Bessingby Road leading to Hilderthorpe Road, emerging out onto the quay and found a small car park in front of the town's Spa theatre that looked out onto the North Sea. As they climbed out of the car they all felt the warm summer breeze with a slight lift in temperature and threw their thin jackets back into the hire car. The North Sea was very calm and in the mood to allow the sun to shine but a slight sea mist had descended on the seven miles of sandy beach, not that it could put Paul and Louise off, they immediately wanted to dip their toes into the cold water, but looked at Marcus first and said. "We won't be long, ten minutes and we'll be back."

"Ok," said Marcus. "Ten minutes no longer, we still have to find Saint John's Church."

Louise squealed with laughter as Paul picked her up and ran barefoot down the beach to the water's edge and as he put her down in the cold salt water, he gently took her hand and paddled as they walked, but Paul also leaned over and romantically kissed her mouth.

Marcus and Chrissie watched them both from the side of the quay and looked at each other. Marcus said with an ache in his voice. "We missed all that Chrissie."

Chrissie pulled at Marcus's hand. "Come on get those shoes and socks off, were going for a paddle as well."

"Don't think," said Marcus laughing. "That I'm going to carry you down, I'll put my back out."

Chrissie swung her shoes at him and laughed. "Oh, Marcus Hoag, you make me feel so young."

Marcus cupped her chin with his hand and groaned. "I'm still not carrying you down there." They both slowly walked hand in hand down to the edge of the water and paddled in the cold North Sea, trying to forget all about Dean Graham, stain glass windows, Cathedrals, Minsters and secrets yet to be revealed, just enjoying the time together and not allowing anything to upset the mood they were all in.

Feet eventually dried and shoe's back on, they enjoyed the sun and fresh air of the coastal Town and walked through the shopping centre down Quay Road towards St. John's Street.

The smell hit them as they entered Saint John's Burlington Methodist Church. It was the scent of polished wood, roses and carnations all mingled into a wonderful bouquet. The walls were painted in a soft creamy white, almost as if someone had used milk on them and the fragile stain glass windows were like painted mercury. Marcus had never seen such detail on an arch window; nothing had prepared him for such beauty all in one place and his thoughts once more returned to the virtuous Saint with the beautiful pale blue eyes and long white beard.

Montecassino Monastery C524 – 543AD

A few months had passed since Benedict and Romanus had travelled to Rome and the Abbot, nearing his seventieth year was easily fatigued and retired to his cell early in the evenings, while Romanus delivered most of the Abbot's meals there, but would also join him for occasional prayers.

On hearing of the death of his twin sister Scholastica, the Abbot sent Romanus and a few other monks to bring her body back to Montecassino where she was to be interred in the burial plot which Benedict had provided for himself and her body was placed in Saint John the Baptist chapel, to rest there until the time came for Benedict to join her.

One month had passed since Scholastica had been buried in the chapel, and Romanus worried about his master, found Benedict sitting contemplating the loss of his sister in his favourite cloister overlooking the valley and the River. The Abbot, feeling vulnerable and weak could sense his time on earth was coming to a close, and sent his faithful monk to bring his successor Constantinus, to administer Holy Communion. Assisted by the old monk and Romanus, Benedict raised his arms to the heavens and with a gentle smile on his face, peacefully passed away in the arms of his friends.

Constantinus immediately sent his monks, with the exception of Romanus, to visit every monastery in the surrounding municipalities, also sending a runner to St. Peter's in Rome, to inform his Eminence of the Abbots demise.

For three days and nights Benedict's constant friend, stood guard over the Abbots corpse while awaiting clerics of all status to enter and file past Benedict's casket, before internment in the burial plot in Saint John the Baptist Chapel next to his beloved sister Scholastica.

Romanus, in deep prayer, wept for the first time in his life, overwhelmed at the death of his friend, he felt he could no longer stay at Montecassino and within a few days he would travel to Rome, entering the Great Basilica of Saint Peter to accept one of the variety of posts available as a cleric to the many deacons there.

St. Johns Church Bridlington

It was Paul that broke the long silence between them and said quietly, almost in a whisper. "Where do we start dad? Dad, where do we start?"

Marcus abruptly brought out of his melancholy quickly replied. "A Font is usually placed next to a western door and symbolises entry into the Christian faith. I think the door we came in is south facing so I guess if we split up we'll cover more ground."

"Toss a coin to decide dad?"

Marcus looked at Paul and shook his head thinking, will the boy never learn, but calmly said. "Paul your in a church, you and Louise go left, Chrissie and I'll head right and try not to make a noise."

Paul turned to Marcus and pressed his finger to his lips and signalled. "Like a mouse dad."

"I'll give him mouse!"

"Come on Marcus," said Chrissie. "He's winding you up."

"I hate it when he does that, it's so childish and why can't he be serious for once!" As they approached the back or east end of the church Chrissie said. "He's more like you than you think." But Marcus wasn't listening to Chrissie his attention was taken up by a small corner chapel window.

"Look at that Chrissie, isn't that something to behold?"

"Yes, but what do the words underneath it mean?" Marcus read the Latin words, and then read them again just to make sure he'd got it right and said. "Oh my God Chrissie, I think I've cracked the code."

"I didn't do anything, never touched a thing."

"No, I mean the black dots, it's all here right in front of me, and I was right all along, I just needed to confirm it."

"What do you mean you were right all along? You know where Saint Benedict's Rule is hidden?"

"Of course I do!"

"Is it here, in this church?"

"No!"

"Then why are we wasting time here?"

"Like I said, I just needed confirmation and what makes you think were wasting time?"

"I thought Dean Graham was following us? He found the photo of the last window."

Marcus narrowed his eyes and smiled at Chrissie as he said. "Don't worry about Dean Graham he's nowhere near here." Marcus, about to say something else to Chrissie, but Paul and Louise came hurrying down the aisle towards them.

"Dad, we've found a font, its moveable and there was this Latin inscription on it."

Paul handed the note to Marcus and he compared what he had written down from the corner chapel window and said. "Well done you two."

Chrissie still didn't understand what was going on, and sat down in one of the pews. "Explain, will you explain, I don't understand what you mean."

Marcus looked at her and said eagerly. "Ok, let's sit down, back up and I'll go through what just happened here. When we were in York Minster I saw the Dragon's Head as soon as we walked in, but the font underneath it was missing, that's why we searched the Minster. I went off on my own purposely to find another clue from the Jesse window."

Paul about to ask his father about the Jesse window, but Marcus had already anticipated his son's curiosity lifted the palm of his hand up. "I'll explain the Jesse tree later son," then carried on saying. "I found the name that should be on the scroll under the last window's blazon and I wrote it down on the back of the photo. The one Paul forgot to pick up from the seat when I passed it to him."

Paul looked at his father, reached into the back pocket of his trousers and pulled out a slightly crumpled photo of the eighth stain glass window with Saint Hilda of Heretu (Hartlepool) written on the back and handed it to Marcus and said. "I thought I'd picked it up, it's a bit crumpled, but I forgot it was there."

Marcus a little lost for words looked at Paul. "The photo I saw Dean Graham looking at, which one was it, because I have the other two and we threw away the others."

Louise suddenly began to laugh as she opened her shoulder bag and produced a second copy of all the photographs, minus the last picture. "I'm sorry, but like you Marcus. I like to have back up as well. Just in case. Oh! And the name I put on the back of the photograph was Whitby, North Yorkshire, famous for its Synod, Whitby Abbey, and black Jet jewellery."

Marcus' face dropped at the mention of Whitby. "Louise, tell me you didn't write Whitby on the back of the photo."

"Yes, but why? I thought the further north Dean Graham was the better."

Marcus sighed deeply. "The black dots on the heraldic blazons, I deciphered them." Marcus wrote down on a new page of his notebook to allow Louise and the other two to understand his frustration:

A<u>D</u>A<u>M</u>   Sowing window Canterbury   D (II) M(VIII)
TRANSFER OF RULE
TRANSLAT<u>I</u>O IMPERII   Jesse tree window York I (III)
WITH GOD WILLING
DEO <u>V</u>OLEN<u>T</u>E Corner chapel window Bridlington V (VII) T (V)
THE KEYS OF SAINT PETER
<u>C</u>LAVES SANCT<u>I</u> PETRI   Font Bridlington C (IV) I ((VI)

DMIVTCI

D=12:30	M= 8:15	LI= 09:35	V= 12:25	T= 11:00	C=11.30
2nd SGW	8th SGW	3rd & 6th SGW	7th SGW	5th SGW	4th SGW
(II)	(VIII)	(III) (VI)	(VII)	(V)	(IV)

Marcus revealed that the black dots were called semaphores. An old system of sending messages by one's arms or two flags in a certain position or you could use lanterns.

Paul with a confused look on his face glanced up at his father. "What has time got to do with these letters, they don't make sense?"

"Your right son," said Marcus. "But if I were a Roman General in the first or second Century and stationed on the coast of Diera/Yorkshire as it was known then, the letters could be rearranged into the name of a small fishing port or Roman Fort."

Louise looking truly shame faced said. "The Roman Fort wouldn't be positioned at Whitby would it?"

"Sorry Louise," said Marcus. "But yes, it takes its name from DICTIVM, the Roman station name (the place of speeches). You weren't to know, so don't beat your self up about it, it's done now and maybe Dean Graham won't understand exactly what he's looking for."

"But why?" said Paul. "I still don't understanding what time has to do with it all."

"Absolutely nothing," said Louise. "They could have used the idea of semaphores to let ships know where they were or what time high tide was."

"Good girl Louise," said Marcus with a grin. "I never thought of that."

"Yes!" said Louise sarcastically. "Write that in your little notebook Marcus."

"Come on lets head on up to Whitby, and you can drive Louise, seeing as your so clever today." Marcus passed her the car keys and said. "Last one back to the car pays for dinner."

"Wait a minute," said Paul with a lost look on his face. "I haven't any money." They all looked at him and began laughing, then Marcus started to back-up to the church entrance and just as he was about to run out the door he cried out. "You better not be last back then." Marcus disappeared out the church door with Chrissie and Louise, and eventually Paul chasing after him.

CHAPTER 11

Whitby, North Yorkshire

Dean Graham parked the hire car in a parking space next to a row of telephone booths and picked one of the receivers up, dialled the usual number and waited what seemed an age, but was in fact a mere few seconds. Gabby picked up the call and asked where he had been yet again, but before the Dean could give her a snappy answer back a man's voice echoed down the line. 'What in hell are you playing at Graham, the auction has been rescheduled for tomorrow, and I could lose a sale as a result.'

"I'm in Whitby and on my way to the Abbey at the top of the cliff, but why's the auction changed? I have the Benedictine within my grasp."

"Within your grasp is not good enough," said the caller. "I need it here now, if you don't get it here by noon tomorrow, you can forget it and no-one will ever hire you again and any bonus will be forfeit." The telephone went dead.

Dean Graham knew there was no way he was going back to London without the Rule, he casually walked back to his car and set of into the modern port of Whitby, winding his way up to the top of the cliff, which overlooked the harbour's vast array of deep-sea fishing vessels and colourful sea-side shops and houses.

John Graham parked his car at the cliff top car park and made his way along the gravel path towards the ruins of Whitby Abbey which stands on the site of a 7th Century monastery which was almost destroyed by Vikings in the 9th Century. The present ruins are of a 13th Century Benedictine Abbey. He walked past the Abbey ruins and carried on towards the now famous Saint Mary's Church. The church was built in the 12th century; although it has had many features added, it remains as it was from that time until now.

The Dean entered the quiet dimly lit church and sat down in one of the box pews, and often rented by families who had their names engraved on the side panels. Dean Graham could feel his exhaustion beginning to take hold, and was about to stand up and move around the church, but his legs felt like lead weights and his head started to droop forwards, shaking his head the Dean lifted his legs up onto the pew and lay back with his head resting on a pew cushion. The Dean's strength was completely gone and he lay peacefully asleep, dreaming of his ranch in Argentina.

Bridlington/Whitby, North Yorkshire

After having eaten the seaside town's famous fish and chips, 'al fresco', next to the promenade, Marcus' new family walked back to the hire car.

As they walked, Chrissie asked Marcus. "How did the Dean get to York so quickly? I thought you said he would be kept occupied for a few days?"

"Dean Graham's very resourceful, he probably asked someone for help in solving the simple clues I left him." Marcus quickly thumbed at Louise.

You left clues," said Chrissie as she threw her arms in the air. "Why on earth would you do that?"

"The clues I left him in the notebook had nothing to do with York, Bridlington or Whitby, my guess is he got lucky, as York is on the main railway line from London to Edinburgh, and I'm hoping he won't know exactly where we'll be going in Whitby." As Marcus spoke they passed a telephone box and he looked at Louise and said conspiratorially. "I need to make a call Louise; will you two take Chrissie back to the car?"

Marcus squeezed Chrissie's hand and whispered. "Don't worry, I won't be long."

Chrissie with a grim look on her face said. "Marcus this cloak and dagger stuff."

Marcus lifted his hand, palm upwards and stopped Chrissie speaking and said in a cool tone. "Chrissie, don't interfere. This is what I do!" Marcus turned around and walked over to the telephone box.

Chrissie hurriedly caught up with Paul and Louise. "Come on, we might as well get in the car, the weather has turned a little cool now." She quickly looked up at the sky and intimated. "The almighty has spoken."

Paul puzzled, looked at Louise and quietly mouthed. "What is she talking about?"

Louise and Chrissie started to laugh as they pushed Paul into the back seat of the car and Chrissie said. "You're dad can tell you all about it when he gets back from 'what he does'."

Marcus picked up the phone and fed the meter with some loose change then dialled the number. The call was picked up immediately, but not by Danny Firth's son.

"Hey Danny," said Marcus. "You manage to do that little job for me?"

"Sure thing Marcus, nobody suspected a thing."

"I've got another favour to ask?"

"Fire away mate."

As Marcus finished asking his second favour he said. "Don't go feinting, but I've a surprise for you and Simon. I'm getting married again."

"Wow! You old dog, kept that quiet didn't you?"

"Well, to be truthful it kind of happened sudden."

"Do I know the unlucky lady?"

"You bastard!" cursed Marcus at his old friend. "'Unlucky lady' indeed, ah Danny you remember Alice; well it's her half-sister Chrissie, Chrissie Greenwood Connor. It's a long time since I felt like this man, so I'm grabbing the advantage while I'm still young enough."

Danny was silent, and deep in thought at the mention of Chrissie's name. He knew Christine Connor and wanted to warn Marcus, but the telephone began to beep, beep as Marcus's money was running out.

"Marcus, Danny shouted down the phone, don't do anything hasty, think about it first." It was too late, the phone went dead, and Danny Firth replaced the receiver and thought to himself, I need a babysitter.

Marcus didn't hear Danny as he shouted back down the phone, but just as the beeps started he understood his silence. He then put down the telephone and stepped out of the box, he was deep in thought as he strolled along the busy promenade to the car.

Marcus silently climbed into the back seat with Paul. Louise was in the driver's seat and Chrissie trying her hand at map reading. "We want the Scarborough Road A165 and then Whitby A171." Chrissie, thinking that her map reading ordeal was over, closed the book, sat back, relaxed and watched the green verges and wonderful sea views going swiftly past.

Within the hour they had arrived at the centre of Whitby and as Louise manoeuvred the hire car into a parking place next to yet another bed and breakfast, she cut the engine, but before getting out of the car she turned round to face Marcus. "Did you call Danny Firth again Marcus?"

Marcus tried to hold back his annoyance and not wanting to alienate Paul by letting Louise know just how much she had caught him off guard said quietly. "Yes, I asked for his help in London and he managed to get the auction put back until tomorrow."

"Thanks for being honest with me Marcus, I appreciate it, I know you're not telling me everything but at least we can trust each other now."

Marcus feeling a little annoyed with himself for giving in to Louise's question, took his temper out on the passenger seat in front of him and pushed it a little too hard and it shot forward, making Chrissie trap her foot as she got out of the seat and resulting in her falling over. They all heard the slight crack as Chrissie screamed in agony and Marcus jumped out of his side door, and tried to sooth Chrissie, but she wasn't in the mood and vented her anger on him.

"You fool Marcus Hoag, always in a hurry, can't you just slow down and stop getting angry when people get too close to your secrets. If this is, 'what you do!' Then I want no part of it." Chrissie, with the help of Louise picked herself up and hobbled over to the B&B entrance and disappeared inside.

Marcus slowly sat down on the guest's summer seats surrounded by a haven of colourful bedding plants and hanging baskets dripping with colourful fuchsia pendulums. Marcus, with a glazed look on his face said to Paul. "She's right, I can never get it right can I, first your mom, then you, now Chrissie, what is it with me son?"

Paul knelt down in front of him and said with a firm tone. "Pull yourself together dad, go in there and tell her just how much you care for her, and stop feeling sorry for yourself, she's the one injured, not you!" Paul stood up and walked away from his father then entered the B&B hoping Marcus would heed his advice and follow him.

Marcus got up from the outdoor seat turned as if to follow Paul but changed his mind and turned again, walked down past the car and on to the path heading towards the town centre, his thoughts still on Chrissie and what she had shouted at him; 'What you do! And I want no part of it'. Over and over again he thought about it in his head until he came to a shopping arcade, walked under a large whalebone arch, which commemorated the once busy whaling industry that was thriving in the 18th century. The very first whaling ship set sail from Whitby harbour to Greenland; as a result it set Whitby firmly on the world map.

Louise had mentioned earlier that Whitby Jet (Black Lignite) was very popular with the locals and in the 19th century it was favoured by Queen Victoria as mourning jewellery. Captain James Cook who sailed from the town on the bark Endeavour to search the globe on his high seas adventures also made Whitby famous.

Mike, the Bed and Breakfast proprietor examined Chrissie's foot and concluded that he thought she'd broken her right ankle and suggested they go to the casualty unit, which was a short trip to the end of the road and five hundred yards further on down the main road. He insisted on taking Chrissie and Louise in his own car, and Paul said he would wait for Marcus to return and tell him where they'd gone.

As Paul sat outside on the summer seat he thought to himself, at times like this I can't believe dad would just walk away, not after the way I cautioned him. Some times I just don't understand how his mind works, but he's gone too far upsetting Chrissie, and I won't let him off this time.

Marcus was walking up past the hire car with a bouquet of flowers and a weary look in his eyes as he called out. "Paul where is she, where's Chrissie? Is she still inside resting?"

Paul had wanted to shout at his father, but instead pulled him down onto the summer seat and informed him where they were. "Chrissie and Louise have gone to the hospital with the proprietor of the B&B he's taken them in his car."

Marcus immediately threw the flowers at Paul and shouted. "Which way did they go?"

Paul caught the flowers, but grabbed his father's arm and said. "No dad it's best to wait here, the proprietor thinks her ankle's broken but I think it's just badly bruised, she's having it x-rayed and Louise is with her, so for once will you just let go and wait for them to come back, after all, she won't break."

Marcus and Paul both looked at each other and Paul realising what he had said, they both begun to laugh and Marcus said. "Son, you come out with the daftest things, but your hearts in the right place, I'll wait."

One hour later they were still waiting. Marcus groaned. "Something must be wrong; it shouldn't take this long for an x-ray." Just as he spoke a car spun into the driveway and parked next to the hire car. Marcus swiftly crossed the gravel drive ahead of Paul and opened the passenger door.

Chrissie looked at Marcus and said with a soft tone to her voice. "Marcus, I'm sorry, I didn't mean what I said, I was just in so much pain, forgive me?"

"Forgive you," said Marcus with a high-pitched tone. "You shout abuse at me and tell everyone what you think of me and you want me to forgive you. No, I won't forgive you, not until..." Marcus put his hand inside his jacket pocket and pulled out a small box, and Paul quickly gave him the flowers. Marcus quickly knelt down and opened the small box and passed it to Chrissie, as his voice softened he said. "Not until you say you'll marry me, please Chrissie before I go off and 'do my thing' as you so nicely put it."

Louise and Paul looked on as Marcus took the ring from the box and placed it on the third finger of her left hand.

Chrissie looked down at him with soft eyes. "Yes, you crazy man, now get out of my way."

Marcus hugged and kissed her until she pushed him away again and with a painful squeal she shouted. "My ankle, my ankle get off me you old softie, the Doctor said it's not broken but I need to rest, come on, and help me get out of this car."

Once Chrissie was settled in the B&B lounge and a cup of tea in her hand, a cushion under her bandaged foot and Louise fussing round her, Marcus said. "I want to stay, but I really need to do this Chrissie."

"I know, but please be careful love."

Marcus looked at Louise and asked if she would stay with Chrissie.

"Of course I will, you don't need me now Marcus."

Marcus quickly turned fully round and looked at Paul. "Come on son I need your help." He then turned back to Chrissie and lifting her left hand; he gently kissed it. "We're going up to the Abbey, I'm sure that's where the Benedictine is buried."

"What makes you so sure it's there Marcus?"

"Do you remember when I went to look at the Jesse tree in York Minster; well underneath the window were the words 'TRANSLATIO IMPERII (transfer of rule)'.

I assumed the underlined letter 'I' meant exactly that a Latin letter, but when I read Hilda Abbess of Heretu/ Streanaesheath (Harlepool/Whitby Abbey), it became obvious that it meant Hilda 1st Abbess of Whitby Abbey and 2nd Abbess of Hartlepool, because there were two II's and I'm fairly sure I've pinpointed almost exactly where it rests."

"Where?" asked Chrissie.

Marcus looked at her and put his finger to his nose. "Ah! You know I can't tell you everything all at once. If we find it, we'll be straight back."

"When you get back Marcus, I have something I must tell you."

Marcus kissed her forehead stepped back from her and winked. "I know all about it, so don't worry."

Louise put her arms around Paul and whispered. "I'm sorry I put you all in danger with Dean Graham."

Paul held her close and nuzzled her nose and cheek saying. "No worries, we can handle him, that's if he turns up. He hasn't any clue to where we'll be."

As Louise let him go and waved to them both, she thought to herself, I have a terrible feeling that Dean Graham, as Marcus said was more resourceful than they all thought, and Chrissie, well her secret would just have to keep until Paul and Marcus returned safely.

Paul and Marcus walked out of the B&B and into the hire car, then drove out of the car park heading for the ruins of Saint Hilda's Abbey which sat at the top of the grassy east hill cliff overlooking the town of Whitby and out onto the dark brooding North Sea.

CHAPTER 12

Manchester
13th June

Danny Firth stood in the antique shop that he'd owned for almost twenty years, just looking out of the window and planning his trip to the east coast and thinking he'd better get a move on. His son Simon had been deposited at his favourite aunt's; Danny's sister Helen loved to have Simon and Danny knew his son would be safe.

Danny was a dark haired 5ft 10in fifty six year old Mancunian by birth. He'd lived in Manchester almost all of his life, except for the few years he spent in the army.

Danny had become separated from his British unit during the Cassino, Italy conflict in WWII and decided to shelter in a tiny chapel. As he stumbled with exhaustion through the entrance and collapsed just inside the archway, he was aware of a few American soldiers who sat with their backs to the east chapel wall trying to relax, with one or two just leaning on their rifle's chewing gum, almost as if they were just passing the time of day, oblivious to the noise of the bombs and sniper fire all around them. Danny, always prepared to be friendly rather than hostile, asked one of them if they would like a cigarette in exchange for some gum, it just so happened that Marcus Hoag stepped forward and gave him a full pack of the stuff, but refused the cigarettes that Danny offered. Marcus made a comment that smoking would stunt his growth, and asked how he got into the army. Danny said they were desperate for bodies and he was healthy so he had no choice, the draft board gave him the once over and stamped him fit to die for his country. From then on Marcus laughed at Danny's never ending jokes, they tripped of his tongue so quickly he had trouble catching the beginning of the joke he was laughing so much. All too soon they had to depart and go their separate ways, Marcus advancing up the mountain and Danny wanting to try and return to his unit. They shook hands and exchanged names and addresses.

It was five years before Danny or Marcus made contact with each other, but they both knew they would be life long friends from that horrible day in the chapel at the bottom of Montecassino hill.

Danny locked the antique shop door and walked to his parking bay, climbed into his car and set off for the East Riding of Yorkshire, but not thinking of Marcus, his thoughts were of Chrissie Connor and how they would feel at seeing each other again.

Saint Hilda's Abbey

Marcus pulled into the same car park as Dean Graham, but at the opposite end and closer to the Abbey. Paul with a tremor in his voice, groaned fearfully. "Why do we have to come to these places when it starts to get dark dad, did you read that brochure about, of all people, Bram Stoker, and Dracula? This is where he was supposed to be washed up on the shore at Whitby. St. Mary's church and the graveyard are just past the Abbey, I don't like it one bit, it makes me shiver."

"That's because you haven't got Louise for protection, you big scary lump."

Marcus opened the boot of the car and pulled out two large torches handing one to Paul he whispered. "Don't turn it on until we get to the Abbey. Come on, let's get moving."

Father and son hurried across the grass avoiding the footpaths and eventually reaching the east wing of the Abbey, Paul mused. "Where do we start to search? It's just a maze of small walls and boulders scattered about."

"These boulders as you loosely call them are an orderly part of the Abbey nave. The broken pillars would have been the slender vertical structures used to support the roof, and if you remember I told you that a font..." Marcus never got to finish his sentence because Paul finished it for him.

"A font is usually placed next to a western door and symbolises entry into the Christian Faith."

Marcus stood stunned by what Paul had recited and said. "You remembered, I don't believe it, for once you were actually listening to me."

"I always listen to you dad, but I sometimes don't agree with you, that's when I keep quiet, I don't want an argument."

"I prefer to call it a heated discussion rather than an argument."

"What ever you call it dad, I don't like to argue, heated or not, ok."

Marcus backed off and said quietly. "Ok son, point taken, lets look at the west wing. Huh!" Marcus was puzzled for a few seconds and said more to himself than to Paul. "Which way is west?"

Paul glanced out to sea. "If we look at the sea are we looking east or north?"

"North," replied Marcus. "Because of the way Whitby sits on the coast line, west is looking up the coast."

"I would have thought looking out to sea we'd be looking east and up the coast would be north?"

"Son, I thought you didn't argue?"

"I'm giving my opinion."

"Your opinion is wrong, trust me! Whitby faces north and up the coast is west, you can just catch a glimmer of the sun setting behind those clouds."

"Hey! Your right, I never thought to look for the sun, good thinking dad."

Marcus wasn't sure if Paul was winding him up again, but he didn't have the time to challenge him about it, so he let it go for now, he had more important things to think about and finding the exact spot where the Rule could be buried was going to be more difficult than he thought.

While Marcus searched the northeast wing, Paul, taking Marcus's advice, switched his torch on and began searching near the west wing of the Abbey behind what looked like the shape of a doorway, he shone his torch upwards onto a large central stone, above which, he was certain would have been the west doorway, and carved above it was the letter 'I'. Paul turned quickly and in trying to catch his father's attention, he tripped over one of the huge nave pillars yelling out. "Aah! Ooh! Ouch!"

Marcus came running over and helped his son to his feet, as he raised his arms he quietly admonished him. "Why don't you advertise to everyone, 'look we're here', have you found anything?"

Paul shone his torch up at the letter and said. "The letter, it's a sign, it has to be."

"Good lad! I think your right, come on search around for anything that might look like an entrance."

Paul couldn't help but be intrigued how the dying light of the sun shone through the window above the doorway and said to his father. "Dad, the time, what was the time next to the letter 'I'? Hurry up dad, before it's too late."

Marcus pulled his notebook out and shone the torch on to the page and said. "09:35 pm. Why?"

Paul quickly asked another question. "What time do you think it would be in Rome around 7th century? Come on dad quick."

Marcus did a quick calculation but wasn't sure so he guessed. "It would be around the same time 09:35 pm but I'm not 100% sure. They used sundials to ascertain the time of day then."

"That's close enough dad. What time is it now?"

Marcus looked at his watch, and couldn't believe his eyes. His watch was almost on 10:35 pm.

"It can't be," said Paul. "If your watch is right, the sun should have set an hour ago, but it's almost dead on the horizon."

Marcus looked again at his watch and recognition was written all over his face as he cried out. "I'm such an idiot! I forgot I turn my watch forwards one hour, because of British summer time. At certain times in the year, the British set their clocks forward one hour, usually around March and put them back in October. That makes the time now at 10:35pm, but the actual time would be 09:35 pm."

Paul listening to his father but also watching the dying sun quietly said. "Turn your torch off dad and watch where the last rays of the sun fall." Sure enough, just as Marcus turned off his torch, the sun cast its last beam of light through the small window above the west archway and rested on one of the orderly pillars. Marcus and Paul looked at each other with anticipation in their eyes they hurried over to the grey form. "What do you think son can we move it together?"

As Marcus waited for a reply from Paul, his senses told him Paul wasn't listening, but was preoccupied with something or someone. Marcus was about to ask Paul what was wrong, when a voice echoed along the south perimeter wall.

"Don't be a fool Hoag; anyone can see you're too old for lifting weights."

Marcus, recognising the voice, spun round and with a huge grin on his face at hearing and seeing his good friend Danny Firth walking towards them, he immediately offered a handshake, and it was reciprocated with a bear like grip from Danny, but he released it as quickly as he had offered it saying. "We don't have much time Danny. Let's get this thing shifted."

The trio heaved and pushed the heavy pillar until they felt something start to give-way. Paul and Danny rolled the nave perimeter marker on to the open grass. As they stepped back they saw Marcus disappear down the small oval shaped opening. Paul was about to follow his father, but Danny pulled his arm back as he said. "Try and hurry him up Paul, I'm staying up here to watch your backs, I'm also going to cover the entrance with this cardboard sheeting I found, it might stop any glare from the torches."

"Thanks, I'll try and hurry him, it won't be easy, but I'll try." Paul disappeared down through the burial entrance into complete darkness but switched his torch on before Danny could completely cover the aperture. Danny instantly cursed and hoped nobody of note had seen the torchlight glinting a few times off the Abbey wall. Once the entrance was covered Danny melted into the background and hoped that Marcus would find what he'd been seeking for as long as he could remember.

St. Mary's Church

As the last rays of the sun shone through St. Mary's western stain glass window on to the face of Dean Graham, the light woke him up and for a few seconds he wondered where he was, when realisation kicked in he gradually sat up swinging his legs from the uncomfortably hard pew seat. As he stretched, his body muscles started to awake and he could feel the chill of a church with it's heating turned off, even though there was a working stove that was sitting amongst the pews. Dean Graham stood up and walked back down past the box pews and passed through the archaic doorway and out into the now fast fading light and thought, where can they be? Or was this just another of Marcus Hoag's carefully planned enticements.

He was completely at a loss what to do next and decided to make his way back along the gravel path towards his hire car, when he saw the beam of a flashlight over towards the ruins, and thought to himself, there it is again, someone is skulking in amongst the remains of the old Abbey, and I'm going to find out who, but gently does it Morgaan, nothing gained by going in guns blazing. The Dean pulled his gun out and attached the silencer as he crept silently across the grassy mounds, coming up along the north-west wing.

Pressing himself firmly against the wall, he decided to sneak a quick look at whoever it was. Seeing no sign of anyone in sight he crouched down, and staying low quickly slipped past two of the nave pillars. He waited for at least two minutes listening for the slightest sound. Dean Graham wasn't the most patient of men and he thought, whoever it was they had either gone or he just couldn't see them. He decided to wait as he wasn't in any hurry and sat down on the grass. As he leaned his back against the pillar looked at his gun his thoughts went back five years to Alice Connor. Why did she always bring out the worst in me? I hadn't really meant to kill her only scare her; I loved her with the kind of love that should have lasted well into our retirement. Oh! Alice, Alice, if only thing's had been different, this is what I'm reduced to and the blame was all yours. If you'd only supported me all those years ago, who knows what our lives could have been like? Dean Graham's eyes were moist with the memories of what he'd done; as he hung his head in misery, he didn't hear Danny Firth come stealthily up behind him.

Danny was in the commandoes during the Second World War and never lost his sneak tactical touch, as his hand slipped underneath the Deans left arm and relieving the gun from his loose fingers, he thought, like taking candy from a baby.

Burial Chamber

Paul's feet followed his father down the uneven stone steps into the dark burial chamber, his mind racing as he thought aloud. "This has got to be one of the worst places on the planet dad, dad! Where are you, oh damn! I've lost him already."

"Mind your language lad."

"Where are you?"

"I'm at the bottom of the second set of steps, be careful they're not exactly made for someone running up and down."

On reaching the bottom, Paul commented on how many steps there were. "There are eight on each flight down. Are they connected to the infinity loop?"

"Looks like it," said Marcus. "But that's not important just now, these three empty stone coffins are."

Paul shone his torch on the almost unreadable names scrolled across the top of the stone cavity and tried with difficulty to read them. "I read Oswine King of Deira, Lady Osthr – something, and Bishop Aidan. Who were they dad?"

"Around the 7th Century Oswine and Lady Osthryth were second cousins, both having the same great grandfather who was Aelle King of Deira? Bishop Aidan and Oswine were reputedly to be good friends, they both died in the same year, 651AD which brings me to conclude that Edmund must have carried out his promise to transfer Oswine, Aidan and Hilda's relics down to Glastonbury. I wonder if his monks made a mistake and removed Lady Osthryth instead. They were probably afraid to go any further into the chamber than they wanted to." Marcus turned away and looking for the next set of steps that would take them further down into the heavy darkness.

"Paul, shine your torch above this sarcophagus I can't quite read the name." As both torches conjoined, Marcus took in a sharp breath as he read the name. "Edwin, King of Northumbria, whose lands stretched from Lincoln up to Edinburgh and as far west as Manchester. My God, we've hit the jackpot son, he was the first Pagan King to be Baptised a

Christian at York by Bishop Paulinus, and this was the beginning of the line that stretched down through the ages, starting with his daughter Eanfleda who married her second cousin Oswiu, who eventually became the longest serving King of Northumbria and the only Royal King to actually die of old age in his own bed."

Paul taking the lead and Marcus following turned right and walked away from King Edwin's stone coffin and passed through an archway leading to a different set of steps. "Be careful dad, these steps for some reason are steeper than the others." Father and son taking care not to slip emerged at the bottom unscathed with another set of steps to their right, but Paul noticed another stone coffin inside the large sarcophagus to their left. "Dad you mentioned Oswiu had married, what was her name?"

"Eanfleda," Paul turned his torch onto yet another name carved above a stone sarcophagus and read. "Oswiu, King of Northumbria."

Marcus could hardly contain himself as he said. "This just gets better and better."

"Come on dad lets go a bit deeper."

"I can't son my legs won't move, I think my age is starting to catch up on me."

"Or fear," said Paul.

"It's not fear son, I've never felt like this before, and I need to sit down. Just give me a minute." Marcus sat down next to the stone sarcophagus to catch his breath and spoke softly, "it must be the stale air or the thought of being so close to Saints and Barbarian Kings."

"I'll go down first," said Paul. "Follow me when you catch your breath, ok?"

"Ok I'll do that son."

Paul entered the lower chamber to find four coffins inside their separate blocks with names above, but no sign of a book or Saint Hilda's coffin, so he returned to where he'd left his Father, only he wasn't there, he'd disappeared.

Paul climbed the fungus covered large steps two at a time, as usual, always in a hurry to get to the top, but just in time to see his father descending yet another set of steps to the left of

King Edwin's sarcophagus. Paul followed him across the room and down the slime covered steps, catching up with Marcus and giving him a running commentary of the lower level. "Dad there were four stone coffins containing four Kings."

"What! Four Kings, oh, I don't think I can take much more of this, go on son can you remember who they were."

"Sure," said Paul, as he reeled off all four names with perfect pronunciation. "There was Eahlfrith, Eaifwine, and Ecgfrith all Kings of Deira."

"I thought you said there were four."

"Err!" Paul thought for a minute, knowing his father was in for another shock, as he told him the last name. "Oswald, King of Northumbria."

Marcus visibly paled in front of Paul and almost collapsed with the knowledge. "Have you any idea of exactly what we have found son. Saint Benedict's Regula Monachorum has no significance compared to all this."

Paul asked why they were all here. "Son, they're a family, whether they are kings or commoners they are basically a family. Oswiu and Oswald were brothers and the three Deira'an Kings were Oswiu's sons, and I have something else to show you." Marcus shone his torch onto the first two coffins next to the steps. "These two princes, Osfrith and Eadfrith were Edwin's sons. Osfrith died with his father in battle and Eadfrith was taken prisoner and was subsequently killed, but one of the best bits is, I've found Hilda's coffin."

"I thought she was a saint?" asked Paul.

"She wasn't a saint then, her title was Lady Hilda the first Abbess of Whitby, and look, she's laid next to her friend and first cousin, Lady Eanfleda the second Abbess, but the piece de resistance is, she's the keeper of Saint Benedict and Saint Columbanus Rule." Marcus looked at Paul. "Give me the Latin translation son?"

"Regula Monachorum, old man."

Marcus gave Paul a sly look as he noted the quip 'old man', but let it pass. "We must let the English authorities know of this find, after all it's their heritage, and I need to have a detailed look at these books."

"Will they be ok," said Paul. "I mean up top in the air, they won't disintegrate will they?"

"No son, not if they're sealed properly." Marcus pulled out three fairly large self-sealing plastic bags and handed Paul two. "Take out both books and place each one into a separate bag and seal it, make sure you seal it tight." Marcus emphasised the tight seal and continued. "Handle them very delicately son, they're a bit older than you or me. Take them up to the first landing and lay them in one of the corners and wait for me, don't forget to turn your torch off."

Paul was about to ask why, but Marcus told him to just do as he asked and he would explain later.

When Paul had gone, Marcus picked up the Irish Satchel, which was still in reasonable condition and climbed the stone steps, as he reached the second level he crossed over to the open coffins. Marcus reached into each of the empty stone coffins and pulled out what he hoped would be pieces of heavy cloth and bits of debris. He carefully placed the pieces of cloth into layers inside the satchel and then scattered the debris in the bottom and gently placed it into the plastic bag, sealed it and carried it up the steps to where Paul was waiting for him.

"Are you ready son, I just want to take a tiny peek first." Marcus eased the heavy cardboard up a couple of inches just in time to see Danny Firth collapse unconscious to the ground. Marcus turned to Paul and said. "Come on Paul lets put on a show for Dean Graham."

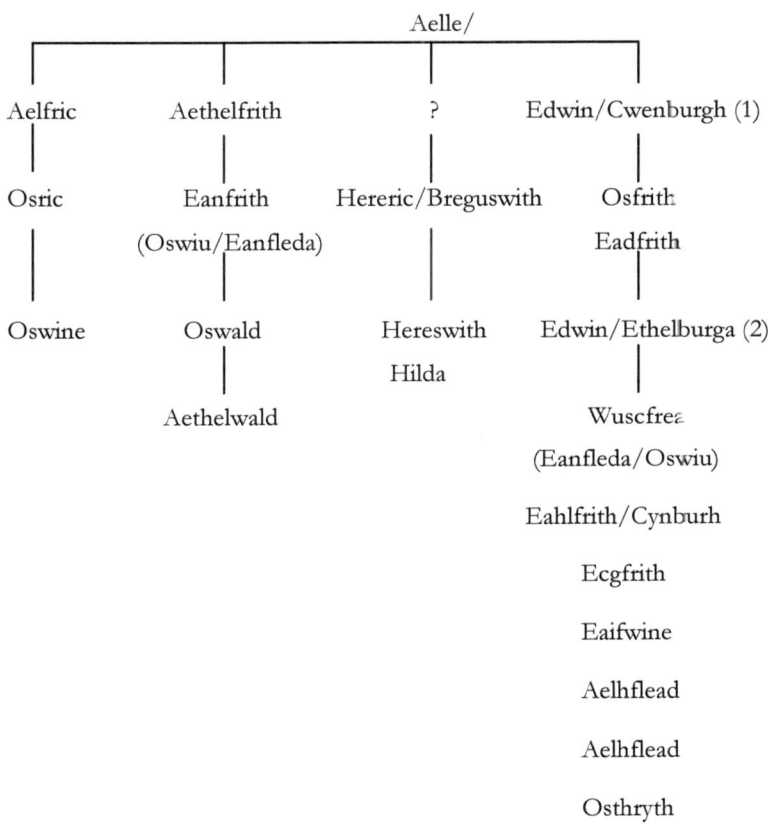

CHAPTER 13

Saint Hilda's Abbey
13th / 14th June

The rotors of the helicopter silently whooped as it hugged the fishing bays, shadowy inlets, and coves of the North Yorkshire coastline. The pilot using the updraft of the east hill cliff face, hovered for a few seconds surveying the Abbey ruins and looking for the best possible landing site, decided to gently manoeuvre and settle his metal bird down on a grassy mound east of the Abbey, close to the small pond.

The expensively suited man climbed out of the helicopter and ordered the pilot. "Under no circumstances do you leave here until I get back. This shouldn't take long."

The pilot with his night visor pulled down, answered with a wave of his hand, and said. "You're the boss."

The suit walked across the grass to the Abbey ruins and immediately took in the situation of Danny Firth pointing a gun at Dean Graham and trying to tell him exactly what he thought of him when suddenly a rock struck the back of his head. Danny was knocked out cold and fell to the ground oblivious of what hit him. The suit had picked up a heavy rock and took aim. He had been a great baseball pitcher in his time and knew he hadn't lost his touch when the rock struck home.

Dean Graham picked up the gun and as he pulled Danny's limp body behind one of the broken columns he said to the marksman. "What are you doing here? I told you I would see you in London tomorrow. It's too risky for you to be here and the fact that Firth is here, Hoag must be coming to meet him but I'll be waiting for him instead."

"Wrong Graham, we'll both be waiting for him!"

Seeing that the visitor meant business, the Dean decided to roll with it and said hurriedly. "Try and make yourself invisible and we'll surprise him together." They stepped away from each other, and melted into the ebony black recesses of the Abbey ruins.

It's beautiful Chrissie," said Louise as she admired the Whitby jet and diamond engagement ring on Chrissie's finger. "You're a lucky lady to have two admirers."

"I don't have two admirers," said Chrissie as she withdrew her hand. "What made you think that?"

"Danny Firth. Come on Chrissie, you can tell me, after all we've been through, I thought we were friends."

"I've known Danny for a long time," said Chrissie. "But the affair we had ended a long time ago and there's nothing to tell."

Louise wasn't easily put off and persisted with the same line of conversation as she said. "I'm intrigued to know why you stormed off when we were walking to York Minster; it's the first chance I've had to ask you about it?"

Chrissie leaned over conspiratorially and whispered to Louise. "What I'm about to tell you Louise must go no further than you and me." Chrissie spoke softly as she looked at Louise. "I met Danny when I was on assignment here in England almost twenty five years ago, it doesn't matter what the assignment was, and we enjoyed each other's company, and I fell pregnant with two of Danny's children."

Louise sat back, and thinking she had misheard. "But it's not on your file at the agency?"

"Let me finish will you! I miscarried them both, they were twins, and a miscarriage is never recorded on a file, especially if no one knows about it. That's the little secret between Danny Firth and me, and it's not to be broadcast." Chrissie lifted her hand and pointed her finger at Louise as she warned. "This is important to me Louise, Marcus and Paul must never know."

"Don't you think He has a right to know Chrissie? After all you're going to marry the man."

"Yes, but it'll be my decision if and when I tell him, and you have your own little secrets Louise, I couldn't begin to guess who your working for or why, but I do know that it's nothing to do with the FBI."

As she was momentarily taken by surprise at Chrissie's revelations about Danny Firth, Louise coloured slightly when her friend mentioned that she was ignorant as to who her other employer was, and thought, this is something Chrissie will have to wonder about for a while longer. The Irish wouldn't take too kindly to me broadcasting their interest in the Saint Columbanus' Rule.

"I can't confirm one way or the other," said Louise. "Not even to you Chrissie."

"Funny," said Chrissie as she got up and began to limp towards the door. "I thought we were friends, apparently not." Chrissie limped through the open lounge door and headed for the guest bedrooms.

Louise stood up and looked out at the Abbey ruins through the B&B lounge window. Everything looked as it should; lights were twinkling across the harbour inlet and the bells from the fishing fleet sounding in the warm evening breeze. She couldn't help but be envious of Chrissie, but most of all she was in awe of Marcus Hoag and his son Paul. She could see that Paul might follow Marcus into his world in search of secret ancient artefacts, she wanted her own relationship with him to flourish, but knew that a conflict of interest would eventually get in the way and she thought, better to finish this job and end the relationship now. Louise sighed deeply then thinking again of how Paul Hoag could instantly make her heart flutter, oh how can I, he's everything I ever wanted and I'm in love with him. She knew that her heart would ache for years to come if she followed through with her decision.

Saint Hilda's Abbey

Out of sight of Dean Graham and the unknown visitor, Marcus and Paul crawled out of the burial entrance and replaced the heavy boarding, they immediately crept around by the east wall, trying to disguise which way they had exited the Abbey and eventually emerged through a fissure in the Abbey's north wall, they then crossed over to where Danny Firth had fallen unconscious. Marcus bent down and tapped his friends face with his hand and said. "Come on Danny, wake up."

Paul knelt down and examined the back of Danny's head as he said. "He must have been hit with something hard; there's a great big lump on the back of his head. He could be concussed dad." Paul, turning away from Danny, sniffed the air then put his hand on his father's arm, he could smell something other than the sea air.

Marcus looked at Paul conspiratorially and placed his finger to his lips as he gently nodded and twitched his nose and quietly mouthed the word, 'Lavender'.

Marcus felt the presence of his adversary behind him and thinking quickly, said. "Danny, Danny I found it, Saint Benedict's Rule, it was hidden under Saint Hilda's font."

Paul, about to question his father, but realised he was creating a ruse, kept quiet as he focused his attention on the pounding headache and nausea he felt as he bowed his head next to the prostrate body of Danny Firth, who was just beginning to come round.

"Marcus!" bellowed Dean Graham with forced pleasure. "You found it for me?"

Marcus swung round and smiled sweetly. "Why do I keep getting the feeling you're following me Dean, did you enjoy your trip to Lincoln and Durham, fascinating Cities, don't you think?"

The Dean stepped forward and grabbed Marcus's collar and pushed the gun under his chin, but held back as the suit stepped forward. "Graham! I don't want any harm to come to Dr. Hoag. I warned you about those types of tactics, release him."

Dean Graham pushed Marcus away from him. "The Rule, give it to me and no tricks this time."

Marcus looked at the suit and with sincerity in his voice he handed over the plastic bag with the Irish Satchel inside to the Dean and feigned alarm. "It must be kept at a constant cool temperature and handled very delicately or it will disintegrate."

"Don't worry Dr. Hoag," soothed the Suit. "It'll be well looked after; I'm not in the habit of spoiling masterpieces, merely exploiting them. I'm sure the Vatican will be pleased to have their prized original Regula Monachorum back, but before that happens I must, as I said; take advantage while it's in my possession. It's a pleasure to do business with you Dr. Hoag."

Dean Graham and the suit turned and walked away. Paul watched as the helicopter took off and disappeared into the night sky, and said with a touch of attitude. "Do you know who the other guy was dad?"

"I haven't a clue son; I've never seen him before."

"Dad, the other guy was Dean Alexander."

"What! I thought he was in hospital, an accident, or something."

Paul, with sarcasm in his voice said. "He must have signed himself out early."

Marcus looked at his son and thought; at last, he's learning.

Paul knelt down again next to Danny and said. "I'll stay with him dad; I think he's still in shock."

"Ok son, I'll get the books and then we can get back to the B&B before they realise exactly what's inside the Irish Satchel and plastic bag."

Paul looked up at his father and with a level tone to his voice said. "They won't be looking inside the bag until they get to a controlled environment, so we have a few hours to get Danny to hospital before we even think of going to the B&B."

Marcus had listened to his son as he walked over to the thick boarding, removed it and climbed down to the first level, picked up both books wrapped in the thick plastic bags and thought, I think this could be my last daring enterprise, I'm tired and Paul has taken to this adventure lark like a duck to water. He climbed out of the burial chamber and called Paul over to help close the entrance.

Danny Firth was sitting up and feeling very groggy as he stammered. "What – what ha – happened? My head feels like a balloon about to pop, where's the Dean? Does he have the..." Danny never finished his question as Marcus and Paul slipped their arms through his and lifted him up, trying to walk and drag him to the hire car. Marcus wanted to drive straight to the hospital but Danny refusing point blank, said. "Go to the B&B, I'm ok, just a bit fuzzy that's all, I want to have a look at those books."

Paul said, earnestly. "We can't, we must look at them in a controlled..."

Marcus interrupted his son and said. "Paul, don't worry we have the perfect place."

Paul a little flummoxed asked. "Where, I thought we were going back to the Bed & Breakfast?"

Danny and Marcus looked and pointed at each other and said together. "The B&B, I own it. He owns it. We own it."

Marcus looked at Paul's surprised face and said. "That was wrong of me Paul, I should have told you everything, but sometimes, you learn, not to divulge everything all at once, it's sometimes a case of who do we trust."

"Are you saying you don't trust me?"

"You know, I don't mean it that way son, but you should always listen to the facts and work it out in your head before you open your mouth."

Danny looked at Paul and started to smile as he tweaked Marcus's ear. "Your dad, he gets so intense and boring in his old age, eh, mate. Don't you just love him?"

Marcus swiped Danny's hand as he said. "Get off my ear you big girl."

Paul began to laugh at the good-humoured pair, but also curious as to why his father chose to buy a B&B at Whitby. Marcus explained that when on a visit to Rome twenty years ago he was privileged to be able to view some of the Dialogues of Pope Saint Gregory, and noted that he was fascinated by the different dialects of the Angles and Saxons whom had visited the city of Rome some reputedly came from Whitby. Marcus finished off by saying. "Well! I put two and two together and hoped that this was where the Rule would be buried."

"You mean you looked that far ahead?"

"In this game son you have to always be one step ahead of your adversaries and it's a lovely town."

Marcus pulled into the B&B driveway and parked next to the abundantly packed flower boxes and borders. The three companions exited the hire car and entered the front door of the co-owned B&B.

"It looks like everyone is asleep," said Marcus. "What say we all turn in and convene in the cellar first thing in the morning?"

"Good idea," said Danny. "I'm bushed."

Paul took a quick look at Danny's head and said. "You really should have gone to hospital Danny."

"I've a scull thicker than a Manchester ship canal lad, don't fuss, I'm off to bed, goodnight!"

"I'm coming too," said Paul. "I'll walk up with you Danny, night dad."

"Night son, before I turn in I'm going to put these books in the cellar to keep them cool."

Chrissie heard the men come through the front door and climbed out of bed, quickly slipped her slippers and dressing gown on and as she limped along the hallway she came face to face with Danny and Paul. As she said goodnight to Paul her eyes never left Danny's face. Paul walked past her and nodded as he whispered. "Night Chrissie, dads still down stairs, I think he's making a cup of tea."

"Ok Paul, get some sleep."

Paul carried on down the hall and disappeared up the next flight of stairs. Danny hung back and leaned on the wall with one hand in his trouser pocket and the other held up in front of Chrissie. "Chrissie, I don't want a confrontation, but I'd like to know. Why Marcus? I know we have history, but I don't want him hurt."

"I would never hurt him, what we had has been finished with for years, and if I remember it was me that got burned."

"Yes Chrissie, but all those years ago, I just wish... Oh I know what we decided, but... did you ever stop and think when you returned to America, of the one's you left behind." Danny pushed himself away from the wall and took Chrissie's hand. "Ah Chrissie, I don't mean to rake up the past, and you're right, who am I to criticize."

"Danny, it's what we decided was best for them."

"Aah love, I needed you back then, I just didn't realise it until it was too late and I blew it." Danny looked at her with soft eyes. "Make him happy Chrissie, I know he's crazy about you, but I also know he's no fool. I'm fairly sure he doesn't know about the boys, so I think you should be the one to tell him as soon as possible."

Danny leaned over and kissed Chrissie on the cheek as he thought. I'm a bloody fool, and I should have made her stay in England and Married her, he then quickly whispered. "Goodnight love."

As Chrissie continued to slowly limp along the hallway she calmly said. "See you in the morning Danny."

Marcus stood watching and listening at the bottom of the stairs, feeling that he'd heard enough crossed over to the open cellar door and pulled the light switch cord but nothing happened. "Damn and blast," cursed Marcus. "The light bulb must have blown." Deciding not to descend the cellar steps, he walked into the extended kitchen and opened the wall fridge door, pulled out a large salad box from the bottom, placed the books inside, and pushed the box back into the lower part of the fridge. He was just about to close the door when Chrissie limped into the hallway, glanced across into the kitchen and spotting Marcus next to the fridge with a bottle of milk in his hand.

"Make me one too will you?"

"What!" Exclaimed Marcus, taken a little by surprise.

"Tea, make me one as well, that's what your doing isn't it?"

"Yes, yes of course, won't be a minute, I'll bring it into the lounge."

"What time is it?"

"It's about half past midnight." Marcus made the tea and put a couple of biscuits on a side plate, carried the tray through to the lounge, and placed it on the occasional table in front of Chrissie. He sat down next to her and handed her a cup and saucer as he asked. "How's your ankle, still hurting?"

Chrissie lowered her head and said. "My ankles not too bad, but before you went up to the Abbey Marcus I said I had something to tell you."

Marcus shook his head as he moved closer to Chrissie and giving her a peck on the cheek, he said. "I know all about it, I told you not to worry just now, just get better and then we can talk."

But Chrissie was adamant she wanted to talk about it now and said. "I need to tell you everything now because tomorrow I won't get the chance, Danny Firth and whatever you've found will take up all your time, so please Marcus I just need five minutes."

"Drink your tea," said Marcus. "And listen to me. I know all about you're relationship with Danny, and I also know it was finished with years ago. Come on Chrissie, its no big deal and Danny has a wonderful ten year old son now, so don't worry about it."

"He has three wonderful sons." Marcus almost spilt his tea as he looked at Chrissie and said. "No, no way, I would have known."

"You think you know everything Marcus Hoag. Oh Marcus, Danny, and I had two babies, twins. I wanted to tell you, but the opportunity never seemed to be right."

"Does Danny know?"

"Of course he does."

Marcus placed his teacup on the tray and snuggled himself further into Chrissie's ample bosom and said with a sleepy voice. "I hardly know what to say Chrissie, only how did you manage to keep it all so quiet and keep your agency job. That must have been terribly difficult." Marcus thought for a few seconds and when realisation hit him he spoke softly as his eyes almost closed. "Don't tell me you had them adopted?"

Chrissie with tears trickling down her cheeks cradled Marcus' head. "No I didn't have them adopted Marcus. I didn't have to. Oh it's a long story and our two sons; well it was for the best." Chrissie never finished what she was about to say as she could hear a feint snoring sound coming from Marcus and thought, am I doing the right thing telling him, and what will Paul think. She shook Marcus awake. "Come on lets get upstairs to bed your exhausted."

"Your bed or mine," said Marcus sleepily.

CHAPTER 14

Auction House, London
14th June

Dean Graham stood with Dean Alexander in the basement of the auction house and watched the young antiques authenticator. "I would prefer to be in there next to that amateur, instead of behind this screen."

"Patience John," said Dean Alexander. "Let him do his job, he's suitably qualified."

"But can we trust him to keep his mouth shut?"

"I think our friend Dr Conroy is uninterested in what he's testing as long as he gets paid, so go and get yourself a cup of tea or a coffee and be patient."

Dean Graham crossed over to the drinks machine and poured himself a coffee, sat down and waited for the young scientist to finish his tests while Dean Alexander stood; casting his mind back on all the planning that had gone into the culmination of this moment.

Six months ago at the university, he was overseeing the workmen who were converting the first floor storeroom in St. Andrew's hall to a new library and they had uncovered the three stain glass windows. The Dean found out about Marcus's interest in them and knowing that Hoag's son was a student there thought this was his chance to do as much research into the windows as possible, and have Saint Francis of Assisi's window re-commissioned without anyone becoming suspicious of his underhand dealing at the auction house. A little accident, the perfect alibi, install John Graham as his replacement for a few months while he prepared the auction, and when Hoag made his move he would announce his decision to leave the university, feigning illness. Perfect, thought Dean Alexander, it was all going to plan.

The young scientist with a plastic hair net covering his head, a face mask, white gown fastened at the neck not too tightly and surgical gloves clinging to his tanned hands, slit open the thick plastic bag and gently removed the almost deteriorated satchel and laid it down on the cold white marble slab, he sliced a tiny sliver from the strap and placed it in a glass culture container and closed the lid, he then slowly and tamely tried to remove the contents but to his dismay, instead of removing a book cover and writings he extracted what looked like strips of cloth. Unsure what to make of the cloth and knowing he had a captive audience in the viewing booth, he decided to repeat exactly what he had done with the satchel and complete his examination. All he needed to do now was to place the materials into the conveniently placed carbon dating testing equipment and wait one hour. While he waited he found that there was quite a lot of what looked like fragments of bone, fur, leather and the most interesting thing, why would the tip of a dagger be inside a seventh century Irish satchel and he thought, there's more to this satchel than their telling me. I think I'll measure it and have a look under the microscope at the dagger tip, but I wonder where it came from. Dr. Conroy placed some of the tiny fragments into their separate receptacles and measured the tip of the dagger and found it to be almost three centimetres, he slid it under his microscope and looked at it, then lifted his head away from the viewer, thought for a moment then had another look. He couldn't believe what he was looking at and thought, my god, it can't be, but it's unmistakable, as he cast his mind back the year before he went to Oxford, he attended a course at Durham University on ancient daggers from the seventh Century, he remembered one especially, as it had been found at Gilling near Oswaldkirk, North Yorkshire and decided to search the databases and came up with Oswine, King of Deira around 644AD in Northern England. According to the famous Bede, he was slain with his own dagger by his cousin near Gilling.

A treasure hunter with one of those metal detectors had found a dagger with the inscription of OSUINE (Oswine) of DEIRA on it and the tip was missing, the guy handed it to the University for an 'above board tax-free fee'.

Dr. Conroy slipped the dagger tip from under the microscope and placed it into one of the receptacles, then laid it on the bench next to the others and picked the tiny bone fragment up and placed it under the microscope, as he looked through the viewer he placed his left hand over the glass container with the dagger tip inside and surreptitiously picked it up and slipped it into his left side pocket, hoping that no one had seen him. After about an hour the young artefact specialist completed his findings and looking at Dean Alexander and Graham he tried to explain the computer graphs.

"There's a ninety one per cent chance that the leather satchel and contents date back to around 530AD to 650AD. I'm sorry I can't be more specific but I thought you might like to know that there was no book inside, not as we understand a book."

The co-conspirators looked at each other and Dean Alexander said with a frown. "What was inside the satchel if not a book?"

Dr. Conroy, determined not to leave without the two scientifically uneducated pair standing in front of him off without paying him his fee, decided to tell them exactly what they wanted to hear and said. "Strips of writing cloth, whoever you picked this up from, it was so poorly packed that it's completely unreadable and it was an immense task to try to authenticate it."

Dean Alexander and Graham looked dejected and were about to ask another question. "But," Dr Conroy said. "At least it is from the Century you asked about and they used cloth as paper in those days, so what does it matter if you're nine per cent out, my findings will be accepted in any auction house in the world."

That was what Dean Alexander was waiting to hear, and crossed over to his intercom and switched the 'on' button and said. "Gabby, Dr. Conroy is about to leave the building, please make sure his cash is ready."

Gabby, the Deans Daughter, as usual was totally bored with the whole idea of her father using her as a secretary said. "Yes sir, right away sir."

"Gabby, cut the crap and get on with it, Dr Conroy's on his way through to the reception now." He switched the intercom button off and crossed back over to the exit. Dr. Conroy proffered his hand and Dean Alexander accepted it, but as he shook his hand, Alexander said. "Don't forget Dr Conroy, discretion."

"Of course, I'm always discreet." Dr. Conroy left the building through the side entrance with the cash firmly secured inside his suit pocket next to the culture receptacles, as he patted his pocket and thought; I must get myself as far away as possible from here. David Conroy exited the building and making sure he wasn't followed, hailed a taxi.

"Ok, where to governor?" called out the taxi driver.

Without hesitation Dr David Conroy replied. "New Scotland Yard please."

B & B Cellar Whitby

Hold the ladder Paul, while I change this light bulb." Marcus climbed the rickety ladder and vowed to tell Mike, his friend and joint proprietor of the B&B to buy a new set of ladders as soon as possible.

Mike Winterbottom and Danny were war buddies and during a sortie Mike had apparently pulled Danny out of a building just before a panzer tank blew a few big holes in and half demolished it, somewhere in Italy. Neither of them would talk about the war years, they said it had been too traumatic, and Marcus only found out about the deed because Mike let it slip when they first met, he'd received a medal and it was sitting in one of his drawers upstairs, amongst the rest of the junk he threatened one day to throw away. Marcus liked Mike and knew that he was secretly proud of saving his friend's life; he was very much like Danny, maybe a little more reserved, but pretty much down to earth. After the war Mike went back to working down the coal mines near Newcastle, and Danny wanting to go into antiques decided to study archaeology and history at university, while Marcus studied at Saint Peter's, which was the reason there was no contact between the three friends for five years.

When Marcus's grandparents died, they had willed everything they owned, money, investments, stocks and shares all to Marcus, but he couldn't touch his inheritance until it had all matured around his twenty first birthday. It was a natural thing for him to do, to help his friends and he still remembers the day he wrote to Mike and Danny with his plans. They both wrote back to Marcus advising him to buy property and that's exactly what he did. Mike jumped at the chance to be a proprietor, if not his own business then someone else's would suit him fine, as long as it was in the fresh air. Danny had some of his own money saved and knew exactly how to advise Marcus, and that's how his life of secrets and intrigue had started.

"Ok Danny lights please."

Danny was standing at the top of the stairs waiting for Marcus' call, as he pulled the light cord he said. "At last, now we can have a look at those books."

Marcus shouted up the half lit shadowy stairs. "Go into the fridge, I left the books in the cool box."

Danny with incredulity in his voice called back. "You left them in the fridge? Marcus you're crazy, what if..."

Marcus shouted up to him again, saying. "Just go and get them, you worry too much Danny."

Sure enough, they were inside the salad box at the bottom of the fridge; Danny carefully pulled them out, trying to keep the books level as he closed the fridge door. He descended the cellar steps, entered the first chamber, and passed the treasures to Marcus.

Dressed in white overalls, a mask over his mouth and surgical gloves, Marcus carried the books wrapped in the thick plastic bags into the prepared enclosure and closed the door behind him. Mike, Chrissie, and Louise stood at the second viewing window, while Danny and Paul stood at the viewer next to the outer door, both would have loved to be inside the room with Marcus, but knew that he wanted to do this alone, so they waited with bated breath outside the small room, watching every move he was about to make.

Marcus slit the plastic across the top of the small book and then continued to all four corners, eventually lifting off the plastic sheet and discarding it to the cold stone floor. Marcus didn't need to read the words on the front he knew exactly what he was holding in his gloved hands. The Saint Columbanus ten chapter Rule, but the date, well, he would have to wait an hour for his carbon dating equipment to reveal the results.

Marcus gingerly lifted the hard cover of the book and knew immediately he wouldn't have to wait for the equipment to give him the results Louise wanted. She thought no one knew of her involvement with Irish Artefact Recuperation but Marcus's associates in the Government gave him all the information he needed, but that side of his life he kept very secret and above all would never reveal a source even to Danny and Mike.

For reasons known only to monks of the early centuries Saint Benedict's Rule and Saint Columbanus' Rule were religiously practiced jointly in monasteries around the $5^{th} - 7^{th}$ Century and possibly to this day, therefore Marcus wasn't surprised when he discovered both Rules together in the burial chamber.

He picked up his pencil and wrote on a piece of paper for Louise:

Louise,
Saint Columbanus 10 Chapter Rule is not an original, but looks like a 7th century copy, but probably written by a very intelligent Monk. This is still a very exceptional find. Don't you agree?

Marcus folded the paper and turned to look at Louise, as he motioned for her to go to the large post box at the side of the door; he pulled it open and dropped the letter inside then closed it immediately. Louise did the same, as she retrieved the letter she thought to herself, do I read it upstairs or here. Huh! What do I have to be so secret about, I'm certain everyone here has worked out that I pander to the one that pays me the most money, and right at this moment it's the Irish museums.

Marcus watched to see what Louise would do with the information, as she opened up the folded paper and read it out to the group, he smiled and thought, between Louise and Paul, they'll make a formidable pair of investigators, and turned away to place the small book into a new heavy plastic bag, sealed it and placed it onto a stone shelf for later examination.

Marcus turned round to face the others and hunched his shoulders, as if to say. What's next? They all looked at him with wide eyes as Mike in his Geordie accent said. "He's in one of his funny moods again; he's having a laugh at your expense the old bugger. Get on with it man."

Marcus turned away with a smile on his face, but thinking and hoping that the book he was about to look at was the real thing. Just then he heard a tapping on the side-viewing window, it was Chrissie mouthing the words. "A cup of tea love?"

Marcus simply nodded and thinking, she picks the oddest times to put the kettle on, as he carried on slitting the plastic bag exactly the same way as the first book and discarded the plastic sheet onto the floor. Marcus' eyes scanned the book cover, then the emotions inside him began to rage and he could feel the energy drain from his legs and he thought, what on earth is wrong with me. As he cast his mind back to the burial chamber at the Abbey, this is exactly how I felt then, weak and cold as if something or someone had a hold of my body squeezing me, and didn't want me to go any further. With a strained look on his face, he turned and pulled his mask from his face mouthing the words. "Danny 'hells fire'!" Suddenly Marcus collapsed in a heap on the floor next to the small cut plastic between the viewing window and marble table.

Danny quickly grasped the door handle and entered the small changing room and was about to open the sealed chamber, when Paul stopped him as he said. "Wait, we must get suited up first the Rule is exposed."

"We don't have time," said Danny.

Paul began to get suited up and said calmly but firmly. "We make time!"

Danny nodded saying nothing, but thinking, bloody hell, the lad's right, if I'd gone in there the different air pressure could have ruined the find of the century.

Paul and Danny entered the pressurised room and ensured the door was closed behind them before Paul lifted his father up in a fireman's lift and heaved him on to his shoulder, while Danny resealed the book in a plastic bag and left it on the stone marble slab.

Marcus's lips were starting to turn blue as Paul carried him up the steep cellar steps, laid him on the kitchen floor, and administered first aid. Paul cupped the back of his father's head and blew into his mouth twice and then placed his hands on Marcus's chest and pumped his heart several times, he did this for what Chrissie felt was an age, but it was only a matter of a few minutes before Marcus started to come round, unable to speak he looked at Paul and Chrissie and nodded the 'ok' sign.

"Damn it Marcus," said Danny. "Why did you say 'hells fire,' you know we only agreed to use that Yorkshire expression in emergencies."

"I was poisoned."

"How were you poisoned? You were fully suited up." They were all speechless, and looked at Marcus and Danny, waiting for an explanation. Chrissie had made a cup of tea and with a shaky hand, handed it to Marcus as she said. "Come on, do we take you to hospital to see a doctor or is this one of your little games again."

Marcus eased himself up with the help of Chrissie, then sat down on a kitchen chair and started to sip the hot tea as he explained how he had felt in the burial chamber and said. "Paul did you feel any different when you came out into the fresh air or just before we were confronted by Dean Graham?"

Paul started to think quickly and said. "Now you come to mention it. When I knelt down next to Danny, my head was pounding like I had a bad migraine, but it lasted only a few minutes and then I was ok. The air in the chamber must have been poisoned."

"Or those chambers haven't been opened for at least thirteen hundred years."

"So! Mr clever Hoag," said Chrissie. "How come you passed out downstairs?" Just as Chrissie said it, she realised her mistake and said. "Of course the air pressure, so you weren't really poisoned only starved of fresh air."

"Got it in one," said Marcus. "But I needed to get out quickly and that call sign did the trick. Well now, as that little mystery is solved, let's get back down there and have another look."

As Chrissie pulled Marcus' arm back she said in a positive manner. "Oh no you don't, one, no two fainting attacks is more than enough for you." Chrissie looked at Louise and said. "Go on it's your turn now."

"Me!" said Louise. "What about Danny or Paul or even Mike."

Mike backed away and said. "I'm needed to cook dinner I can't afford to be passing out next to a hot stove. What about Danny."

Chrissie looked at Danny and tweaked his cheek as she said. "You're too old and you've a bump on your head, and you Paul, you've already been in contact with this bad air, so it looks like it's you Louise." Chrissie nudged Louise and said gently. "Like I said before, go on Louise show them what you can do."

Louise looked at Marcus. "Marcus what do you think of Chrissie's hypothesis? Do I qualify?"

"I hardly think qualify is the word, but you've shown over the last few days that trust could be the word, so like Chrissie said, go on, you earned it. Have a look at Saint Columbanus' Rule as well; see what you make of it?"

Louise didn't need telling twice, she was through the cellar door, into the first chamber and suited up before any of the others got to the bottom of the cellar steps.

New Scotland Yard, London

Dr. Conroy passed through the locked door of Scotland Yards Metropolitan Police station and was shown into an interview room by a young police constable who asked him if he would like a cup of tea and told that a detective inspector would be there directly to take his statement.

Saying no to the tea Dr David Conroy sat down and waited, feeling just like another cog in the wheel of the lucrative business of antiques, in fact he didn't look like a specialist at all. At five foot ten inches and looking rather thin, almost skinny, his only attributes were his Fair hair, attractive hazel eyes, and sweeping eyelashes. He sat in the interview room wondering if anyone was watching him behind the double mirror on the wall and thought, if they're watching me, I'm going to tell them everything I know, but not about the broken dagger piece. He felt in his pocket and another thought occurred to him, what if they ask about how much the auction house paid me, would I have to give that up as well. As he laid out the individual glass containers, a piece of fur, shard of bone, pieces of cloth and the sliver of leather from the satchel on the table the door opened and two tall detectives entered the room.

Dr Conroy had decided to tell them everything even going as far as producing lastly onto the table; his fee from the auction house, the three thousand pounds wrapped in one thousand pound bundles.

"Good Morning Dr Conroy, we apologise for keeping you waiting, it's been a busy morning. I'm DI Kent and my colleague is DC Logan. Now sir, what can we do for you and what have we here?"

"I'm not sure where to start?" said Dr. Conroy nervously.

As DI Kent opened his notebook he said. "The beginning is usually the best place."

Dr David Conroy left nothing out of his statement, from beginning to end. DC Logan picked up the glass container with the sliver of leather inside and about to open it, asked David. "What's this from?"

David immediately reached out and held it closed as he said. "Let me explain. I took that specimen and analysed it from a type of Irish satchel, and all these other pieces were also inside that same satchel."

DC Logan looked at the young man with suspicion as he asked his next question. "How old would you say this satchel is Dr Conroy?"

"I'm not sure if you'll believe me, but I measured it to be around the seventh century."

Logan and Kent looked at each other and almost asked the next question together, but Kent the more senior officer asked his question first. "Where is this auction house? Can you show us?"

"Of course I can."

"Would you," asked DC Logan. "Be prepared to stand up in a court of law, under oath, and repeat exactly what you've just told us? The fact you came straight here gives us the edge on these, so called auction dealers."

David Conroy hesitated for a few seconds, but nodded his head and said. "I guess I can say goodbye to my cash?"

DI Kent crossed over the room towards what David Conroy thought was a double mirror, flicked a light switch and the mirror changed to a concentration of inner City London streets as he said. "For now sir, but first of all show us on the map exactly where it is?"

Dr Conroy obliged and was told he was free to leave the station, but before he left, informed officers to place their evidence in a cold storage container or an ordinary fridge to preserve the delicate chemical balance.

David walked out of the London Police station and pulled out the other glass culture receptacle which contained the dagger tip and thought, this is getting dangerous, he crossed over the quiet street to a telephone box, closed the squeaky door behind him, then dialled a Manchester code and continued to dial Danny Firth's antique shop, only to get an answer phone, he thought to himself, come on dad, pick up the phone.

B&B Cellar, Whitby

Louise could feel the eyes of her peers, resting on her as she repeated the same procedure as Marcus, casting the sheet of cut plastic to the floor, and extracting the ancient book from its temporary home. Louise looked at the front of the book and hoped to see valuable gems embedded in the fragile cover, her feeling of disappointment on further investigation was replaced by elation as her observations revealed, not valuable gems, but a beautiful dull gemstone embedded in the heavy embossed cover.

As Louise looked at the front cover, a thought occurred to her, I've seen this colour before, and then it hit her, the eighth stain glass window, of course, the blazon was the same colour, how amazing, and I must tell Marcus.

Marcus unable to contain himself any longer tapped on the window, as Louise turned and looked up she could see Chrissie admonishing him. She thought I better let them know I'm ok, as she lifted her thumb up and made the ok gesture, she could almost hear the sigh of relief from them all. While she continued her investigation, Louise thought to herself, well, here goes, she removed a sliver of leather bind and placed it in the small glass receptacle, stepped over to the equipment and slotted it into the carbon dating machine then typed the details into the computer to start the programme. Louise turned back to the marble table and lifted the heavily embossed cover to reveal the first page of what was undeniably Saint Benedict's Regula Monachorum.

Outside the small chamber, the air was heavy with anticipation as Marcus whispered. "What's she doing? Why doesn't she tell us what it says?"

Paul put his hand on his father's shoulder and tapped it gently as he looked at Louise in admiration, and slowly said. "Patience dad, Patience, remember, timing is everything, and right at this moment Louise has the reins."

Marcus nodded his head as he smiled to himself, folded his arms and looked at Louise and said to Paul. "Louise has got guts going in there, so watch her closely son?"

"Don't worry dad; my nerves are almost shattered just watching her outside of that chamber never mind in." Paul could hear the guffaws of laughter, and he wasn't sure what everyone thought was so hilarious, but he couldn't take his eyes off Louise, not even for a second.

As Louise cautiously lifted back the book cover, all her training and resolve were meaningless, it hadn't prepared her for what her eyes beheld across the beauty of the first page, as the words written in perfectly formed Latin scroll started to overwhelm her. Louise looked up at all the people that had come to mean so much to her over the last few days, and the tears flooded her face as she gently nodded her head in confirmation, and tried to hold her concentration as she wrote down Saint Benedict's dedication.

As Mike looked at Louise almost in tears himself, he made the harsh comment, directed at Marcus that everyone was thinking. "Poor lass, Marcus she's obviously not prepared for what's written on that first page, I think you should bring the bonny lass out of there, quick!"

Marcus unsure what Mike meant, began to question his friend. "What the devil do you mean Mike?'

Danny unused to Mike being so forward looked at him and almost in slow motion nudged Paul with his elbow and said. "Get suited up lad and bring her out, she's been exposed to the low density air long enough."

Paul didn't need telling twice as he hurriedly entered the first chamber while Louise, still emotional slipped the note she had written into her white suit pocket and re-sealed the book once again inside a plastic bag. She turned and pulled open the inner chamber door, then closing it behind her she walked into Paul's open arms and as he embraced her she wept uncontrollably.

The rest of the party climbed the cellar steps and left the couple inside the inner chamber to comfort each other, and give Louise time to recover from her ordeal.

Within fifteen minutes Louise and Paul breezed into the dining room as if nothing had happened and Paul feeling hungry, called to Mike in his native Geordie tongue. "What's for lunch, man?"

Mike popped his head around the kitchen doorway and with a huge grin on his face, looked at Paul and holding a meat cleaver in his hand, said menacingly. "French fries and tongue bonny lad, beginning..." As he brought the meat cleaver down on the table he once more said menacingly, but still with the grin on his face, "beginning with your fingers and mouth youngster."

Paul began to laugh nervously, but soon saw the funny side when Mike retreated to the kitchen laughing his head off.

Louise slightly embarrassed by her emotions was pleased that Mike played the fool with Paul; it took the attention away from her and gave her time to pass on the Latin note she had written in the chamber to Marcus. As Louise sat down at the dining table she said to Marcus. "I'm not very good with Latin verse, but that first page Marcus, it really overwhelmed me, and I'm sorry I broke down in front of everyone."

"It happens to the best of us," said Marcus. "Don't give it another thought."

"Another thing," said Louise. "The embossing on the book cover, did you notice the colour?"

As Marcus opened the note Louise had passed him he said. "What do you mean colour?"

"The colour on the embossing, it was tawny, don't you remember, the Dragons Head."

As Marcus glanced at the note he looked up at Paul and said. "Don't you dare sing," then he turned to Louise. "Do you remember what the meaning of the symbol was Louise?"

She thought for a few minutes, but try as she might the meaning eluded her. Then Paul came to her rescue. "Louise, the meaning of the symbol was joy and if there's a gemstone embedded in the embossing it should be Jacinth."

"There is a stone of some sort there," said Louise. "But I wasn't sure what to make of it."

"A gemstone?" said Marcus surprised. "I never saw any gemstone!"

"I almost didn't see it myself," said Louise. "But it was embedded in the cover. I think the copy of Saint Columbanus' Rule must have been resting on the top and over the centuries it must have been pushed further and further into the book cover."

Marcus stood up and without saying a word pushed his dining chair back, and walked out of the room clutching the note Louise had passed him.

Paul called after his father. "Dad, are you ok?"

Danny looked round and about to get up and follow Marcus, but Chrissie knowing exactly why he had walked out of the room, held Danny's arm. "Let him go Danny, he needs time to let that note Louise gave him sink in. He'll come back when he's hungry," but Chrissie knew Marcus didn't want any one to see, what he would class as, his weak emotions.

Marcus walked out of the B&B front door and sat down on the summer seat next to the flower borders and car park, and as his tears ran down his face Marcus' memory returned once more to the final pages of the university library book and what the virtuous Saint had left behind.

St. Peter's Basilica Rome C524 – 543AD

Romanus entered the Basilica for the second time and remained there for the rest of his natural life. Deacon Pelagius, as Pope Vigilius' representative, sent Romanus and a few other monks to the vaults to work on the original copy and Papal Brief (Pacus Nuntius).

The Benedict's Rule remained in the vaults, and this was where it rested for nearly fifty years, until Pope Gregory The Great, a Roman Magistrate turned monk had the monastic rule retrieved from the vaults and informed Augustine of Canterbury on his return journey from Britain, to remove the Rule or a copy and travel back, to try and convert the many British Pagan Saxon Kings to Christianity.

A few months later, biographer deacon Paul, a friend of Pope Gregory went to the vaults to retrieve a separate document, he noticed the short note of guidance (Pacus Nuntius) for Benedict's monastic Rule lay open on the viewing table, but the large Rule book itself was missing. He searched all the viewing tables, but unable to find it and thinking it strange that it hadn't been returned and filed away and he could possibly be blamed for carelessness. He closed the file and placed it back on the shelf, then walked briskly out of the vaults and locked the door. Deacon Paul never spoke of, or was ever asked about this incident; keeping it to himself he took what he knew to his own eventual grave.

The Scholars of the modern day assumed Benedict's Regula Monachorum was lost forever.

B&B Whitby

Marcus sat on the summer seat outside lost in his thoughts, but said in a whispered voice. "Was it lost because of Deacon Paul's carelessness, or cunningly misplaced? No matter now, it will be returned to its rightful owner, The Vatican Museum."

Marcus' melancholy instantly took him back to the year 1944 and the Montecassino monastery ruins, of two people in a picture under an altar, quietly sitting near each other and smiling in conversation. These two gentle saints thought Marcus would be embedded in his memory for the rest of his life, and in Saint Benedict's own words Marcus re-read the simple but poignant dedication, and wrote down the translation:

Corum deo	In the presence of god
Noster nostri	our hearts beat as one
Pax tecum Scholasticam	Peace be with you Scholastica
Ab imo pectore	from the bottom of my heart
Non omnis moriar	not all of me will die
Haecolim meminisse invabit	One day we'll look back on this and smile

Marcus leaned back on the flower-adorned seat and once more spoke quietly to himself. "One day we'll look back on this and smile, if that isn't a fitting dedication and epitaph for retirement, then my names not Marcus Hoag." As Marcus was about to get up, he slipped the note into his jacket pocket, and once more gave vent to his memories of twenty years ago, to the time when they all bought the B&B. Mike was chuffed to bits, but Danny was never happy until he was back in his home town of Manchester and never once told Marcus why, but now Chrissie's revelation about having Danny's two Sons, twins, began to make him uneasy and he wondered at what other secrets they were both keeping from him. He'd known about their liaison years ago, but thought it was dead and buried, but Marcus saw the way Danny looked at Chrissie on the stairway and instantly his heart and head was full of jealousy, but he was unsure why, until now.

CHAPTER 15

Auction House London
15th June

As the auction was about to commence, the auctioneer stood on the dais in front of the lectern with a gavel in his hand. In front of him were the eight people who had been sent an invitation informing them of the auction?

Six suited dealers were sitting quietly waiting, while three antique dealers with telephones to their ears also waited for the beginning of the auction, and all from different parts of the world. Dean Graham stood at the entrance with the invitation cards in his hand; he discarded them as Dean Alexander walked in through a side doorway holding a glass container in front of him. The Irish satchel lay on the cold marble inside the glass as the Dean; also clutching Dr. Conroy's authentication papers, laid the container down on a long table, and beckoned the dealers to view the satchel in the glass container. For obvious reasons the container couldn't be opened so he passed the authentication papers to one dealer, and as he read them, he duly passed them to the next dealer and so on.

The auctioneer called for everyone's attention and asked the group who would like to start the bidding at £500,000. There were no hands showing and an eerie silence hung over the small room. Dean Alexander with sweaty palms almost raised his own hand, but brought back to his senses when the first bidder clicked his pen and the bidding started.

The second bidder on the telephone waved his hand in earnest.

"£1million," called the auctioneer.

The pen loudly clicked again and the auctioneer registered. "£1.5million to the gentleman seated at the back."

Another seated bidder lifted his eyebrow.

"£2million," called the auctioneer.

The room quietly buzzed and the auctioneer solemnly called out. "Going once, going twice."

Instantly the pen clicked again. "£3million," the auctioneer pointed his gavel at the seated bidder.

Once more the telephone bidder for the second time waved his hand firmly in the air and aggressively called out £5million. This time the room went deathly quiet.

"Going once, going twice, sold to the caller on line one," announced the Auctioneer.

Dean Alexander and Graham looked at each other and smiled as they rubbed their hands together they knew the money would be immediately deposited into their bank account in Switzerland.

DI Kent whispered to his five officers. "I want quick and clean arrests, no messing about, just get them into the Police vans as soon as you arrest them, and don't forget to read them their rights. Let's go."

Meanwhile DC Logan had made a quick check of all the exits and decided there were only two, front, and back. He placed himself at the back and sat in his car until his colleagues went in the front, he didn't have to wait long. His plan was to stay low and follow the stragglers coming out the back door.

The antique dealers were petrified as they were arrested; with the exception of three others; the auctioneer, the line one telephone bidder, and the guardian of the glass container who were undercover police officers, but the two men they were hoping would make a run for the back door Dean Alexander and Graham were falling into the police trap.

The back door of the run down building clattered open and Dean Alexander and Graham rushed out almost falling over each other. DC Logan slunk down in his car seat, not wanting to be seen hoping that the pair would rush past him and make a run for it. He hoped they would eventually lead him to their place of business or home address. DC Logan spoke in a whisper. "Come on little girl show yourself."

As a small green Mini spun round the corner of the building and Dean Alexander and Graham hurriedly climbed in. Gabby accelerated away, passing the unmarked police car and into the busy London traffic. Nice one Kent, whispered Logan again. "Now to let them think they've got away."

Unknown to Gabby, DI Kent had placed a homing beacon under her green Mini hopefully she would do exactly as they expected and DC Logan would be able to follow her at a reasonable distance with the receiver turned on in his car.

Logan's radio crackled and he picked it up. It was DI Kent. "Logan, come in Logan!"

"Logan here sir, I'm following at a distance, I'm certain they didn't suspect a thing."

"Ok, keep in contact, and don't lose them."

"Don't worry sir, I haven't come all the way from Ireland to go back with nothing, and the information Pendleton gave us, will, I hope reap a good reward."

As Logan drove up Tower Street on the south bank heading for Tower Bridge, the homing beacon suddenly stopped beeping and just continued to flash on and off on his console. Logan pulled his hand radio from its housing and called in the location of the stationary Mini, hoping that it had stopped at its final destination and had not been abandoned at an empty parking lot or on open derelict ground.

Logan's prayers were answered as he turned his unmarked police car into a dead end street; there in front of him was the green Mini, as bold as you please, parked next to a painted white mews house with an elegant black door and brass door handle.

DC Logan with a smile on his face and a nervous ache in the pit of his stomach picked up his radio again and called DI Kent. "Inspector, I think we have to do this softly, softly. I'm parked in a dead end street with a church on my right and the Mini is parked across the road in front of a mews house, the number is 88 Saint Benedict's Street. I'm guessing the church is the same name."

"Keep cool Logan we've pinpointed you and we're one minute away."

True to his word, within a minute DI Kent turned up the dead end street sirens wailing and tyres screeching, Logan thought, what happened to softly, softly. He abandoned his thoughts and jumped out of the car and ran to number 88 pushing the door open and catching Gabby and Dean Alexander as they were trying to pack as many antiques as possible into a few large trunks.

DI Kent looked at Logan and said. "Son, that took some guts to keep those bastards under surveillance on your own, well done!"

Daniel Logan was pleased at the praise being thrown at him but as he searched the other rooms with his uniformed colleagues there was no sign of the third suspect. As he ran outside he shouted to DI Kent. "Inspector there's one missing and I've a feeling I know exactly where he is." Logan headed across the street to the open doors of the church, but stopped as he came face to face with Dean Graham, a Nagant revolver with a silencer fitted, was pointing straight at Logan's head.

B&B Whitby

Mike answered the telephone, and shouted through to the dining room. "Danny, call for you."

"Who is it?"

Mike looked at Danny knowingly and said. "A young man called David."

Chrissie heard what Mike said and got up from her seat and followed Danny through into the wide reception area; she looked at him and mouthed the words. "Is it David?"

"Give me a minute to speak to him and I'll hand him over to you."

"Right son, that's great news. Your mother's here, I'll put her on." As Danny passed the phone to Chrissie, she held the phone to her ear and said with quiet affection. "How are you lad?"

Danny walked back into the dining room and sat down to finish his lunch and as Marcus walked through the B&B front door he could see Chrissie on the phone, he continued to walk into the dining room and sat down next to Danny, and started to eat his lunch and asked. 'What's going on Danny, I know you're up to something, but I've been so wrapped up in this book I've had no time for a discussion.'

"Marcus I didn't want to risk going to do the authentication of the Irish satchel that you gave Dean Graham, so I had someone else do it for me. The contents of the satchel turned out to be lots of pieces of cloth plus bits and pieces of bone and such, but there was something else inside, and my source tells me that it could be a great find, and the London Police have raided the auction house and made a few arrests."

"What was it that your source found inside the Irish satchel?"

"Ah, well that's the mystery he can't understand. He found a three-centimetre tip from a dagger, which he dated back to the seventh century and he thinks it belongs to the dagger that was used to murder King Oswine of Deira. It's absolutely amazing and he wants to know how you came by this Satchel."

"Before I tell you that Danny, I want to know who your source is."

"No way Marcus, you have your secrets, and I have mine, remember that's the way we work."

"Danny I'm going to marry Chrissie and I want to know everything?"

Just as Marcus spoke Chrissie walked in from the reception and said to Danny. "We have to tell him Danny, it's not fair to keep it quiet anymore."

As Danny looked at Chrissie with affection in his eyes, Marcus visibly winced as his mind began to whirr into place and he thought, my god, he's still in love with her, but is she in love with him?

"Sorry Marcus but maybe I should have told you this years ago, but I never thought in a million years that you and Chrissie, well to cut a long story short we have two grown up sons and I have or rather we have just spoken to one. Dr David Conroy, we decided to register them in my middle name to keep anyone from finding out about them. David and his brother grew up in Manchester with my Sister and both went on to study at Oxford. David is a freelance authenticator and he has covered a few assignments for me."

Marcus could hardly believe his ears at hearing his friend and his fiancée's revelations and asked. "What about you're other son is he doing assignments for you as well?"

Danny was about to give Marcus the truth, but Chrissie quickly interrupted and said. "Marc is still studying at Oxford." She then turned to Louise and with a pained look on her face she said. "I'm sorry Louise; I should have been truthful with you."

Louise stood up from the dining table and standing with her back to the window, said to Chrissie. "You didn't have a miscarriage? The twins were born in Manchester. I don't know how you've managed to keep them a secret all this time, but what I don't understand is why you felt it necessary to keep them a secret."

"We kept them secret," said Danny. "Because of Chrissie's inheritance and work at the agency and of course while Marcus and I worked together, the twins would have been a prime target for kidnap, this way seemed the easiest solution and the longer it went on the harder it became to bring them to light, so between the three of us, me Chrissie and Helen my sister and of course the boarding school and after that they went on to university."

Louise could understand Chrissies reasons now and the last few years they worked together, the furtive phone calls and sudden flights to England all became clear, but Louise had some revelations of her own and decided to come clean as she nervously glanced at Marcus. "I want to tell you all something, some of you may have already guessed. The Irish Government approached the agency and asked if we would help in locating the Saint Columbanus' ten chapter Rule, needless to say I was chosen, and decided to start with Dean Graham, I dug a little deeper into his past and came up with you Dr Hoag, you were the key and Saint Peter's University, you all know the rest."

Paul thinking Louise had finished and about to make a disclosure of his own, kept quiet as he realised Louise hadn't finished with her revelations. Louise continued by saying. "I informed Scotland Yard, namely DC Daniel Logan from the Irish Garda to look out for the satchel and anything it might contain. They confirmed the raid on the auction house and found the Irish satchel under a glass container, also a little factory in the basement crammed full of artefacts ranging from expensive paintings to Ming Pottery, all forgeries. They must have staged the auction, invited one genuine buyer in and the other bidders were hired to be there, when the sucker bid the highest, the rest stopped bidding; they would then switch the real thing for a forgery and return the original to wherever they stole it from. Poor sucker gets home and realises he's been duped, what can he do? He's not going to report it because it's illegal to buy the artefacts in the first place."

"What about the dagger tip, David didn't disclose it to the police?"

"I'm sorry Danny," said Louise. "Did you say something?"

Danny smiled and kept his mouth shut and thought, your alright Louise, yes, your alright.

"Marcus," said Louise. "I informed the authorities of the existence of the burial chamber as well, so we will probably be getting a visit from them in the next twenty four hours and that's my little bit said, does anyone else want the floor."

As Louise sat down on Paul's knee she whispered in his ear. "Let's go for a walk I have something personal to tell you."

Paul squeezed her tight as he remembered about his revelation, but for now, decided to keep quiet yet again about what he knew, but turned to Chrissie and said. "Louise and I are going for a walk to stretch our legs and get some sea air. Will you be ok Chrissie?"

"I'll be just fine lad," said Chrissie softly. "I'll keep your dad busy making me cups of tea; go on enjoy yourselves for a few hours."

As the young couple walked out of the B&B entrance they could hear Chrissie shouting to Marcus and him shouting back. "Get me a cup of tea Marcus Hoag and I'll consider keeping this bit of glass on my finger."

"Bit of glass! She calls £580 pounds worth of diamonds and gold, glass? Give me strength, and don't you laugh Danny Firth, if you ask me, you had a narrow escape."

Danny looked at Chrissie and laughed along with his three friends, but he decided to leave Mike to his kitchen and allow Chrissie and Marcus to enjoy some relaxing time together as his head suddenly became painful and he said he wanted to lie down and catch up on some sleep.

As Louise walked close to Paul he slipped his arm around her shoulder and she pushed her hand into the back pocket of his denim jeans, and said happily. "Chrissie really winds your dad up, doesn't she?"

"I think he secretly loves it," replied Paul.

"Did you see the way Danny looked at Chrissie earlier?"

"Yes, I think he wishes he'd married her instead of letting her dictate how the twins were brought up, but it sounds like they did ok."

They both made they're way down to the quay and stood leaning on the promenade railings looking out over the colourful array of fishing boats, Louise snuggled in to Paul's warm body and as she tilted her chin up to him he gently kissed her, but Paul's voice almost croaked as he spoke an endearment to her. "Louise I – I love you, and I know I'd be lost without you."

"Oh Paul I feel the same, I love you my darling."

Paul circled his arms around her, but as his mouth, not so gently this time, smothered hers, they could hear the happy laughter of the holiday makers all turning their heads and watching them, but began to 'ooh' and 'aah' at the passionate way the young man was kissing his girlfriend.

Ignoring the passers-by, Louise steered Paul to some vacant promenade seats and indicated they sit down. "You know I called Scotland Yard this morning?"

Paul placed his arm around Louise's shoulder and said. "Yes, the auction house, and burial chamber, what about them?"

"No, this has nothing to do with either of them." Louise, trying to compose herself, hesitated for a few seconds, but said with a lowered voice. "It's about your mother."

"Louise I don't think I want to hear this."

Louise was adamant, and knew that Paul was the only one that could tell Marcus, so she continued with her revelation. "Paul, you need to hear this because you have to tell your dad, it's far too personal for me to just blurt it out in front of everyone."

Paul nodded his head in agreement and leaned back waiting for the unwanted news. "The authorities have found your mother, she was, or rather a large trunk was uncovered by a hunter out shooting, and his dog must have picked up the scent of some wildlife they were tracking, but uncovered the buried trunk instead. Forensics matched DNA to Dean Graham and right at this moment they have him under surveillance in a mews house in London."

Paul removed his arm and placed his hand in hers; he then quickly stood up, pulled her away from the promenade seat and said. "Come on Louise, while we walk back to the B&B I've something to tell you about one of Chrissie's sons."

Saint Benedict Mews

Dean Graham held the revolver in front of DC Logan's face and told him to move further into the church entrance. "That's right, a little bit further so nobody can see us. Keys! Give me your car keys?"

Logan loathed to obey but pulled his ignition keys out and handed them over to the guy with black and blue eyes and a nose that looked like he'd gone twenty rounds with a boxer.

Logan was still looking at the guys nose when he was thumped on the back of his head by the butt of a gun, and crumpled to the floor, not quite out cold, but with blurred vision he watched as the two guys, one was short and thin with dark hair and the other tall and heavily built ran to Logan's unmarked police car. That was all he remembered as he lost consciousness behind the church door.

Ten minutes passed before DI Kent realised he was a man short and always heeding his intuition he shouted to his PC's. "Logan! The church! Damn it! The church, come on Logan's been gone too long, he could be in trouble." Sure enough, as they crossed the street DI Kent could see a leg sticking out from the entrance. He knelt down next to Logan's prone body, trying to administer first aid then placed his index finger below Logan's left ear to try and find a pulse, unable to feel anything, he screamed at his uniformed officers to call an ambulance, pronto!

DI Kent held his head in his hands and vowed to catch the bastards that had taken the life of the young Irish DC Daniel Logan. As Kent started to stand up he noticed letters written on the dusty floor and bent down again, picking up Logan's left hand he noticed the young detective's index finger was covered in dust, confused as to what the letters meant he re-read them again.

2 – SEAT – MSR – CHAIR

DI Kent watched as the mature female medic worked quickly on Logan's body and by what Kent could only hazard as a miracle, young Logan came round, but before Kent could speak to him the medic whisked him off into the ambulance and quickly transported him to the nearest hospital.

DI Kent, in hot pursuit of the speeding ambulance, thought who would know what the letters meant. Logan obviously meant those letters for someone other than me, so who does he know in England? Of course, it hit him like a lightning bolt and his car almost careered into the back of the ambulance as the brake lights in front of him screamed. Red! Red!

Kent cursed loudly. "Damn that was a close one, I almost ran into that ambulance."

DI Kent pulled into the hospital car park, silenced his mobile siren, and placed it on the front passenger seat. He pulled out the small radio receiver and called control. "This is DI Kent to control."

An unknown voice answered his call. "WPC Wallis here Sir how can I help you?"

"Put me through to Scotland Yard."

"Already done sir, they were waiting for your call. You're through now."

"This is DC Johnson sir."

"Johnson, get me the telephone number of that American agent Pendleton."

DC Johnson was always on the ball and looking for promotion, he'd heard what happened to Logan, so he had anticipated what his DI wanted and had the number ready.

"Good man Johnson I'll speak to you later regards Logan, but it looks like he might be ok." Kent could hear the sighs from the open plan detective's office as he switched off his radio.

DI Kent walked over to the hospital reception kiosk and picked up the phone, dialled the Whitby code and number and waited for the ringing tone.

Mike picked up the phone and asked whom the caller wanted.

"I believe you have a Miss Louise Pendleton staying there. Would you mind telling her DI Kent would like to speak to her, it's important."

Mike waved to Louise as she walked up the driveway, just getting back from her walk with Paul and she hurriedly walked in through the front doorway, crossed over to Mike and asked. "What, for me?"

"It's DI Kent from London," said Mike. "Not the one you spoke to earlier."

"Thanks Mike. Hello Pendleton here."

DI Kent explained what had happened to Logan and asked her opinion on the message that he had left. "Give me your phone number sir and my colleagues and I will get to work on it."

As Louise replaced the phone on its cradle she wrote the number down in Mike's phone book and walked into the lounge sitting down next to Marcus.

"Problem," said Louise. "DC Logan's been concussed and he's in hospital and I'll give you one guess who's involved."

"Dean Graham," said Marcus. "But what's the problem?"

"Before he was taken to hospital, Logan left a message for me, for us to solve. I think I understand the message but thought I'd let you have a look, just to confirm my suspicions."

Louise handed Marcus the slip of paper, he studied it for a few seconds and smiled at her as he said. "Two clerics from the Vatican, is that what you thought Louise?"

Louise couldn't lie, not at a time like this and said. "I honestly thought it referred to two Cathedrals, you know as in Seat and Chair."

Marcus looked at her and said. "I told you I was smarter than you. Seat and Chair in this instance refers to the Vatican and two MSR means Monsignors. This DC Logan is he ok?"

Louise rose from the sofa and answered. "It was touch and go, but I think he'll be ok." She quickly walked back to the telephone and called DI Kent with Marcus's supposition.

As Louise replaced the phone, Paul had just finished telling Marcus and Chrissie about his mother Alice, Marcus held Chrissie's hand as she agreed with him that nothing anyone could say would bring her back, they would all travel back to the

States to attend her second funeral as soon as the authorities released her body.

"Dad, Louise, and I are going to Ireland; she wants to return Saint Columbanus' Rule to Phoenix Park in Dublin."

"That's ok with me son; it'll need to be wrapped properly and placed in a cool box for transporting. When do you leave?"

"Early tomorrow morning, were booked on a flight from Newcastle to Dublin and that should give us a couple of days to organise ourselves."

Louise slowly walked back into the lounge and flopped down on a sofa and said wearily. "DI Kent has just given me information on Dean Graham and his accomplice. They found the unmarked Police car parked near a local harbour, and assume the pair must have hired a motorboat and crossed the channel to France. He's spoken to Interpol but doesn't hold out much hope of catching them, who knows where they're headed, it could be anywhere."

"Oh Louise, Louise," said Marcus. "It's obvious where they're headed."

Louise stared back at Marcus and rolled her eyes. "I know I'm going to regret saying this, but where?"

Marcus helped Chrissie up from the sofa and with a smile across his face turned to Louise and Paul and said. "See you both in Rome."

CHAPTER 16

Whitby Yorkshire
16th June

Once Paul and Louise had eventually packaged the Irish Rule and set off on their journey to Ireland via Newcastle, Danny informed them he wanted to get back home, he didn't like to leave Simon any longer than necessary, and asked if Marcus and Chrissie would like a lift to Manchester airport, they could book their tickets from the various booking desks there. Marcus asked Chrissie what she thought, and Chrissie said she would like to spend a bit more time in Whitby. Marcus wanted to stay a little longer also but his motives were different to Chrissie's, he wanted to wait for the authorities to investigate the burial chamber and hopefully return to York to have another look inside the Minster at the Jesse window, but Chrissie had other ideas.

"Marcus it's a beautiful building but no way am I going back to York, we need a rest before going to Rome, and I want to do a little bit of shopping and planning."

"Planning, what sort of planning?"

Danny started to walk out of the lounge but stopped, turned and looked at Chrissie as he said in a joking manner. "I told you Chrissie, you should marry me instead, and he's a wonderer, always has been, and always will be." Then Danny turned serious as he looked and nodded to Marcus. "Make sure you put her first Marcus and make some wedding plans; don't shelve her away like some artefact. I'm going before I say anymore."

Marcus walked over to Danny and shook his hand. As he released his hand he put his arms around him and held him as he whispered. "Thanks Danny, I owe you big time."

"Don't forget," said Danny. "Take my advice and do it when you get to Rome, you old romantic."

Chrissie and Mike stepped forward and waved to Danny as he threw his overnight bag into the boot, then climbed into the car and waved as he drove out of the B&B car park.

Marcus turned and walked back into the B&B and began to climb the stairs, but half way up he turned and shouted to Chrissie. "I'm going to pack; we're going to Rome first thing in the morning."

Mike and Chrissie stood at the bottom of the stairs in the reception area and looked at each other; suddenly they shook their heads and laughed together, and Mike expressed his true feelings for his friend. "Ah bonny lass, isn't he just the damndest romantic you ever did see."

"Yes and he's mine, all mine Mike."

Rome Hotel/Museum/Mancini Villa
17th – 21st June

Chrissie hobbled over to the Rome hotel's 5th floor bedroom window and opened it, stepping out on to the balcony, she breathed in the fresh morning air and stretched her arms out then relaxed, her ankle was much better now, and she decided to keep the strapping off. Marcus followed her out on to the balcony and put his arms around her ample waist and held her tight.

Chrissie was very self-conscious of her weight but Marcus assured her that she was fine as she was, he loved to cuddle her, and then he pulled her round to face him and said. "You're not having second thoughts about marrying me are you?"

Chrissie put both her hands on Marcus's face and looked at him with love in her eyes and said. "You're not getting out of this one, I have your commitment on my finger, and it's staying there."

She pushed him back into the beautifully decorated pale green bedroom and white marble floor. As they fell back on the sumptuous king size emerald green quilted bed, Marcus allowed Chrissie to kiss him passionately and decided this wasn't the time to argue.

Within a few days Paul and Louise were booked into the same Rome Hotel and Paul; emerging first for Breakfast deciding to give his father and Chrissie an early morning wake-up call crossed the marble hallway and stood in front of door number 554 knocked once and shouted. "Come on you two, we've no time to waste the sun is up and it's a beautiful day." Paul knocked again and walked back to his own bedroom. Louise was perched on the end of the bed and giggling like a schoolgirl.

"You enjoy getting your own back on Marcus don't you, you wicked man."

Paul laughed as he pushed Louise back on the bed and instantly feigned eating her neck.

Marcus and Chrissie, sat in the huge breakfast room, enjoying their continental breakfast when Louise and Paul walked in, Marcus looked up and said. "Late down as usual, he never learns does he?"

"Marcus," said Chrissie sternly. "Just eat your breakfast."

Paul sat next to Chrissie with his mound of toast, butter, and jam, while Louise lingered at the cereal counter. Paul glanced at his father's bedroom key, which read number 553 and said. "I thought you were in number 554?"

"Why? What has our bedroom to do with you?"

"Eh! Nothing, I was just curious." He then looked at Louise as she sat down across from him and they both began to laugh hysterically.

Giovanni's chauffeur, Angelo deposited Marcus and the other three passengers outside the Grand Museum doors. Because of Marcus's association with the museum they didn't stand in the long queue that meandered along the high Vatican walls. Marcus had already telephoned his long time friend Giovanni Mancini, the Curator, to tell him of his great find and would be given another free tour of the museum.

Every time Marcus returned to Rome he would normally stay with Giovanni in his private villa on the outskirts of Rome with his wife Valentina and their seven children, but this time Marcus decided to book into a hotel as he knew Giovanni didn't have the facilities for keeping the Rule at a constant temperature and his Children wouldn't be able to resist taking regular little peeks at the historic works.

The hotel on the other hand had a vast underground cold storage vault, which was under secure lock and key and Marcus wouldn't have to worry, he could concentrate on making Chrissie happy.

The party of four entered the museum double doors and were soon confronted by a small round immaculately tailored gentleman. Marcus immediately threw his hands up in the air and gave his friend a bear hug as he conversed in Italian. "Giovanni, you get younger looking each time I see you, what's your secret?"

"Ah Valentina, my bambino's and of course my work, but how are you Marcus?"

"Benissimo Giovanni. Allow me to introduce you to Chrissie, Louise, and Paul."

Chrissie was a little taken back when she heard Marcus speak in fluent Italian and received another surprise when Giovanni spoke in excellent English.

"No, this can't be little Paul?"

Paul's hand was almost shaken from his shoulder as Giovanni gripped it tightly and shook it vigorously, then went to Louise, lifted her hand to his lips and caressed her fingers as he lapsed momentarily into Italian and slowly whispered. "Aah Bella! Bella!"

Louise pouted and blushed as she said. "It's nice to meet you, sir."

Giovanni turned to Chrissie and threw his arms around her, as he kissed both her cheeks and about to kiss her full on the mouth Marcus pulled him off and quickly laughed as he said. "No Giovanni, remember Valentina?"

"I get so carried away, excuse me, such beautiful ladies, you lucky man Marcus."

Marcus changed the subject as they walk through into the museum, but asked Giovanni if he'd received the special package that morning. The little Curators hands were constantly moving as he explained how they had collected it from the armoured courier and how it was just as Marcus had packaged it, and was the perfect temperature; they returned it to the museum vaults for safe keeping and would put it on show as soon as the time was right. The party continued on their tour and Marcus was fairly sure that Saint Benedict's Regula Monachorum would never see the light of day. It would be hidden away, and nothing

Giovanni Mancini said would change Marcus's mind in that regard, but he was just happy that it was back where it belonged.

At that very moment in the vaults of the museum, and as Marcus stood watching Chrissie and Giovanni chatting for a few minutes, his thoughts and the thoughts of a young slightly built fair haired cleric by the divine name of Monsignor Benedict had entered the vaults and walked briskly down past the heavily laden bookcases, finding the compartment he wanted he extracted the Pacus Nuntius and inserted the ancient Rule of Benedict of Nurcia into the file. Quickly returning the same way, closing, and locking the vault door behind him, his thoughts mingled with Marcus' and going back to deacon Paul and the year 660AD. You can rest in peace now my friend, but Marcus' senses held more than the young priest as they told him someone was watching from the stairway above.

Almost out of sight, Dean Graham stood at the top of the winding staircase and watched Marcus' party as they climbed the circular stairway, his mind racing as he remembered how much money he had lost and the uneventful journey across the English Channel to France, from where his accomplice had stolen a large non descript vehicle, with the driver safely tied up in the sleeping cabin, they crossed over the border of Switzerland and entered Italy over the Dolomites, then down through Florence and on to Rome.

There was no way he wanted anything to do with the Benedictine now, but before he left for Argentina he would take care of Marcus Hoag for good.

As their day wasn't over yet the family group returned to the hotel to freshen up. Unbeknown to Marcus, Paul had made his own special arrangements for his Father and new Aunt soon to be stepmother. Giovanni had invited them all to his villa as a special surprise for Marcus and Chrissie.

As they travelled through the busy streets of Rome in the back of Giovanni's four-wheel drive Range Rover, Louise, curious to know why he thought Dean Graham would come to Rome asked Marcus. "Dean Graham has no connection with Rome, so why would he come here?"

"Louise, Dean Graham needs to blame someone and I just happen to be the one he hates most in the world." As Marcus leaned over to Chrissie and held her hand he said. "He was in the museum, standing at the top of the circular stairway watching us, so now we definitely know he's here in Rome and Giovanni said his name was Monsignor Morgaan, which entitles him entry to the museum and the Vatican, he must have an accomplice with connections, therefore we must be on our guard."

Giovanni drove the Range Rover expertly out of Rome and up into the mountains arriving at a large secluded villa surrounded by fruit trees, olive and wine groves. The estate was Giovanni's family home and with pride in his voice he told Chrissie and Louise that there had been Mancini's living on the estate for over five hundred years. With craggy mountains on both sides and overlooking a beautiful green valley it made a veritable safe haven for his children to grow up and study without outside influences.

The Range Rover pulled up outside the front door of the flower adorned imposing two stories, six bed roomed villa and the party alighted. Marcus sensing something was not quite right said to Giovanni. "Where are the children and Valentina? They are usually all over visitors."

"Ah!" said Giovanni. "They must be at study period."

Suddenly the front doors flew open and a gaggle of screaming children ranging from three to twelve descended on them, shouting. "Surprise, surprise, we have a secret surprise Uncle Marcus."

Marcus half expected the cries of the children, but Chrissie was a little overwhelmed as the children grabbed their hands and clothes and pulled them along. They entered the villa and crossed through the beautiful hallway emerging out the back door and into a huge garden adorned with coloured garlands, bunting, and balloons dotted about. Standing to the right of the villa were two terraces with outdoor tables, chairs and parasols to keep the hot sun off, and a huge stone barbeque with steaks, savoury sausages and all manner of wonderful food, the aroma of herbs and spices sent Paul's nasal senses wild.

Giovanni's wife Valentina a tall elegant raven-haired former Italian beauty Queen, her hair now cropped short, welcomed

Paul and Louise warmly into the hallway and were very surprised when they emerged out into the back garden.

Paul looked at Giovanni and said. "Giovanni, this is wonderful, when I telephoned you I didn't expect all this, your family and children have done a wonderful job decorating the garden." Paul stooped down as he whispered to Giovanni and said. "Did you manage the other thing I asked for?"

Giovanni smiled from ear to ear and said. "Of course, anything for Marcus, but that event will take place in about one hour; we have to wait for the Monsignor to arrive."

"Ah yes!" said Paul. "The Monsignor, how is he these days? I haven't seen him for a few years."

"He is much the same."

Paul pulled a sour face and said. "I guess as sombre as always?"

"Of course, but the Order he chose makes him seem that way, we must all accept that fact and admire his tenacity."

Paul stepped away from Giovanni and glanced over to where Chrissie and Louise were standing, his thoughts taking him back to his first year at St Peter's University and how he had befriended a young man called Marc Conroy, of medium height and fair haired with striking hazel eyes and long sweeping eyelashes, he wanted he remembered, to become a Missionary and travel the world, but his fellow students whether out of jealousy or ignorance or simply because of his reticence, had tied him up and put him in a boat, rowed out on the lake, pushed him overboard and dragged him along behind the boat. By the time the students reached the shore young Conroy had almost drowned, he was ill for almost six months after that and was taken away from the College, Paul had tried to keep in touch and remembered Marc had been sent to Oxford.

Paul was brought back to the present when his father called to him. "Do you want a Penny for your thoughts son?"

"What? Oh, sorry dad I didn't hear you."

"You still dreaming son?"

"I guess."

"What do you have to dream about, Louise is over there?"

With a wry smile Paul stuffed a barbequed sausage into his mouth and chuckled. "You'll soon find out old man."

"I'll give you 'old man'," said Marcus as he chased Paul around the garden and the children seeing the fun started to join in. Marcus shouted to Chrissie. "Save me! Save me, from these little bambinos," which made the children squeal even louder and everyone enjoyed the fun.

Giovanni took Chrissie's arm as he watched Marcus and Paul with the children. "He is a wonderful man my dear, and that is the first time I have seen him so relaxed with his own son. It's good to see his fun side don't you think?"

Chrissie thought about Giovanni's words for a moment and was about to agree with him when Giovanni's eyes darkened as he continued. "But I would not like to be on the receiving end of his wrath if he was trapped or deceived."

Chrissie a little lost for words, merely nodded, and couldn't get Giovanni's words out of her head, 'trapped or deceived'.

CHAPTER 17

The Vatican City/Mancini Villa

Dean Graham knew he would be seeing Marcus Hoag again, but didn't think it would be so soon. As he stood at the top of the museums spiral stairway he stepped back from the railing just as the artefact specialist looked up and Graham wasn't sure if he had been seen, his only defence at the moment was to keep in the background and try to follow Hoag, bid his time and wait for the right moment. His accomplice was an old friend from his past and with his help Marcus Hoag wouldn't live long enough to enjoy the rest of his retirement.

Dean Graham and his accomplice had followed Giovanni's Range Rover at a safe distance out of the City of Rome and up the valley to the villa Mancini. Leaving their small car at the bottom of the hill hidden among a dense thicket of bushes, the co-conspirators exited the car and keeping well away from the main road, trekked their way up the winding dusty track towards the villa. As they approached the perimeter fence, both could hear the sound of Giovanni's children squealing with laughter and decided to wait under the shelter of a vine workers lean-to until evening when hopefully the children would be tucked up in bed asleep. The plan was to surprise Hoag while he was on his own and then finish him off for good with the gun and silencer.

Villa Mancini

The taxi wound its way up the mountain road towards the villa and passed through the open gates to deposit two young men of approximately twenty-three years of age. Both men of medium height, fair haired and striking Hazel eyes, walked through the archway, but instead of passing through the front door they decided to surprise everyone by heading around the side entrance. When they eventually emerged from under the hanging flower baskets and trailing red geraniums, David Conroy saw his mother first and then to his amazement Marcus

Hoag being chased by screaming children and the tall young man talking to Giovanni must be Paul Hoag. David didn't know Paul, but his brother Marc knew him from his time at Saint Peter's.

Marcus ran around the trees trying to shake off the children until Valentina came running over and bustled them away from him as she said. "We have visitors Marcus and I think Chrissie has someone she wants you to meet." She took the children over to the food table and gave them orders to stay at the table and enjoy their meal until the grown ups had a little chat and then they could play some of their games.

Paul, seeing the twins first, hurried over throwing both his arms out and shouting jovially. "Marc, what a wonderful surprise, did you get my letter?"

Marc Conroy offered his hand to Paul as he said. "Yes, about a year ago." They both began to laugh as Paul explained how he knew Marc but not David, and also realised now why he was so morose at the university, he was missing his twin brother.

"Yes," said David as he put his arm around his Marc's shoulder. "Like two peas in a pod, we're in agony when we're separated."

Marcus, relieved of the children, walked across the grass with Chrissie and said. "I feel sure I've seen David before and Marc, he's a priest."

"Yes, they both studied at Oxford, but Marc had to do a year at another university and Danny and I chose Saint Peter's to be close to me. It didn't work out so he returned to England and finished his studies at Oxford with David."

"But you said he was still studying, you lied!"

Chrissie drew in a sharp breath, remembering Giovanni's words, 'trapped, or deceived', but undaunted she carried on and said coyly. "Just a little white one, they might be identical twins but Marc's nature is not the same as David's, and he didn't want anyone to know that he was working in the Vatican, we had to allow him his anonymity, it was the only way that Danny could carry on helping you."

Marcus quickly shook Marc's hand and then as he slowly shook David's hand, but whispered conspiratorially in his ear. "David, you keep my secrets and I'll keep yours son." David's head came up in recognition and instantly smiled and Marcus looked at Chrissie. "It's incredible the facial likeness to Danny, apart from the fair hair, and they're slightly taller."

Just then Giovanni and Valentina came over to the group and said. "We have a big surprise for you both."

Chrissie looked at Marcus with suspicion across over her face. "I'm getting the feeling we're being Shanghai'd. Marcus, what's the big surprise? Do you know?"

"Chrissie I swear I have no idea."

As Chrissie was pulled away from Marcus by Valentina and led indoors, she shrugged her shoulders and allowed Giovanni's wife to escort her upstairs to a bedroom, where Valentina said she wanted to show her something special. While Marcus was given the same treatment and Giovanni led his friend indoors to explain what they had planned.

Louise had been very quiet, but Paul pulled her close and said. "Do you think everything will work out the way we planned it?"

"Of course it will, why shouldn't it, it's the perfect setting for a wedding, Marcus's friends, Chrissie's sons and of course Danny's family and Mike will be here soon so don't panic, everything will fall into place, you'll see and I'll keep my eye on Marcus."

The stage was almost complete, but unbeknown to Marcus and Chrissie; Danny and the others had arrived but wanted to stay out of the way until the last minute. The children had planned to sing an old folk song and Marc had been given a special dispensation allowing him to conduct the service.

Marcus eventually emerged from the villa sporting a black morning suit, white shirt and tie, silver brocade waistcoat and polished black shoes everyone looked and applauded as he walked down towards the family group, and with panic in his voice he groaned. "Where's Chrissie? Hasn't she come out yet? Oh I'm getting the jitters. Paul, what if she says no?"

"Dad, she won't say no, you know she won't, just try and relax."

"I'm going for a walk to calm my nerves."

"Don't go far dad, Chrissie won't be long."

"Ok son, I'm just over there where the children are sitting." Marcus walked across the grass and down through the pergola and out to the terrace where three tables were heavily laden with food and soft drinks. Marcus thought to himself. No Jack Daniels I see, oh well soft drinks will have to do. As he picked up a bottle of orange juice and started to pour it into a glass, he could have sworn he saw Danny Firth down by the vineyard next to the lean-to and, oh my god, no, it can't be, Dean Graham. If Chrissie happened to see them both together she would probably pass out. He decided to take a closer look and crept down to the second terrace, crossed over the dirt path and emerged as close to the lean-to as possible, expecting to see Dean Graham and Danny, but there was nobody there. Marcus thought he must have been seeing things when he suddenly felt a gun pushed into the back of his neck.

Dean Graham's accomplice had spotted Marcus skirting the vineyard and decided to keep out of the way until the Dean was in position. This was exactly what Graham wanted; Marcus Hoag out in the open and none of Hoag's trickery would help him now.

Louise, always alert, spotted Marcus disappearing across the lower terrace and creep past the vineyard, but instead of following the same path she decided to excuse herself, making the old 'I must visit the ladies room' excuse to Paul and quickly saying to him. "Entertain Chrissie when she comes down, I won't be long."

Louise hurried indoors, passing through the hallway and out the front door, she made her way towards the road and thought, trying to run in high heels is not to be recommended. She then skirted down past the heavy fruit laden bushes and trees that surrounded the villa emerging almost next to the vine workers lean-to. Louise pulled her agency issue Beretta out from under her thin jacket and held it in her right hand across her right breast with her index finger hovering over the trigger and her left hand cupping her wrist for stability. She watched as Dean Graham held his gun at Marcus's head, but kept silent and hidden as a second person appeared next to the Dean.

"Oh my God," she gasped and began to shake as recognition crossed her beautiful face. "This can't be happening, where did he spring from and why would he team up with the Dean."

As Louise was momentarily distracted, Marcus confronted Dean Graham and tried to goad him into telling him why he was here, shouted. "The invitation didn't include, quote, 'your wretched fat ugly mug', unquote. Why don't you just admit defeat and retire like the arrogant bastard you are, I'm tired of running into you everywhere I turn, if you intend shooting me, then you better get it over with because my fiancée is waiting, Ok!"

Marcus stepped back from the Dean and was about to walk away when Dean Graham fired a silenced warning shot into the air.

Marcus immediately froze, turned around and said. "Look Dean, why don't you go down to Argentina and retire to that piece of dirt you call your retirement home and stay there, permanently, who's to know your there?"

Dean Graham was next to take a step back. He thought no one knew about Argentina and the surprise showed on his face.

Marcus feeling he was getting the upper hand said. "Ah! You thought no-one knew about Argentina, no-one does, only me." Marcus realised he'd said the wrong thing and could see the Dean's eyes begin to distort with hate and anger, and pointed the Nagant revolver and silencer at Marcus and pulled the trigger.

In the split second that Dean Graham pulled back his trigger finger Louise emptied her Beretta, two shots to the hand gun in case she missed, the rest hit his body, the heart first and she didn't much care where the rest ended up.

Dean Graham as if staring in a his own silent movie, slumped to his knees and hovered there for a few slow seconds before gravity took over and he dropped face down in the vineyard soil causing a dust cloud. Louise unclipped the empty magazine and replaced it with a full clip all inside of two seconds ready for the Dean's accomplice, but he just stood, as did Marcus gasping at the speed with which Louise had coldly applied her mental and physical training to the full.

Louise spoke first and said with authority. "Give me a reason to shoot you, you bastard!" The accomplice simply dropped his gun then knelt down with his head bent over and hands in the air in surrender.

Giovanni, Paul, and the twins were running down the dirt pathway towards the lean-to and shouting together at Marcus, while Paul went straight to Louise and asked what happened and who the other guy was. Louise ignored Paul for a few seconds until her heightened senses began to return to normal, she then holstered her gun and grabbed the accomplice asking him why he was with the Dean and what could he gain by being involved with him.

Before the Dean's accomplice could say anything, Marcus shouted. "Danny! Mike! What are you two doing here?" Marcus edged past Paul to confront his friends whom he could see running past the fruit trees towards them.

"I've called the local police," shouted Danny. "They should be here soon, are you ok Marcus."

"What are you doing here you old fox and you Mike, you Geordie hero?" Marcus shook Danny and Mike's outstretched hands.

Danny looked up at Mike and they both laughed at Marcus' description of them. "Mike, my sister Helen, Simon, and me, we're here for the secret wedding you old romantic."

Marcus pushed his fist into Danny's shoulder and held his friends gaze. Danny was the first to look away as he said. "Chrissie needs you mate, go and get married, never mind about him on the ground he got his comeuppance and the other guy. Anyone know who he is?"

"I know who he is," said Louise with a scowl. Paul turned round and looked at her. "How do you know him?"

"He's the guy, you remember, I told you about him, I almost quit the force because of this piece of muck. Go on Lou, tell them how and why you're involved in all of this, this should be a good detective story. Lou Quarry disgraced ex-detective, couldn't keep your hands to yourself could you Lou, tried to seduce all the young rookies including me, I ought to shoot you right here and now." As Louise started to reach for her Beretta again Lou saw her and blind panic took over his small lean body and he slumped to the dusty ground clutching his chest and shaking in agony.

Paul with panic in his voice shouted. "Heart attack, he's having a heart attack." But before anyone could reach him Lou Quarry was dead, struck down by sheer fear.

Paul, with a pained look on his face, looked up at Louise and winced. "He must have been terrified of you?"

"Or what I was going to do to him. Anyhow the world will be a better place without those two." Louise remembering, she had told Paul to look after Chrissie.

"Paul, can you get everyone up to the villa? I'll wait for the local police."

Paul stood in front of Louise, but instead of leaving with the others he pulled her towards him, and as she began to shake, not with fear, but love for this gentle giant standing in front of her, she said. "I need you to hold me?"

Instantly, Paul held her close, forgetting about how she'd disposed of his father's hated adversary, but almost hugged and kissed the life out of her tiny mouth and body.

Marcus watched his son's reaction to Louise as did everyone else and they all shouted. "Amore, they're in love."

Within the hour the Local Police had spoken to Louise and removed the two dead bodies and were satisfied with her explanation of the events that led up to the deaths. Louise was free to proceed up to the villa and join her friends and new family wedding, hoping that she and Paul's wedding would be a little less eventful. Louise and Paul arrived just in time to see Danny frantically searching in his pockets for what she guessed to be a wedding ring. Mike leaned over to Danny and grouched. 'I gave it to you and you put it in your top pocket.' Just in time Danny produced the ring and held it in his shaking hands ready to pass Marcus at the appointed time.

Marc stood waiting at the top of the first row of seats. His family, Helen and Simon sat on the left and Marcus's family; Paul, Louise, and Mike sat on the right. Giovanni, Valentina and the children decided to spread out between the two families. Marcus stood to the left of Marc with Danny next to him, waiting.

Chrissie for the first time in her life not as a bridesmaid but a beautiful bride, stepped onto the flower adorned terrace with her arm linked through her son David's arm, and with the sound of Giovanni's children singing a well rehearsed folk song, she walked slowly towards her groom. Danny tapped Marcus on the shoulder and indicated he turn around and acknowledges his bride. Marcus could hardly move, his body wasn't used to being so nervous but eventually he half turned and almost wept. Trying to keep his emotions under control, he watched Chrissie, dressed in a knee length lilac brocade dress with a small matching bolero, clutching a small bouquet of lilac roses and trailing white gypsophila in her hands, walk in step to the children's voices. She and David eventually stood in front of her Marc and they both bowed their heads in acknowledgment; she then turned to Marcus and smiled at him with moist eyes as he mouthed the words. "You are beautiful my love."

Marc with narrowed eyes turned to Marcus and said with a serious voice. "Do you take this woman, my mother, Chrissie Greenwood Connor to be your lawful wife?"

Marcus stood silent and his mouth wouldn't open until Danny nudged him into reality. "Um, Eh, Yes! I do!"

After the ceremony and the speeches had ended they were all sitting relaxing, and laughing at Danny's terrible jokes, and drinking Giovanni's special wine, Chrissie stood up and announced she had a very special wedding present for Marcus. From beyond the pergola Simon and Giovanni's children emerged carrying a huge flat parcel, wrapped up in brown paper with rainbow coloured ribbon tied in a bow around the middle. The children carried it together and handed it to Marcus. He immediately ripped the paper off with the help of the children, to reveal a huge canvas.

Marcus with tears in his eyes looked at Chrissie and said simply. "Thank you my love." The huge picture was a canvas painting of the York Jesse tree window. While still in Whitby, she had asked Danny if he would commission it from the York Minster and either send it by special messenger or bring it himself to Rome.

Marcus sat and gazed at the canvas, whilst Chrissie put her arms around his shoulders, and as she nuzzled his neck she whispered. "I love you my darling, happy wedding day Marcus."

Marcus not to be outdone quickly clicked his fingers and the children gathered round them, but instead of laughing and giggling they all stood behind Marcus. Suddenly Simon began to sing in his boy soprano voice, a church plainsong. When he'd finished Marcus turned to Paul and said. "Son, that's how it should be sung."

Immediately Paul, Marc, and David began to try their hand at singing, but the happy party all shook their heads and cried out. "No, please no, no more."

Marcus and Chrissie quickly hugged each other and Marcus whispered. "If this is what it's like to be happy and in love Chrissie, then like the virtuous Saint Benedict, I can die with a smile on my face because I'm a blissfully happy man."

Shield  Crest

www.ingramcontent.com/pod-product-compliance
Ingram Content Group UK Ltd.
Pitfield, Milton Keynes, MK11 3LW, UK
UKHW041439180426